Bloody Mexico

a novel of cartel wars

Larry B. Lambert

Niederhauser Andwendungen (Asia) Ltd.

Also by Larry B. Lambert:

WHITE POWDER: A Novel of the CIA and the Secret War in Laos

THE BLACK SCORPIONS: A Novel of Outsourced War

Cover art by *VINCE PETERSON DESIGNS*

Bloody Mexico

a novel of cartel wars

Larry B. Lambert

In dystopian Mexico, the absence of a just and moral government has led to a vacuum where evil runs virtually unchecked. Society festers where an underground empire rules a land in self-destruct mode. Rampant corruption at all levels thrives in an environment where many compromise their principles and their virtue for narco-money. Recent violence as a result of the cartel wars may have topped 100,000 dead—but nobody really knows the numbers and the Mexican government hides the death toll for the sake of 'national credibility'. There are states in Mexico where the narcos rule and the government's efforts to restore the rule of constituted law have been repeatedly thwarted.

Narcotics are not just a Mexican or an American problem. Worldwide people spend more money on narcotics than they do on food. The wars between entrepreneurs who would be king for control of the drug trade are as vicious as they are unrelenting. The Mexican cartels have made billions of dollars by moving cocaine that was grown in Peru and Brazil and refined in Colombia through Mexico and into the world's largest consumer of everything, the United States of America.

The unstable and unsustainable situation in Mexico, caused in great part by the narcotics cartels, is quickly becoming a matter of concern to American national security planners, as the border is not destroyed with a bang, but by intentional neglect. This is only a novel. It's just a flight of imagination. Keep telling yourself that. It will help you sleep at night.

For information about permission to reproduce selections of this book, e-mail   asia.publishers@me.com.

Niederhauser Anwendungen (Asia) Ltd.
Publishing Office
The Lee Gardens, 12th Floor,
33 Hysan Avenue,
Causeway Bay,
Hong Kong

FIRST EDITION

Library of Congress Catalog-in-Publication Data
Title ID: 3561152
ISBN-13: 978-1460900260

Bloody Mexico: A Novel/ Larry B. Lambert – 1st Ed
1. Mexico —Fiction. 2. Drug Cartels—Fiction. 3. Planned Political Kidnapping—Fiction. 4. Central Intelligence Agency—Fiction.
5. Drug War—Fiction

This is a work of fiction. Names, characters, places, and incidents either are the product of the author's imagination or are used fictitiously, and any resemblance to actual persons, living or dead, business establishments, events or locales is entirely coincidental.

Printed in the United States of America

For Amanda, Heather, Kelly and Emilie

The only things that are carved in stone
are stone carvings

And for Jack Willoughby

survivor of large wars, small wars,
and the New Orleans Police Department

Tell me, is something eluding you, Sunshine?
Is this not what you expected to see?
If you want to find out what's behind these cold eyes,
You'll just have to claw your way through this disguise...

--Roger Waters
Pink Floyd, *The Wall*

1

Mexico City, Mexico
Present Day

The single room's massive dimensions dwarfed the mansion in much the same way that a medieval church with its spire reaching heavenward, outsized the village, which surrounded it.

A great clock of indeterminable antiquity covered the entire wall of the spacious gallery. Glittering gold hands over a meter long stood at attention, nearly overlapping as midnight approached, while filigreed wheels turned behind them. Symbols of the zodiac predicted the future of men and the course of the planets. They moved with the hands, as slowly and surely as the stars in the heavens. Iconic gilded statues from Christianity, their expressions twisted and angry, stared with sightless eyes toward a vast painted mural on the wall depicting the vices of men: debauched pleasure, adultery and greed. Demonic gargoyles clung to corbels above and the clawed feet of others gripped the rafters with spread wings like fierce, twisted black vultures preparing to leap onto carrion. The winged demons hovered and menaced those below who gazed on the evil majesty of the clock.

Incense censors hidden in the walls burned and sent their cloying vapor gently into the room, scenting it with aromatic myrrh like a gentle fog, wafting through the spacious, vaulted expanse.

A circular mural of embossed silver skeletons dancing and making merry together around the clock's rosettes were joined by ominous words in blood red enamel: *quod sumus hoc eritis.*

BLOODY MEXICO

Felix Ochoa looked up at the clock with burning eyes, set deep beneath a ridged bony brow and read, *"As we are, you will be."*

The clock had been purchased three decades earlier. Rey del Cielo (King of the Sky) paid a king's ransom to have it reconstructed and housed in the great room. Rey del Cielo received his moniker for flying many tens of thousands of tons of cocaine from Colombia to the United States by way of Mexico. Rivals had killed the great man and he died badly, sealed in an oil drum with rattlesnakes. Some said he forgot his faith and that it had been his undoing. The clock, *His* clock, and the legend that surrounded it were a matter of public conjecture since his death eleven years previously. Only rumors of the great instrument named, The Clock of the Lives of Men, circulated. No photographs had been taken and no eyewitnesses ever stepped forward. That this very mansion, a secret palace in Mexico City, remained anonymous for so many years, could only be attributed to divine providence and condescension.

Felix Ochoa watched the clock with his mouth open, in awe. By all accounts, Ochoa transcended normal standards of ugliness. He could have been the model for an artist seeking to render an impression of Cro-Magnon Man. His skull pushed forward heavily from his spine and massively muscled shoulders. A low forehead, heavy brow, unusually close-set eyes and broad face with a wide, prominent nose completed the stereotype. The black eyes that blazed like coal embers from deep within their sockets, were impossible to read. His hair had once been black. Now time had streaked the ebony with a few silver strands.

A bell tolled clear and pure, silver doors in the clock clacked open and life-sized mechanical demons, apostles, skeletons and sinners in an attitude of supplication appeared, turning on golden platters over three meters in diameter in a ritual dance as the clock struck midnight.

Felix looked to his left and saw that a larger door had opened and it was Death who rang the chime of time. The Dead Saint was familiar to him: A complete human woman's skeleton clad in a long, colorful robe, carrying a crystal globe and a scythe. The dead saint struck the chime with her scythe again and again as it marched to signal midnight.

2

Scales, an hour glass with the sand running out and a golden owl with ruby eyes rotated out of a gilded cavern in the massive clock and stood as totems of the faith.

The scale of the pageant that unfolded, the intricate human figures and the vast opulence in precious stones and metal that went into the creation staggered Felix.

"They call you El Indio, don't they?"

Felix turned to face a man, twenty years his junior, dressed casually but fashionably. The clock continued to chime.

"I'm told you worship Santa Muerte, the Holy Death."

Felix nodded his large, shaggy head slowly.

The man facing him, he who owned the clock, looked like a young Spanish Don down to the sweeping moustache and slicked back black hair. He had that well-connected, well-oiled charisma that made his family famous.

"I too sacrifice to Señora de las Sombras."

"I call her Niña Negra Santa," Felix replied.

"But it is all the same, yes?"

"It is all the same."

"Est autem fides credere quod nondum vides; cuius fidei merces est videre quod credis," The tall, dapper Spaniard gestured toward a chair upholstered in expensive damask, opposite the clock.

Felix sat, watching the clock chime ten, eleven and twelve. Then he turned his attention to the Spanish Don, intoning the words, "Faith is to believe what you do not see; the reward of this faith is to see what you believe. I learned Latin in the seminary." He nodded his head vigorously, "It is the truth." He scrutinized the man, "They call you El León."

"Yes, Felix they do. "

"You are the nephew of the Lord of the Sky."

The young man smiled.

"People say that Señora de la Noche protects you." He shrugged toward the clock and its display that closed back within its golden opulence.

"It is a matter of faith with me."

"Me too."

3

"They say that a man's worth can be judged by what he has or what he owes—it's only the amount that matters."

"You forget Niña Negra Santa?"

El León smiled in pitch perfect petulance, "Many people do because there is more than merely money and property. There is Señora de las Sombras, who holds the lives of men in her hands like grains of sand.

"You were trained by the Cubans." El León made the statement and then he took a cigar box from a table next to his chair and opened it toward Felix. Felix selected one. They not only looked Cuban wrapped, but they were fragrantly Cuban. El León took a cigar for himself, replaced the box and then offered Felix a cutter and a box of cedar matches. Felix fired his cigar and took in a series of deep puffs that caused a glowing ember to appear at its tip.

"The cigar takes me back to those days when Castro was strong. When I lived there on the island."

"They trained you in planned political kidnapping," El León puffed smoke as the cigar took fire. "Don't look surprised. I've reviewed your achievements in Mozambique and Angola. Everyone thought you were Cuban yourself. They called you El Loco Selva. A term of respect."

"Today I am El Indio."

"Of course. There is almost no difference between political kidnapping and assassination in the planning phases. The execution of the plan with a kidnapping is often more difficult because the target must live."

"Sí."

El León asked, "Would you like to work for me, Felix?"

Even though Felix anticipated the question, the reply stuck in his throat. El León did not have an army of assassins and he only recently began to transport cocaine from Colombia to the United States in ton quantities. Felix worked for the opposition that demanded a percentage from people like El León.

El León had become a marked man because he refused to pay tribute to any of the cartels for the privilege of moving cocaine into the United States. That meant that the cartels were all more or less his enemies. Felix didn't think a man would last long who made a tacit enemy of every cartel in Mexico. Working with a man such as that meant that you linked your fate to his.

"And before you decide, let me tell you that I plan to be the most important Narco in Mexico. The Sinaloa Federation won't exist when I'm done. If you help me with my plan, together we will be their undoing."

"If I don't agree."

"Then the sand will have run out of the hourglass for you, my friend. Your bones will rest here, on this ground in an honored place."

Felix gulped and took a long drag on the cigar.

"I'm not so stupid," El León stressed, "as to think that you wouldn't betray me. Under duress you would agree to work for me tonight, at midnight and tomorrow or the next day, you'd vomit my plan to my enemies."

Felix's close-set eyes stared directly under his heavy brows, but he didn't reply.

"So we will swear a holy oath to Señora de las Sombras. And if you betray Her, your soul will be forfeit to Hell."

A bead of sweat dripped from Felix's bushy hairline and ran down over his wide cheek.

"And you will swear an oath to me, as well, El León?"

El León's face registered surprise. "Go on."

"An oath to the saint that you will not betray me, on penalty of your soul."

They both puffed on their cigars for what seemed to Felix to be a long time. Then El León stood and walked to a corner of the clock where a golden altar had been built. On the altar a dozen large candles burned brightly and hot. Pooling wax joined at their bases. The candles illuminated offerings of tequila, coins, cigarettes, and brilliant blue turquoise rocks. El León took the bottle of tequila, snatched two shot glasses from a sideboard and sat down again across from Felix. He poured for each of them and set the bottle down.

El León said, "I so swear and seal my oath with the blood of the saint taken from her altar." Then he knocked back the tequila.

"I am your sworn man until death takes me." Felix pelted down the tequila. The silvery liquid both tasted and felt like nectar of the Gods. "I will remember my faith."

"Then let us join as brothers and enter the world of shared experience, treasure, plunder, bloodshed, and brotherhood!" Pointing to the clock with its periodic passion play, "We have now entered a play in which we are both actors and audience. As with my uncle, the Lord of the Sky, we will make our own mythology with a pantheon of Heroes and enter this doorway, this procession into history that will transcend the ordinary."

El Indio thought but didn't say that the new boss was very full of himself. He liked that. That's precisely how Castro talked back in the old days when he spit in the eye of the Norte Americanos time and time again.

"Have you ever thought of growing a beard, patrón?"

El León puffed his cigar contentedly and looked at the ugly man who had just joined him in a blood oath. He tipped his head with a degree of appreciation. Maybe.

2

The Old Dominion Club
Washington DC

At the age of sixty, Gary Granger retired from the outfit, and began to spend his time as an annuitant, struggling to write the great American novel. He hung out at the Old Dominion Club on Wisconsin Avenue, down the street from the Naval Observatory, far more often than he toiled on his masterpiece.

In the comfortable, dark, musty fastness of the club, he drank more of his lunch than he ate. Though Gary appeared to be convivial to a fault, he found that the same crowd with the same tired stories wore him down. By the time he'd been out of the business for six months, he realized that he'd turned into a bitter hector with a more acutely cultivated drinking problem than he had when he left the CIA.

The novel's outline remained stalled somewhere well shy of the middle. Gary fiercely blamed writer's block and drank more gin in the hopes of generating a Hemingwayesque epiphany. Unfortunately, Gary, for all his exploits and life experience, was not Hemingway.

Missy, his occasional mistress, a forty-something, worn-down, career cocktail waitress at that same Old Dominion Club, managed to coax erections from his weary flesh on Tuesdays and Thursdays. She reserved two evenings for Gary. Missy blithely explained that they were the only open evenings when she didn't play cards or babysit her grandchildren. Missy's apartment smelled like over-ripe cat litter. She smelled like cheap perfume. Her breath had the persistent chalky spearmint taste that one associates with denture adhesive. Gary rationalized that it was the best he could do.

Gary earnestly tried his hand at golf but it had not interested him back when he had worked, and interested him less now that he had retired. His career at the Central Intelligence Agency never even bordered on stellar. Perhaps that could be attributed to his weak interest in golf?

At best, those who didn't know him well characterized Gary as a steady hand with a penchant for independent action, somewhat phlegmatic, and the sort of gray man who nobody paid any attention to. Those attributes are sought after in a spy, but Gary Granger had never been noticed or marked for exaltation or significant management-level responsibility at CIA. What's more, it didn't bother him. As a secret Renaissance man, he marched to the beat of his own drummer.

He had completed a three-year tour as a reports officer in Mexico City toward the end of his career between his second divorce and his third marriage. He had needed a change and the Agency obliged with the Mexico posting.

The Latin America Division's Area Of Responsibility had never been his stomping ground. Granger was an East Asia man throughout most of his thirty-two years in the Clandestine Service. Though he spoke Mandarin, Cantonese, Japanese, Hangul, Filipino, Tagalog, Iban, Yawi and Minangkabau fluently, his Spanish scores stretched hard to reach level 3. He made excuses, but it was more from a general lack of interest in learning the language than from a deficient aptitude. At least that's what the people administering the language test deduced.

After Mexico, there was a three-year assignment as a deputy branch chief in Jakarta and then back to Northern Virginia for his twilight tour at headquarters-on-the Potomac. During his last three years, the Agency more or less ignored him and he more or less ignored them. Though he had been hobnobbing with the diplomatic envoys of friendly Asian powers, dubbed the sweet-and-sour shrimp circuit, he was consistently less than diligent in showing up for work.

On a dismal, rainy Friday, after lunch and before dinner, he sat on one of two dozen tuck-and-roll maroon leather barstools, teetering, considering going home to his wife, but planning to have at least one more cocktail to work up the courage to face her. Vivian stood third in his line of wives, though she seemed to be well on her way to becoming redundant. He lamented absently that there were several days left to endure before Tuesday arrived again, bringing the promise of sexual release.

The serious drinkers joined him at the bar and muttered to each other. Some were boastful, others reminiscent. They looked very much alike: red noses, beer bellies, fat necks, blue blazers, button down collar shirts and slacks. Some wore ties. Most did not. A few were beltway bandits, hoping to make friends with somebody who knew somebody and could put them in touch with a decision maker who would buy their wares. Most had served under the flag at one time or another, in one capacity or another. They were all completely at home in the Old Dominion Club.

Gary spiked another green pimento-stuffed olive with a tiny plastic sword from a white plastic bowl as he slurped down the last of his fourth martini. He waved to the bartender for one more drink and stepped off the barstool, shuffling for the men's room.

He didn't look around or notice anything or anyone, his focus firmly locked onto the task at hand. Arriving at the urinal in time, he unzipped, whipped it out, and shuddered slightly as the stream melted ice that the management troweled into the bowl of the pisser for the patron's amusement. He shrank a few small cubes, with urine that had as least as much gin in it as genuine piss, when he felt somebody staring at him. He looked left and Lieutenant Commander Mike Sirrine looked back at him.

"Hey Mike."

"Is the water cold or deep, Gary?"

Gary Granger zipped up and washed his hands before he spoke again. The gin fogged his brain and it took a few extra seconds for him to put everything in place.

"What happened when you left Mexico City?"

"I came back here to Sodom-on-the-Potomac for a little bit. Then there were two tours as a Naval Attaché in London and Oslo, and now I'm in Mexico again, this time on loan to the State Department."

"The State Department? How'd you land that one, Mike?"

"Mexico, the cartels. The FSO's—Foreign Service Officers—are afraid to leave the Embassy without heavy escort since one of their numbers was beheaded in Monterey about a year ago now. State baited a hook, dragged it through the water and I bit. Now I work at the Office of Bilateral Implementation. They offered hazardous duty pay, imminent danger pay, and promotion to commander after six months. I held out until they threw in a supplemental expense account and tied the package with a bow if I'd go to Mexico. It's not the most popular resort destination on the planet these days."

"State Department?" Granger slurred, "You know that FSO stands for faggot serving overseas?"

Sirrine laughed dutifully. It was an old if not accurate cliché.

"Somebody told me that you'd retired and started working on your memoirs."

Gary said, "Let me buy you a drink and I'll tell you all about my fucked up retired life—and my screwed up retired wife."

"I'll take a rain check on the drink, but I want you to give me a call tomorrow." He fished into his wallet and pulled out a card, forcing it on Granger. "I think you'll like what I'm selling. Maybe you can refresh your taste for guacamole, tequila and muñeca?" Sirrine walked out of the men's restroom.

Gary Granger slid the card next to the cash in his wallet and then he looked at himself in the mirror.

"You look like shit," He observed to the image scowling back at him. Straightening the knot in his tie and then pulling a black plastic comb through his thinning gray hair, Gary tried to make himself a bit more respectable.

Mike Sirrine had been the Deputy Naval Attaché in Mexico City at the same time that Gary worked out of the US Embassy. Gary helped him out of a scrape with a local woman and her irate husband who happened to be a senior official in Secretaría de Gobernación (Mexican Department of the Interior) that could have effectively ended his navy career.

What did Sirrine have to sell? He speculated that it would be an offer to work for the State Department, on contract. They hired more than a few Agency re-treads.

He thought his carrier had ended with a goofy retirement party that two-dozen people attended six months before. Would he go back to the grind, back to the rackets? This time with State—as a subcontractor? Maybe. It hadn't been offered. He and Mike just passed a few words across a urinal privacy screen. Still, Sirrine had been a true mechanic at working the system and maybe he'd turn the crank for an old buddy and add some grease to the cogs.

Gary reasoned that if there was an offer, he still knew a lot of people that he could reach out to if things started to unwind down south. He'd heard rumors that the violence in some states mirrored Beirut in the halcyon days. Yes, he served his career as a nobody, but he did a lot of favors and payback could be counted on. If that wasn't sufficient, he knew where the skeletons were buried. Simply being helpful and innocuous had its graces for a journeyman spy.

Gary worked his way back to the bar for one final pop for the road before he went back to Vivian.

The bartender said, "One more and I'm going to cut you off, Gary."

"But I'm going home to my next ex." Gary snickered, "Marriage is a three ring circus. An engagement ring, a wedding ring, and suffer-ring." He laughed again. "I'll need more than one more to dull the ache."

"Only if I can call you a cab."

3

Office of Bilateral Implementation (OBI)
Mexico City, District Federal, Mexico

Traffic congestion in the area reminded Deputy Chief of Mission Cheryl Osborne-Clarridge, J.D., of the daily commute from Waverly Hills and across the Key Bridge to downtown Washington DC. However, in Mexico, the exhaust fumes were much worse than they were on the Northern Virginia commute. The sun pounded through morning haze and the clotting traffic increased as she passed the Sheraton Hotel and the US Embassy, with its paramilitary guards carrying MP-5 machine pistols and wearing blue bulletproof vests. She pushed her Volvo through the roundabout and drove back toward the Embassy on the northern frontage road. Arriving at the modern office complex, she passed through the Federal Police cordon and then showed her ID to a private security officer who scanned it and cleared her.

Scooter Olsen stepped gingerly into the mahogany paneled elevator with her and then looked directly at her breasts. She mused that women would never be equal to men until they could walk down the street with no neck, a bald head and a beer gut, and still think that they are sexy.

"Good morning, ma'am," Scooter said, still focused on her breasts.

"Scooter, do yourself a big favor and just watch the numbers roll on the read-out."

The elevator stopped and Cheryl stepped out. Scooter stayed on and rode it to the floor above hers. A US Army brigadier general ran OBI. There was symbolism to Scooter's office being higher in the building than hers and she felt offended whenever she gave it any thought.

Cheryl Osborne-Clarridge worked at the Office of Bilateral Implementation as their senior liaison to the State Department's

Directorate of U. S. Foreign Assistance. The Bilateral Implementation Office had been established and funded under the Secretary of State so Ms. Osborne held the purse strings firmly in her claws—sort of.

She lamented that secret intelligence funds did not fall under her aegis. She had been kept out of the loop by the Central Intelligence Agency, and harbored suspicions that the funds directed toward their efforts to promote and support democratic, well governed states in Mexico might not have been spent as wisely as it could have been if she had been overseeing them.

A form of compensating ego came naturally to Ms. Cheryl Osborne-Clarridge, known as Oz, to everyone at the Bilateral Implementation Office. Secretly, she felt as if she spent her life with a sail and no rudder. Achievement had become a replacement for genuine self-actualization and now it felt hollow, like a brass bell without a striker. Usually, others had to pay for her personal inadequacy as they weathered the storms of her mood changes and periodic vindictive anger. While it didn't lead to interpersonal growth, it passed for normal in the federal government's Byzantine society.

She sat down at her desk after browbeating her secretary for not having a draft report to Assistant Secretary of State Jane Hillary ready for review. Oz used the mirror on her desk to confirm that her make-up remained as near perfect as possible. She set the mirror down and decided not to look into it today. The looking glass only served to remind her that the biological clock ticked remorselessly. At forty-one years of age, wrinkles appeared in place of taunt skin, and her pale blue eyes looked tired to her. It had been a long time since she'd slept through the night.

Oz felt profoundly lonely and didn't know what to do to improve her condition.

The secure phone on her desk rang. As usual, there was some sound distortion in the audio quality. The LED screen showed that Commander Mike Sirrine initiated the call. "Mike, how are you doing?"

Her mind formed a mental picture of the tall, handsome naval officer whose looks, manners and charm were the talk of the Mexico City diplomatic social scene. He stood somewhere over six feet,

13

worked out like an Olympian, and best of all, was single and completely heterosexual. His nose was a bit too hawkish, his dark eyes a bit too fierce and his smile a bit too heart-melting. Mike Sirrine was an alpha male.

"Do we need to go secure?"

"Yeah, I guess."

The read-out changed and the message: 'going secure' appeared. Ten seconds later, it was replaced by, 'secure'.

"Cheryl, I've found a couple people here that might fill out the Staff for you."

"Are they cleared?"

"Yeah, Gary Granger retired from CIA six months ago and still has a Top Secret SBI. The best part is that he's a Mexico veteran. He was the interface between the inside and their outside officers." Mike Sirrine referred to the need for non-official cover officers to have a CIA contact inside the Embassy. Non-official cover people lived and worked in the environment without ever walking through the doors of a government office. Granger, as their liaison, would have managed their reporting and would have handled their somewhat peculiar problems.

"Oh, he'd be perfect." Cheryl would have her own clandestine affairs expert. "If you like him, offer him a job, standard terms equivalent to, GS13 Step 10 pay grade, a two year renewable contract with a ten thousand dollar signing and relocation bonus."

Sirrine outlined two other people he recommended for different tasks, but neither of them were as qualified as Granger seemed to be. Though she wouldn't have admitted it to anyone, she had no intention of over-ruling Mike Sirrine. She planned to take him as her own, a prize that would make her the envy of hundreds of other female diplomats from many nations who interacted in Mexico City.

Yes, she had a few wrinkles, and considered Botox. It was also true that she gained weight since she'd been in Mexico City. The first restroom scale ended up in the trash. The second one, confirming the conclusions of the first, remained in her apartment. The only angle she had to play with Mike Sirrine was one of ardent supporter and devoted colleague.

"I'll offer Granger the job then and fast-track him through processing."

"Great, Mike. I need you back here ASAP."

"I'll be back as soon as I can, Oz."

She disconnected the conversation with the touch of a button. A deep breath, a memory of Sirrine and she turned her mind back to work.

Pulling paperwork from her briefcase, she sifted and sorted, throwing some of it into a burn bag, designated for destroying classified material, sitting next to her desk. Oz pivoted on her chair and punched a combination into her small personal safe. She swung the door open with one hand and put the other remaining paperwork from her briefcase in with the other. Then she closed the door, locking it in place.

A chart, marked SECRET, hung on the south wall of her office. The Consolidated Priority Organization Targets consisted of the Sinaloa Cartel, called "The Federation" in Mexico and the Beltran Leyva Organization, referred to by the American as "The BLO". Heading the wire diagrams were the current leaders of the respective organizations. In some parts of Mexico they were more popular than rock stars. Throughout Mexico, they instilled fear.

Another chart, nearly covering the west wall, graphically illustrated narcotics trafficking efforts to import multi-ton quantities of cocaine from Central and South American countries, through Mexico and into the United States. The chart showed the various means of transportation currently in use. Boeing 747 cargo aircraft, submarines and other submersible and semi-submersible vessels, container ships, go-fast boats, fishing boats, tugboats and coastal tramp steamers, busses, rail cars, tractor-trailers and automobiles were all represented.

The remaining wall served as Oz's glory wall. Her diploma from Stanford Law, photos of her with the President, Secretary of State, Speaker of the House, Senate Majority Leader and others demonstrated to one and all that she had connections.

A wall-sized window looked out from the twenty-third floor onto Paseo de La Reforma, the Marriott Hotel and Cine Latino, beyond. She paused to look out and take in the morning rush, not seeing much. Her mind remained firmly on Mike Sirrine.

Scooter Olsen only beat his boss into work by a few minutes. Their relationship in public remained stiff and formal but in private, things were calm and relaxed.

"I rode up on the elevator with Oz," Scooter told Brigadier General Darrell Barton, the Director of OBI.

"She's been packing on the weight," the General replied. "The mere shadow cast by her ass must weight fifty pounds."

"At high noon. Thirty-five pounds when the sun is setting." Scooter mused that even though Oz was getting a little long in the tooth, had indeed put on weight and sagged here and there, he felt certain that he'd have sex with her if he could down a six pack of beer first. He mused that she appeared to have a fine rack under the padding and clothing draped over her breasts.

"I've got to go down and see her, Scooter. Keep an eye on the fort."

Barton walked to the elevator, scanned his ID card, stepped in as the door opened, punched a button and the elevator moved down a floor.

"Hey Oz." Brigadier General Darrell Barton walked through her office door and sat in the nearest chair. He looked at the wall-sized charts "It's remarkable isn't it? The charts are just a mute witness of hundreds of thousands of kilograms of cocaine being moved worldwide. The little bastards are nothing if not industrious." Barton took on the tone of instructor, "The Federation is currently buying from the Colombian Norte Valle Cartel and from the Colombian paramilitary army, Autodefensas Unidas de Colombia."

"And we're doing something about it," Cheryl said proudly.

General Darrell H. Barton, who she had never seen wearing an Army uniform, simply smiled. The smile spoke volumes. Oz knew that the general thought she was at best, marginally stupid because they didn't seem to be making any headway at all and upper echelons in Washington D. C. were beginning to question the effectiveness of the operation and the millions of dollars they threw into it. Cheryl spun the reports to look as if the war had begun to turn in the Mexican Government's direction, but it was all spin and Barton knew it. The truth remained that the Mexican military only controlled that physical space where troops stood, and sometimes not even then. The most popular person in Mexico wasn't a rock star, the president or a sports hero. Ruben Gonzales, El Macho himself, topped the charts. Gonzales ran the Sinaloa Federation, the most powerful cartel in all of Mexico. The Federation's influence had been felt nationwide and they marketed more heavily in Europe than they ever had before. But Oz couldn't tell Washington *that.*

General Barton wore many hats and had many bosses. The US Assistant Secretary of State for International Narcotics and Law Enforcement Affairs pumped in funds overseen by Cheryl Osborne-Clarridge. Representatives from each of nine US Government agencies posted to OBL reported back to their masters in Washington DC on both the progress they made and on his leadership of the center that found its creation with the implementation of the Merida Initiative.

His military chain of command ran to Admiral Walter Norton at Peterson Air Force Base, west of Colorado Springs, Colorado. Admiral Norton commanded the US Northern Command and the North American Air Defense Command (NORAD). Juggling the problems of many men and some women in Mexico required a politician with a deft grasp of what the Mexican and American customers wanted. Admiral Norton picked Barton because he wouldn't make waves and, above all, wanted that second star. Therefore Barton's concern for the down-side potential of any activity or liaison carried out by OBI had absolute priority over any up-side.

Brigadier General Darrell Howard Barton graduated with West Point Class of 1987 and while his promotions had not been meteoric, he'd done all the right things, and in the right order. Prior to his assignment to OBI, he'd commanded a combat brigade in Afghanistan, then moved to Chief of Staff, 82nd (Airborne) Division. Then came the star and the new job in Mexico. He brought bald headed, scar faced, no neck, thirty-five year veteran, Scott (Scooter) Olsen, his Command Sergeant Major from Afghanistan with him. With the new assignment, the Army made Olsen a Master Warrant Officer

(W-5) at Barton's request. There'd been resistance at first but Admiral Norton at NORAD endorsed the promotion and made it happen.

Between his service with then Colonel Barton in Afghanistan and his reassignment to OBI, Scooter Olsen had been slotted into a do-nothing job at the Office of the Army Chief of Staff. He growled at people during the morning hours. At noon and beyond he drank his lunch of Beef Eater's and an occasional bar burger at the Old Dominion Club with his friend, Gary Granger. Unbeknown to Granger, he took his turn with Missy, the same cocktail waitress as Gary did— on Wednesday nights. He would have seen her more often but she said that she played cards on Tuesday and Thursday nights.

4

Lima Sierra 2
The Yucatan Peninsula, Mexico

The aging North American Aviation Aero Commander squatted on the gravel apron like a ruptured duck. Its haze-gray paint peeled here and dimpled there, giving it strange camouflage all its own. Black oil dripped from the starboard engine, forming a small pool on the ground that dimpled and expanded slightly with each successive drop. The oversized nose cone had been removed, revealing the bright metal and anodized aluminum of a radar dish. Track couldn't see all of it because somebody draped it with an old green canvas tarp in an expectation of afternoon rain.

He stood on the airport apron; eyes hooded against an afternoon sun, an isolated man, set apart from all other living things. Track's personality reflected the independence of a gunslinger and the discipline of a soldier, though he didn't hold a weapon or have one visible. There was only a well-worn leather bag with its strap slung casually over his shoulder.

A Mexican kid in a makeshift khaki uniform, two sizes too large, wearing worn out sneakers, stood in the shade cast by the airplane's wing and marked an inventory on a clipboard. Two other kids dressed in civilian makeshift carried military small arms ammunition crates from a shelter and stacked them on the bed of an old oxidized red Dodge pick-up truck by the edge of the runway. Track took a closer look at the crates and the black-stenciled Chinese characters. Though the wooden cases weren't opened, he knew what was inside. Each case contained two sealed metal tins. Within each tin there were 550 rounds of 7.62x39 caliber ammunition wrapped in paper assembled into stripper clips. The ammo was used in Mexico for the Russian and Chinese-made AK-47, fast becoming the favored rifle of the cartel soldiers and, more particularly, Los Zetas. A narcotics cartel at times, enforcers for other cartels at other times, the Zetas were formed by Mexican Special Forces operatives who decided that they could make more money in the drug business.

At a time when the Mexican government had been complaining bitterly of American arms and ammunition showing up south of the border it interested him that the workers seemed to be moving quite a bit of it to the American owned airplane from the pick up truck.

He wore a tan baseball cap; a sun bleached tan safari shirt and Levis, blending with the action on the base precisely because he was just another gringo walking around Landing Site (Lima Sierra) Two. To the dozen or so Mexicans working here and there he was a gringo. The gringos ran the show; therefore he was one of that species, and not to be messed or questioned.

Track walked on and looked into a large white metal shed streaked by rust. Two flat gray Beechcraft King Air twin prop aircraft with humps behind the cockpits and sensor stanchions that made them look disturbingly like a flying cellular telephone towers were chalked in place on the concrete inside the shed – though once he got closer he could see that what he took for a shed was a reinforced hangar with a veneer of rusting steel over it.

Track walked on, taking a self-guided tour.

Everyone called him, Track. It went back a long way because his given name was Llewellyn. When that's your name, you go with something else. Lew would have been logical, but it didn't happen like that.

Llewellyn (Track) Ryder looked as if his likeness had been peeled from a Nazi recruiting poster and made flesh. He stood a shade over six feet three inches, was fit, and handsome. At the moment, he wore a natural, flax colored goatee on his tanned face. Age and exposure to the elements roughened his complexion, but at 39 years of age, he still looked younger than the calendar indicated. The only thing that marred Track's face was light acne scarring from his teenage years. It didn't make him appear ugly or sinister, only human.

Track had been around and had enough dirt on enough people to keep out of headquarters when he didn't want to be there, but it seemed as though he lacked the pull required to stay out of the Latin America Division.

A drug lord bought the land he stood on in the 1980's but the runway and surrounding property fell into disuse when the narcotics trafficking patterns changed in the mid and late 1990's. Eventually, in 2010 the drug lord's estate sold the four thousand hectare ranch in the near trackless Yucatan to Mangrove Cay Rare Woods, Ltd., a Bahamian Company specializing in teak. The new owner rolled bull dozers out of the back of military aircraft and they pushed the runway out from 1,400 feet to 2,000 feet, and knocked the jungle back to 140 feet on the apron area to allow a C-130 Hercules to turn around.

If anyone had bothered to check, and they hadn't, they would have found that Mangrove Cay Rare Woods, Ltd. was owned by Harcourt & Hare Holdings S.A., a bearer share company established in the 1960's in the Cayman Islands.

Harcourt & Hare Holdings consisted of a brass plaque on the polished mahogany door of an attorney's office located in the Cayman Island Seafarers Association building at the corner of Victory Avenue and Shamrock Drive, Grand Harbor, Grand Cayman. Banking and corporate secrecy laws remain a treasured commodity in the Cayman Islands. The person physically holding the shares owns the bearer share company. Usually this is an attorney, representing the true owner(s).

The brass plaque screwed to the office door of Mr. Julius Ramsey, Solicitor, might lead one to believe that he held the company's shares as a proxy for someone else. In fact, the actual share certificate was filed in metal file drawer, locked in one of several safes of the General Counsel to the US Central Intelligence Agency, in Langley, Virginia.

"Dawg Damnit!"

Track's attention immediately pulled back from two odd looking Beechcraft to the Aero Commander he'd just left.

Fisher crawled out of the cockpit where he had been fixing something. He wore a filthy t-shirt that had been white in the distant past and beltless denim jeans that drooped perilously under his potbelly. A busted brim straw cowboy hat with a turkey feather in the band topped his head. Fisher wore hats because he hated people to see his hair, once carrot red, now rusty with age. Track didn't know why graying hair bothered him so much, but it did. A year previously,

21

Fisher shaved his head and bought a red hair piece. Everyone took to calling it a dead parrot. It didn't last long and he went back to hats.

"Track! A Virginia Farm Boy who drifted through here a couple of weeks ago said you'd be coming and I said that it had to be another Track Ryder, because I heard that you were in Paris, far from the cartel rackets."

"I heard that myself, Fish. It used to be true."

Fisher walked over to Track, all five-foot five of him, and he grabbed Track's hand with a paw the size of a first baseman's mitt. He would have given Track a hug, but the big man pushed him back. He reeked of gear oil, body odor, tequila and garlic.

"As you can see, I'm still flying for the outfit." He called the Central Intelligence Agency, 'the outfit'. "You look the same as always. The wars change but the players don't. I missed you in Colombia."

"I didn't make it to that war," Track told him. "I pulled some different taffy for a while."

Fisher didn't ask what the senior man had been up to beyond that. He knew that Track would lie to him if he pushed it. That was how it went.

Fisher joined the CIA as a paramilitary officer back before the World Trade Center Attack, back before being a PM was cool. He'd been shunted around the globe but the duty appealed to him. For the most part, he flew. Sometimes the cover for status in a given country had been commercial cover. As a result, he'd become known as an eccentric transient pilot in nearly every shit hole in the world. Elaborate cover was no longer became. Everybody knew Matthew Fisher, tramp pilot. To all and sundry, he was Fish.

"I'm not in country under the Office of Bilateral Implementation or the Initiative," Track cautioned. "I thought I'd drop in and see if I could hitch a ride all the same."

Fisher looked around, "How did you get here?"

"Long story, Fish. I walked here."

"From where? There's nothing for fifty miles in any direction."

"From *somewhere*–other than here."

"I take it that you don't have orders or a trip voucher."

"I'm not official. No paperwork, you never saw me, no questions or bullshit, you know the drill."

"Yes, I do. Ok, Track, when do you need to leave?"

"If we can get out of here in the morning, that works. This is Mexico and there's no such thing as a schedule. If I arrive on time anywhere they'll think I work for the American government."

"That's a fact. Ok, uh—we're not going to be flying anywhere tomorrow because the bird's busted and I'm waiting for parts."

"How soon?"

"The parts should be in sometime later tomorrow. I'll throw 'em in and we can be gone the next day."

Track looked at the two odd looking Beechcraft in the hangar disguised to look like a large equipment shed. "What about those?"

"Those are US Army RC-12Q Utes"

"They look like a King Airs with a lot of stuff bolted on 'em."

Fish took off his hat and mopped his head with a crusty red bandana. "In point of fact they are King Airs – but they are *Army* King Airs and they call them Utes. They have the improved Guardrail 2000 sensor suite in them and belong to General Barton at OBI. They use the aircraft to track narcos and then they feed what they want from the batch of info they collect to DEA and to the Mexican Government.

"The pilots and crew aren't here. They flew off in a new Piper Meridian that the DEA seized and gave to us to do general hauling with. They're in Mexico City attending some sort of confab and should be back tomorrow sometime late. Sometimes they come back alone and sometimes an official from Homeland Security or DEA comes with them. I don't know how much you don't want to be recognized."

"And nobody guards the Utes?"

A hurt look crossed Fish's face, "I guard them. Well, me and the boys look after them and the base. They had some genuine soldiers down here standing watch on it, but they pulled 'em out six months later because they started to go nuts. There is absolutely nothing to do here in the way your healthy twenty-year old boy would think of things to do.

"There are four retired cops from the LAPD who rotate with four other has-been cops every three months. They're the security force now but we laid on a bender last night and it would seem they're still asleep or detoxing somewhere."

"Who fixes the Beechcraft?"

23

"They'd fly the aircraft north to Florida if they broke but they've worked fine so far," Fish said defensively. "We handle the routine squawks and gripes here on site. We can bring in whatever we need. The runway will accommodate a C-130. Since there are no roads into Lima Sierra 2, everything comes in by cargo plane, usually once a month—at night. I guess if something we couldn't fix happened, we'd pull the wings off and winch them into the C-130."

"Let's walk and talk." Track walked out onto the crushed limestone runway and Fish followed. "I did a once-around the place before I walked in and saw the infrared landing lights."

"If you have IR goggles, the place lights up like a Christmas tree. If you don't, it's pitch black."

"Fuel?"

"Bladders come in on pallets on the cargo drops, fresh food, videos, beer, whatever. We pull water up from the aquifer and purify it. There are a dozen and a half CHU's—Containerized Housing Units, the good ones with showers. We have pressurized water, power from a diesel generator insulated and cooled in a CON-EX box, a glorified shipping container. All the comforts of home."

"Women," Track asked with an arched eyebrow?

"That's why God gave you *two* hands. Everybody needs a bit of variety."

"Who owns the Aero Commander?"

"The outfit. It's on loan to OBI, but we hold the pink slip."

"And what sort of whiz-bang electronics do you have on this old piece of airframe," Track asked?

"We have the same thing the Ute has, the Guardrail 2000 and the High Accuracy Airborne Location System. I fly in conjunction with the Army. They didn't want to send a third Army RC-12 down here. They'd rather keep them waxed and in a hanger up north. There's far less danger of loosing one there." Fish paused, "Is that the end of the interrogation?"

"I'm sorry it sounds like that. I've got to get the lay of the land down here. This is my first time in Mexico with a single-scope mandate. Up until now I've worked Venezuela, Brazil, the Upper Huallaga Valley in Peru on Bush's Andean Initiative, sometimes into Chile. I never really worked narcotics per-se, even there. Usually I

24

was hunting Hezballah, Irish Republicans, and Red Chinese agitators. There was some political work too against Partido Socialista Unido de Venezuela until the new president came into office and spiked the operation. Mexico is a different creature. I've got a lot to learn."

"I concentrate on flying."

"Yeah, I happened to be looking at the list of assets we had in country and came across your name and the nomenclature of this aging lady." Track shrugged toward the Aero Commander. "I thought that with an airplane like the Commander 695A jetprop, you'd need to take it out of service from time to time and fly it here or there to pick up a part, have an expert look at something. You know?"

Fish winked.

"What sort of range are we looking at?"

"2000 nautical miles, depending on altitude, wind conditions, load and so forth. 300 knot cruise speed."

"Cover?"

"De Carga Aérea Occidental, SA, a legitimate charter company in Cuzco, Peru employs me and covers the aircraft registration. It's not an asset company, they simply do it for an exorbitant fee."

Track kicked the dusty runway.

"Can I ask a question?"

Track looked at Fisher sideways, "You can ask."

"Are you on this alone?"

"Yeah, all alone for now. But after all I've been through, that's the way I like it. I'm safer that way. Once I've hammered out the details and have them approved there will be more than just me. Would there be a problem picking up a package south of here and hauling it to the Dominican Republic?"

Fish started to do mental arithmetic, "How heavy?"

"Figure 200 pounds to be on the safe side?"

"Just you and the package?"

Track considered briefly how much he needed to tell Matthew Fisher. "A Deputy United States Marshall to make it legal, two Delta force operators for security, a doctor to insure that the package doesn't expire during the trip, and me."

"Weight won't be a problem, but it will be tight back there with all the surveillance gear I have stowed. We could take out the seats and you could all crowd in."

"Let me think about that."

"Is this nap of the Earth flying, skimming the jungle and dodging parrots?"

"No, whatever altitude you think best. I'll give you a transponder for another aircraft that belongs to someone else and you'll be them officially."

Fish rolled his eyes. He'd flown a lot of those missions over the years. "Can I top off fuel in the Dom-Rep?"

"Do you have to?"

"No, but you know what they say, there are old pilots and bold pilots but no old bold pilots."

"Then be old and bold just this once. I don't want a tower flunkey taking down the tail number. The mission will call for you to put the airplane down on a dirt strip outside Los Patos. A team will meet the plane, take the cargo off and you can fly back on your own unless you need me to sit in the co-pilot's seat and keep you awake."

"Am I coming back to Lima Sierra 2?"

"As if nothing ever happened," Track reassured Fish.

"If I run into a wicked headwind or something unexpected, can I refuel at Montego Bay?"

"Jamaica? Yeah, shouldn't be a problem there."

Fish seemed to be relieved to have the option. "Have you eaten?"

"I had a power bar for breakfast, but that was a while ago."

Fish smiled and tilted his broke brim hat back, "We've got fixings for carnitas burritos over in the galley. They're good. The guys made it up this morning. I'll have the cook scramble you a couple of eggs. You can fold 'em into the burrito if you want."

Track said, "Lead the way."

As he started on the second burrito, Track broached the subject of the Chicom ammunition. "What's with the ammo? Do you guys have a side deal going?"

Fisher looked hurt, "What would make you think a dirty rotten thing like that?"

26

"I don't know, we don't shoot it and the Mexican Army doesn't shoot it."

"It's a secret."

"Really, Fish?"

"Yeah, but I guess you're cleared. It's an Army operation called VECTOR SHRIKE. The President signed a lethal finding authorizing it."

"That means the Commander-in-Chief is growing a spine?"

"Or somebody bent his arm," Fish suggested. It's not unique in the history of warfare. It's a retread operation. During the Viet Nam War, SOG, the Studies And Observations Group, created a classified program called Project ELDEST SON, designed to cause the Viet Cong and NVA to doubt the safety of their guns and ammunition."

"I never heard of it, but I was too young for Viet Nam."

"I was too and I *hadn't* heard of it, but once they decided to reboot the operation, they read me into the program and I learned the history. Green Berets attached to SOG found caches of ammo along the Ho Chi Minh Trail but didn't have the ability to destroy it in place. Demo just scattered the cartridges. They were booby-trapping some of the ammo crates and then somebody hit on the idea of booby-trapping the ammo itself. The British did it first during the Second Matabele War back in the late 1800's so we reinvented the wheel in the 1960's and now we're doing it again.

"There's a building at Redstone Arsenal where people sit around all day pulling bullets and sabotaging the cartridges with an explosive that looks like gunpowder. It generates a quarter million pounds per square inch in that firing chamber and *bloowy!*"

"How do they deal with that lacquer seal around the neck of the bullet and case," Track asked?

"Damned if I know. I really just fly in tainted cases of ammo and sell them to the narcos. There is only one round out of each thousand that has a problem, but when they go, it completely blows up the receiver and the bolt flies back into the face of the trigger puller."

"Aren't you worried that the defective ammo will be tracked back to you?"

"I don't sell them myself. I broker them here and there along with perfectly good, untainted rounds. As I understand the program, there is no particular interest in killing the cartel types that use the weapons. If they mistrust the ammo and rifles, we hope to see the day when they won't use the Chinese and Russian weapons at all. I don't think the banditos know whether it's the weapons or the ammo, but it will certainly limit the weapons available to them if they don't want to use all of the AK-47's that they have."

Track asked, "And you run guns in a plane loaded with high end commo gear?"

"I'll show it to you. It's disguised and I can detonate thermite grenades if we're compromised."

"Why not get a second airplane for the ammo running?"

"The Outfit is cheap."

"Who's running that program—VECTOR SHRIKE—here on the ground?"

Fish scratched his whiskers, "I think it comes from General Barton, the head chignon at OBI."

An older Mexican gentleman wearing a pressed white shirt and striped tie walked up to them, respectfully. "Jefe Fish, it's time for church."

"Ok, you go along, Arturo. I'll keep an eye on things."

Arturo turned and walked away toward the containerized housing units. The young men who had been working around them followed Arturo.

"I'd completely forgotten what day of the week it is. I guess that it is a Sunday, isn't it," Track admitted.

Fisher said, "These Mexican fellas we have working here are all Mormons. Arturo is a bishop from one of several congregations in Campeche and all of the guys here on LS2 are in his congregation. They're hand picked. They don't smoke, drink, cuss and all work hard. They're solid men who know how to keep a secret and they hate the narcos. They're paid very well even by American standards and it all works out."

Track wondered how the Agency kept the nature of what happened at Lima Sierra Two a secret. That helped explain it.

"On Sunday morning they hold a service for a couple of hours, and then again in the afternoon. They'd rather not work during the day on Sundays but make allowances if there's something that needs to be done."

"Like loading the ammo?"

"That, maintenance work and getting ready for next week's ops. The tempo is slow today but when we have aircraft coming in and going out it picks up. Sometimes somebody or other from OBI will have a secret meeting here. Agency and DEA aircraft refuel here on their way to Colombia or Peru and sometimes they overnight because we have secure housing here. Arturo is the gaffer and he manages the labor force. There's an Army captain named Russell Jensen who runs the base. He's in Mexico City with the aircrews right now. Oh, and Captain Jensen is a Mormon Elder so he gets along well with Arturo and his guys."

"I'd rather that the Army and the OBI types not know that I'm here. If it comes down to that, introduce me as a cargo handler or something."

"Can do. Maybe you're guarding the ammo shipments. Sometimes, I take Arturo, hand him an M-4, and tell him to look mean, but you look a lot meaner—Look, Track, am I going to get into trouble if I work with you on this package thing? The press is all over extraordinary renditions. I've got five years to my pension."

"Life is a calculated risk."

"Everything happens once if you live long enough."

Track changed the subject as he checked the time by looking at the sun. "Do you have a spare housing unit where I can crash until you can fly me out?"

"Follow me. We have a couple of 'em and you can take your pick. I think that the politically correct term today is isotainers. They're a solid step up from the tents and Modular Initial Deployment Latrines. This particular species of fancy steel shipping containers has linoleum floors and beds inside. The laborers have versions that house four people. The executive staff," he said with a smile, "have units split into two rooms with a flush toilet and shower in the middle."

5

Riverside County, California

Felix Ochoa sat behind the steering wheel of a stolen Toyota Camry with license plates he'd switched with a clean Camry of the same year and color. He managed the swap personally, at a large apartment complex where nobody paid much attention to comings and goings. It was vitally important that things go well with the kidnapping he'd planned so meticulously. El León, Santiago Iglesias-Aznar, would be riding in the car with him, watching the action.

El León was about to make his first move, designed to bring down the largest cartel in Mexico while propelling himself into the catbird's seat.

Ochoa/El Indio watched a small television, sitting on the front seat of the car, next to him. He scanned the TV news channels. A radio detected and rebroadcast the police frequency on the 800 MHz band. Nothing out of the ordinary had happened *yet* on the sleepy Sunday afternoon in Corona, California.

Assistant United States Attorney José Antonio Melendez-Rab announced that the government rested in the five-defendant case against members of The Sinaloa Federation narcotics cartel. Five defense attorneys would begin with their arguments Monday before Judge Sheila Tonner in the US District Court, Central District of California, sitting in Riverside. The case-in-chief took three weeks primarily because of a line-up of government and informant witnesses. The law required a jury to find guilt beyond a reasonable doubt. José felt confident that he proved proof beyond all doubt and hoped that guilty verdicts would propel him from the relative obscurity of Riverside to the a more prestigious posting in Los Angeles.

The day the prosecution completed its case-in-chief, José seemed pleased as El Indio, watched patiently. The United States Attorney dropped file folders in a box into the trunk of his BMW and then left the secured parking area reserved for employees of the Federal Court. It seemed to Felix as if he intended to do a little homework over the coming weekend.

José Melendez drove straight home to his residence in Corona, a suburban community located west of Riverside along the congested 91 freeway. He drove into his driveway, opened the garage door remotely and pulled the 2010 BMW 535 safely inside. Before he closed the garage door, El Indio watched him take a soft brush to the car, removing the road soil and dust.

"José's BMW is immaculate," El Indo told Santiago Iglesias as they sat together in a motel room, drinking tequila. "He treats it better than I treat my mother. The plan will work the way I have outlined it. Political kidnapping requires planning above all else and this is planned as well as it can ever be. There are always things you can't foresee, but I expect that by Sunday night, José the prosecutor will be ours."

"He has children," El León asked carefully?

"Two children, both too young for school. They stay at home with their mother, a gringa named Bethany." El Indio tensed his gargoyle features. Yes, he explored options, but he had somewhat generic scruples where children were concerned. If children died while he carried the plan out, it was the will of God. He just didn't want to cut them, burn them, behead them, dismember them or do anything like that with his own hands. The gratuitous murder of innocent women and children violated his personal code.

"Relax, I approve of your plan. There is no need to hurt the children. This will be quite enough for the time being."

They sealed the meeting with more tequila and watched a Mexican soap opera on the motel television.

The next day, El León met the other four people who would be involved in the kidnapping. El Indio introduced them. First, Juan Hernandez, a real doctor from Chihuahua, would serve as the bait. He wasn't a normal doctor in the sense people think of a healer. His moniker said it all, El Carnicero, the butcher. El León agreed that he

31

did look like a doctor. It seemed hard to put into words, but doctors simply had a look that came from their experience. El Carnicero earned his name from many surgeries gone wrong. He wasn't a bad man, simply an incompetent cutter that had to resort to being a narco to earn a living.

Next two of El Indio's enforcers took the limelight. El Indio introduced them as los Güeros Diablo, the two white devils. They could play the part of gringos and nobody would think otherwise. The fourth person, Julio Belon a professional driver and US Citizen from National City on the US/ Mexico Border, would be the wheelman. The van that they planned to use belonged to Belon, the Citizen, and was registered to him. If all went well, the van would cross the border with the United States Attorney bound and gagged inside, never to be seen alive again.

On Sunday evening, José Melendez, his wife and two children, attended the Northwest Hills Congregational Church where he served as a deacon. To protect his BMW from damage, he parked on the south side of the lot, far from the nearest car. Gathering his youngest child in his arms, he walked into the chapel. His wife held the hand of their other child.

El Indo drove the Toyota Camry close to the BMW and swerved into the passenger door. Backing, he scraped the paint and transferred paint from the Toyota along the entire length of the sparkling sedan. He laughed to himself. Through the rear view mirror, he could see El León, laughing, trying to control himself as he watched from a distance.

He got out of the Toyota and slipped a pre-printed card under the windshield wiper of the BMW. Then he drove to the corner, picked up El León, and they drove back to the hotel while one of the fake security guards watched with his direct connect telephone/radio in hand.

At the end of the religious service, the radio chirped and El Indio listened with the speaker function turned on so that El León could monitor their progress with him. The fake security guard spoke in English.

"He's so angry. He's stomping his feet, his wife and kids are crying. He just found the card. Now he's calling.

A pre-paid telephone in El León's pocket rang. "This is doctor Guerrero," El León said in accented English.

"My name is José Melendez, and I'm an attorney. I own the BMW you hit. I need your full name and the name of your insurance company."

"I don't need another insurance claim, "El León replied. "There must be some way we can work this out. I'm leaving town in the morning for a conference in Florida and I can pay you cash for the damage right now."

"How much?"

"Twelve thousand, cash."

"That should cover it. What if it doesn't?"

"You know where to find me. Can you meet me at my office in an hour? The address is on the card. I have the money there. It's not far from the church."

"Ok, you have a deal. One hour. If you're not there, I call the police and the insurance company."

"I'll be there," El León assured him. "There are security guards who patrol the building at night. Tell them who you are and they'll bring you to my office."

He turned to El Indio, "Your people will be ready?"

"Yes, it will be as you say, El León."

Freddie Friel had been a janitor at the Corona medical clinic for seven years. On Sunday he did his deep cleaning and each office took about an hour. Since the doctor's offices weren't open he could work whenever he wanted to and on Sunday he liked to sleep in. It meant that he'd end up working into the evening. He secured cleaning contracts with most of the tenants over his tenure and had just entered the office of an allergist when two security guards arrived in an old van. Freddie had never seen security guards there before. Something was happening. Something unusual. So Freddie Friel watched.

An older man who looked the way a doctor was supposed to look, stepped out of the front seat of the van and walked nervously into the medical mall, looking in some of the office windows, waiting. He torched the end of a cigarette. Friel wondered if he really was a doctor. Both the older man and the younger security guards had a tension about them that transmitted fear to Friel, a devout coward.

José Melendez didn't need a map, a GPS or directions to find the medical clinic on Magnolia Avenue. He'd taken his children there to see a specialist. The particular office on the card was located in a medical mall of sorts, constructed in the 60's or 70's and showing its age. The brown paint hadn't peeled off yet, but it looked as if it might at any day. Two rows of buildings formed an 'H' shape with an atrium and walkway that led to the offices in between. Melendez had never been there at night and felt some relief to see that the parking lot and building was well lighted. Two security guards stood near the opening in the middle of the H.

Santiago (El León) Iglesias-Aznar sat next to El Indio, in his Toyota, parked in a deep shadow caused by an overhanging tree at the end of the parking lot. There had been other kidnappings, but they had all taken place in Mexico and none of them were United States Attorneys involved in prosecution of higher-level cocaine wholesalers. This raised the bar and his investment in the success of the operation brought him to this place to watch, and assist if necessary. Things could go wrong. He counted them off in his mind as Melendez drove the scraped and dented BMW into the parking lot.

It looked somewhat anti-climactic from where he sat with the ugly El Indio. Melendez stepped out of his car. The fake security guards met him, escorted him back to the shelter of the offices where the doctor he hired waited. One of the guards stunned Melendez with a taser and the other wrapped his hands, feet and mouth with tape very quickly and efficiently. While they did that, the doctor walked calmly to the van. Belon started the engine and drove the van closer to the entrance to the office mall. The guards threw him in and then they followed him.

Then, almost anticlimactically, the deed has been accomplished. The crew was on the road, headed for the I-15 freeway – Southbound toward Mexico. It couldn't have taken more than thirty seconds.

El Indo looked over and El León nodded. No alarm had been raised. Everything went as planned. He started the car and followed the van down Magnolia Avenue, keeping a respectful distance back.

Freddie Friel didn't know whether he believed his eyes or not. He stepped back, cleared them with his fists and then looked again. The van had gone. He kept a bottle of Old Crow Kentucky Bourbon in his bag and went there first for a long pull. Then he went back to the window and noticed the BMW that had not been there when he arrived that evening. Maybe it had been real? He pulled his cell phone from his pocket and called the police.

Officer Braden Friend had just cleared the station on the graveyard shift when the call came out.

"Units 331, 332 and S10, stand-by to copy an unknown problem at the medical offices, 790 South Magnolia Avenue," the dispatcher's voice had that mundane tone that didn't change.

"Units 331, 332 and S10, it appears to be a 415 between a patient and two security guards – stand by for more."

Officer Friend in Unit 331 responded, "10-4, enroute."

The dispatcher came back on the air again, "Units responding to South Magnolia, it now appears to be a possible kidnapping, vehicle—a dark colored van last seen southbound on Magnolia, Unit 331 the R/P will meet you at the curb."

Officer Friend increased the tempo of his response.

"Be advised that the license plate of the possible victim vehicle comes back 10-35 to José Melendez, 1687 Valencia Grove Way in Corona. Melendez's driver's license and vehicle confidentiality is with the United States Attorney's Office."

Sergeant Ken Bagley in unit S-10 came on the air, "I'll respond to the scene with 331. 332 check I-15 northbound. Notify the Highway Patrol. Break—do we have any more on the van other than dark in color?"

"K9-1, I'm in the area. I'll be checking southbound I-15."

Officer Friend had been with the Corona Police department for the past five years and didn't spook easily, but the details that Friel put together while he interviewed him sent a chill up his back.

Sergeant Bagley asked that Lieutenant Chris Patton respond to the Melendez home after officers who went there determined that the family was safe. The lieutenant would have to notify the Federal Bureau of Investigation that one of the US Department of Justice's Assistant United States Attorneys had likely just been kidnapped.

Assistant Director-in-Charge Chaia Grey ran the FBI's Los Angeles Division. She had just finished her third glass of cabernet when the phone call hit. José Melendez had just rested on one of the largest organized drug cases on the west coast. The media had been all over it. Chaia sat back in her chair, looked over at her husband, a civil attorney with a prominent firm, and said, "Somebody just kidnapped José Melendez."

"You mean *our* José Melendez?"

"From a medical clinic near his home."

"What was he doing at a medical clinic on a Sunday night? Maybe some sort of urgent care?"

"I don't know but I'm going to mobilize resources on this one."

Chaia began to dial numbers, but by that time, the van had crossed the border and was driving south on the highway that led from Tijuana to Mexicali. When the FBI had been fully mobilized, the van and El León were headed south from Mexicali and half way to Los Mochis.

6

Office of Bilateral Implementation (OBI)
Mexico City, District Federal, Mexico

General Darrell H. Barton read the overnight cables at his desk. Because it was Monday, there were quite a few that drifted in over the weekend. The one at the top of the stack had been printed on paper, edged in red stripes, which meant that somebody over his pay grade wanted him to read it first.

He reminded himself as he read that the Office of Bilateral Implementation did not take action on anything. Its charter allowed them to consult with their Mexican counterparts, encourage, pass funding through for the counternarcotics effort and not much more.

CW5 (Scooter) Olsen sat across from him in a padded chair and watched the boss. While General Barton could fairly be classified as a stuffed shirt, he didn't differ from other Academy types that Scooter Olsen worked for over the years. General Barton, caretaker of the Office of Bilateral Implementation, looked at the world through shrewd, intelligent eyes. He tipped his coffee cup and took a long draught.

"You read this?"

"Yes sir," Scooter Olsen said without emotion.

"What's your take on it?"

"The State Department wants us to encourage the Mexicans to find the missing lawyer, providing that he's in Mexico, and repatriate him."

"They want us to offer a reward and throw more cash at the Procurador General de la República and demand that they find the lawyer and insist that in doing so they can't violate anybody's human rights. Don't those numb nuts in Washington know that giving these guys more money is like pouring perfume on a pig?"

"If these guys from the Mexican Justice Department make it to heaven, they'll steal every last harp."

"Goddamned right, Scooter."

"I know that there's not much chance of them finding him, but we could always go a bit rogue and see what might be out there ourselves."

General Barton looked closely at Scooter. "What are you thinking?"

"A new guy arrives today to work for Oz on compliance issues with the Mexican Army."

Barton racked his memory, "Yeah, Feldstein, a Pakistani whose name escapes me and Granger."

"I thought we may want to put Granger on it—strictly liaison."

"Tell me about Granger," Barton prompted.

"Everybody who knows Granger says that he is fucked up. Granger would tell you that himself if you asked."

"Give me the gouge, Master Chief. I don't have time to dance with you."

"Granger is a CIA retread, and he has shoe leather time in Mexico. We could always ask him to focus on this issue in his spare time, when he's not insuring that the money we dole out to these thieves is being used to fight narcotics trafficking."

"Meet him at the airport, let the other mopes take a cab. Explain what we need and why. I don't like the idea of these bastards snatching our people. If—" Barton consulted the cable to confirm the victim's name, "Melendez is here in Mexico, let's do our bit to find him."

Scooter Olsen walked across the hall to his office, an interior room without a window. He picked up Gary Granger's itinerary from a folder. They'd scheduled him to leave Washington Dulles at 1110 HRS, he changed planes in Miami and would arrive in Mexico City at 1840 HRS on American Airlines, flight 2115.

Scooter thought it through. Granger didn't have a diplomatic passport so he'd have to stand in line through immigration and customs. Because he would be bringing belongings for an extended stay, it could mean a customs inspection, but it wasn't inevitable. Olsen did the math. He'd leave for the airport early just in case Gary's flight caught a tail wind, and he'd bring a novel to read while he waited.

Two of the new State Department contractors, Asfandyar Mustapha Jatoi, CPA and his travel companion, Morris Feldstein, CPA, CFE, sat in economy class. The third, Gary Granger, spent his own money for an upgrade to business class both because he wanted to ride in more comfort and because Jatoi, a Punjabi, was recovering from a cold with a nasty cough and spit repeatedly into his handkerchief. Gary didn't want to sit near him. Feldstein casually mentioned that he didn't drink. He struck Granger as a snitch and Gary planned to drink as much as the airline would pour. He looked like a lush if he did that in economy. In business class, both the other passengers and the airline almost expected it.

On the flight from DC to Miami, he sat next to a woman whose husband left her. After a few drinks went down the chute, she wanted to talk to him. He paid attention because she had breasts built like howitzers and he possessed a natural inclination not to turn away on that account alone.

"I thought our marriage would last forever."

"That's what I thought," Gary commiserated, "every goddamned time I got married."

Then he listened for nearly an hour. The thirty-something lady now knew what he learned through the school of hard knocks and cheap pops. It does not matter how honest, nice, humbled or forgiving you are. You will still be dragged through the mud and chewed up. It doesn't matter how ignorant or less than honest the former spouse is, they'll still have that family, moral support, close 'true' friends and love that you've always wanted.

As her rant intensified and became shrill, he felt certain that Vivian would be saying the same nasty things about him to a close circle of her friends as they spent his pension money on an overpriced bottle—or five of cabernet and a fourth course of fattening appetizers.

Finally, when he had all that he could take, he abruptly stood up, looked down at her and said, "Madam, I think I know why your husband left you." And he changed seats to an empty, two rows back on the other side of the aisle.

The somber, pinched-face gentleman he sat next to asked, "Is that your wife?"

"No, I never met her before the flight. She's somebody else's wife."

"Poor bastard."

Gary spent the rest of the flight and the next flight on to Mexico City with nothing to disturb his drinking but the background whine of the jet engines and a prompting from the flight attendant to move his seat back to an upright position and lock his tray table.

He'd shipped his baggage the week before and so deplaned in Mexico City with the clothes on his back and what little he needed for incidental use stuffed into his carry-on.

Immigration posed no problem. He presented a diplomatic passport from the Republic of the Philippines.

Gary stroked the dip passport from the President of the Philippines before he was deposed on corruption charges—*that didn't* stem from him slipping Gary Granger the credentials.

Before he took the job in Mexico, Gary called the Philippines Ambassador, who he knew from his time in the P. I. The name on the passport, Emmanuel Joel Romano was quickly and quietly added to fill an open slot in their roster as First Commercial Secretary. The name matched Gary's photo on the passport and the roster kept at the immigration kiosk for diplomats. Technically, it granted full diplomatic immunity to Emmanuel Joel Romano/Gary Granger. They passed him through with smiles and gestures of accommodation. It didn't matter that Gary didn't look the least bit like a Filipino. The paperwork was in order and if questioned in either Tagalog or Filipino, he could have responded fluently.

While Gary had no intention of testing the limits of the Ambassador's largess or of Mexican jurisprudence, he learned a long time before that waving the completely legitimate (sort of) diplomatic passport and claiming immunity occasionally came in handy. Now that he'd officially arrived in the country as Emmanuel Joel Romano, any check would confirm his status completely.

The sight of Scooter Olsen standing with the huddled crowd waiting for international arrivals surprised him. He planned to deplane innocuously, jet through the short diplomatic line and vanish to an apartment, currently unoccupied, where the Philippine Ambassador usually kept a mistress.

"Scooter, fancy meeting you here."

Scooter looked at the roll-aboard luggage that Gary trailed behind him. "Is that all you brought with you?"

"That's it. I sent everything else ahead."

"I don't recall anything arriving from you."

Gary winked.

"Oh, yeah, I get it." Scooter wasn't really sure where Gary would have sent his baggage but he didn't want to look stupid.

Scooter led Gary out and they talked quietly as they walked through what felt more like a cheesy shopping mall than an airport terminal. "Something big happened over the weekend up in the States. We think that one of the cartels snatched a US Attorney in California and he may be down here."

"Why do you think he's in Mexico?"

"I don't know that he's here. Nobody knows where he is, but General Barton, the boss, wants us to try and find him."

"Nobody knows where in all of Mexico that this kidnap victim may be, and they want *us* to find him? Two frigging gringos?"

"Yeah."

"Does the kidnap victim stand eight feet tall with blue skin and red hair?"

"He's Mexican-American."

"I see. This general that you work for—how many stars?"

"One."

"And he'll be wanting to add to the collection?"

"In the worst way."

"But I don't work for him, do I?"

"Not directly. You work for a lady named Cheryl, nickname Oz, as in living in the land of."

"And my new boss won't care that I'm showboating around Mexico looking for a kidnapped Mexican-American in a sea of Mexican-Mexicans?"

"She knows you're ex-Agency and she's intimidated."

"About what?"

"Ex-Agency means something to her."

"My first question would be how that could possibly be, but then again, I've been told that there's mystique to it if you've never been on the inside. Unfortunately, I have an intimate knowledge of the ugly side of the craft."

They arrived at the armored black Chevrolet Tahoe that Scooter checked out from the OBI motor pool. Scooter disarmed the alarm and opened a back door for Gary's wheeled travel bag. Gary tossed it in and then opened the passenger door, sitting in the 'shotgun' position.

"Did you pick the ride, Scooter?"

"Full Level A-Ten protection, turbo charged engine—It's the most fortified thing we've got. I thought we might want to drive something like this if we're going out *there*."

Gary lifted his cell phone, punched a pre-programmed number and spoke rapid fire Bahasa.

"What language is that?"

"Indonesian." He dialed another number and his voice became very commanding.

"It's a dialect of Riau. I've been speaking it for years. If we're going to be flathatting round the Mexican hinterland, I think that you should leave this tank in a parking garage at your office. I called in a favor and we'll get a ride that fits in a little better." As Gary spoke, he programmed the Tahoe's navigation system. "Drop me here, pack a bag for a week and take a cab back to this spot," Gary pointed to the navigation system, "where you're driving me now."

Admiration showed in Scooter's eyes. "You really do have your shit wired air-tight, Gary."

Gary didn't quite get it. "I just had things set up for a comfortable stay while I worked here. You know, Scooter, things have been like this my whole life. I fly by the seat of my pants. I try to run defensive, in *Bohica* mode. If I don't, somebody will prang me."

"Bend-over, here-it-comes-again," Scooter translated, absently. One couldn't ever operate with too much situational awareness when the federal, and in particular, the military bureaucracy was involved. "Got to be defensive—absolutely goddamned always."

Scooter dropped Gary in front of the gleaming new high-rise glass and steel apartment in the Santa Fé District, across the street from the Centro Comercial Santa Fé, shopping mall. The choice of location reflected the Ambassador to the Philippines' love for opulence and his profound devotion to the women he entertained. As *the* high-end shopping mall in Mexico City, Centro Comercial Santa Fé, provided a temple of greed where the high priestesses of Gucci, Rolex, Tiffany and Bulgari peddled their wares just a few meters from the Ambassador's special apartment. Gary thought privately that it was a lot of work and expense to go to for a blowjob.

He handed Scooter an access key. "The key will get you up to the penthouse."

The privately keyed elevator took Gary to the thirty-sixth floor of the high-rise condo that overlooked the shopping mall. The Apartment building was one of many surrounding the mall—luxury in the sea of Mexican squalor, constructed with narco-dollars.

As Gary walked around he found that he had the entire top floor, four bedrooms and half a dozen special purpose rooms: a gym, steam room and sauna, library, and large entertaining area. Half a dozen balconies branched off the rooms. The ambassador confided that there were two apartments, this being one of two used to house ladies he had an interest in. Since he reduced the stable of women he kept, as opposed to those he currently slept with, to one, Gary could have it as long as he wanted to use it. Favors were favors and the Ambassador was in payback mode to an old friend.

Three large trunks, sent ahead to the Philippines Embassy, waited inside the master bedroom.

Gary sat on a sofa in the living room and unpacked the carry-on bag he'd brought with him from the States. He pulled a notebook computer from a padded sleeve and plugged a telecom transponder into the USB port. In an instant, he was on-line.

It didn't take long to get the official version of the kidnapping, as reported by the press. They'd interviewed the distraught wife, loyal and caring neighbors and co-workers. He took notes on a ruled pad.

(1) José Melendez, Assistant United States Attorney, kidnapped from a medical clinic parking last (Sun.) night.

(2) Drug case, five defendants, Sinaloa Federation.

(3) No <u>known</u> corruption involvement. That meant that the victim hadn't gone back on a deal with the bad guys as far as anybody said. (Sometimes corrupt government officials went back on a deal with the crooks and suffered their wrath. This didn't smell like that.)

(4) 24 hours so far.

Gary pulled out the telecom USB from the computer and replaced it with a printer cable. The other end connected to a small travel printer that he pulled from his bag. He slipped in a sheet of paper, hit return on the computer keyboard, and the printer buzzed out a map of Mexico. He assumed 40 mph, at least twenty driving hours. That meant they could easily be eight hundred miles from Corona, California. Maybe they were in Sinaloa, maybe only close, and maybe it was far fetched to think that the Sinaloa Cartel snatched the guy and were taking him to their turf. It made sense to look in Sinaloa first. Even if they only made a pass-through, they could say that they tried to look for one particular needle in a mountain of needles.

Scooter arrived within twenty minutes after the Indonesian Embassy delivered a compact gray 2010 Volkswagen Bora (lightly armored) with diplomatic license plates.

"Damn, Gary, you do know how to live," Scooter said as he made a self-guided tour of the apartment. "I'm fucking impressed! You have your brain housing group firmly attached to your shoulders, my friend."

"It's just largess from an old friend," Gary said. "It's nothing. Just a place to rest my weary bones while I'm in town." He unstrapped and unlocked one of the steamer trunks containing his goods. He lifted the lid to an array of cables and exotic graphite components.

"What is all that?"

Gary smiled, "Once I put it together, it will be a crossbow. I designed it myself."

"Why do you have a crossbow?"

"It's a hobby. I build them, shoot them and find some solace in the historical context that they represent." Gary displayed a long wickedly tipped metal bolt, over a foot long. "They fire silently and they'll drive a two and a half inch tunnel through whatever they hit."

"Don't ever go medieval on me, Gary."

Gary looked lovingly at the projectile and Scooter turned his attention to the opulent penthouse.

As Scooter finished his second tour, he offered, "Ok, I'll buy. I know a place not far from here that burns a mean steak and pours a wicked drink."

"We're going to Sinaloa tonight."

Scooter cocked his head at an angle as if he didn't hear correctly, "Sinaloa if off-limits. It is *Indian country*, as in you'll get beheaded if you go there."

"Yeah, but if the prosecutor from California was handling a Sinaloa Cartel case and if we presume that they snatched him, it makes sense that they'd take him there."

"Sinaloa is a big place. It would be like driving from New York City to Philadelphia looking for a kidnapped guy when we have no idea if he's there and if he is, where he is."

"Your boss wants us to try and find the unfortunate, so we should start somewhere and I can't think of any other place to begin.

"We can't go there without the permission of the Mexican Army and half a dozen other people."

Gary smiled like a sphinx, "Better to ask forgiveness later than to ask permission now. Besides, your boss won't want to stick his neck out like that. When these admin types say that they want you to find the guy, they don't expect you to go and do it. They expect you to sit around, eat a steak, sip a drink and bullshit about it in theory. Finding nothing, you have done your bit for Queen and country—the old college try with no useful results. I had a boss whose philosophy was; do nothing. If you do anything, it will be assumed that you could have done something."

"That's what I had in mind," Scooter said. He opened a briefcase and displayed a Heckler & Koch MP-5K sub-machinegun. "But I brought this just in case."

"We can't go to Sinaloa, fangs-out. If we're smart we won't need a machinegun."

"But it doesn't hurt to have one."

Gary reflected on his diplomatic immunity in a nation where the penalty for possession of a machinegun is life in prison. "I guess you can bring it along, but don't use it on anyone."

Scooter smiled broadly and taunted, "Don't tell me you're too old to fight, Gary."

"I'm definitely *not* too old to fight, but I *am* too old to lose a fight. And in Sinaloa, we'll be out-gunned no matter how much hardware you bring."

"What will we do if we find Melendez?"

"I doubt that we'll find him. If we do, we can worry about that then." Gary summarized and then lifted his still-packed carryon bag, "Ready to go?"

7

Twelve hours later

Mike Sirrine handed Oz the cable that he proposed to send out as soon as General Barton approved it. "Congratulations are in order! The State Department found the kidnapped US Attorney. Not an MQ-1 Predator. Not an MQ-9 Reaper. Good old gumshoe investigation and observation saved the day. It's only unfortunate that they were too late to save the lawyer, but we can't have everything."

Oz, coffee cup in hand, basked in the glow of political triumph as she made the rounds on all three floors, stopping at every office to crow how her guy, Granger, found the dead man. General Barton reminded her that Scooter Olsen had been with her new guy and it was a group victory. At the same time, he also reminded Oz that the cable would go out under his signature.

She cornered Mike Sirrine in her office. "Mike, I really owe you big on this. You're going to need to find a way for me to repay you. It was brilliant to bring Granger down here to help us out."

Sirrine smiled broadly and she gave him a hug that lasted about three beats too long.

"Maybe dinner tonight, on me?"

"Ok," Sirrine conceded, "but shouldn't we send somebody other than Gary out there to deal with the Consul General from Guadalajara and the Mexican Army? I could go with one of the FBI legats."

"Ejército Mexicano hasn't called us in and according to protocols, they need to do that explicitly. OBI isn't the State Department and there is scrutiny when we do anything."

"We found the corpse."

"And we're taking credit for that back in Washington, but it doesn't rule out having our own private little celebration here. You and I can get to know each other better tonight. Granger and Scooter Olsen seem to have things well in hand in Sinaloa."

Sirrine changed the subject because Oz sounded as if she intended to rape him. "What's the reaction from Washington going to be when they find out that the cartel hung him from a shitty, tagged up overpass in Los Mochis?"

"The President will have to say something. I expect he might even take some of his talking points from my cable." Oz showed Sirrine The cable that he had authored. It carried her name and that of General Barton. She'd already forgotten that he had a small role in the creation of what she clearly considered to be her own masterpiece.

Los Mochis- Navojoa Highway (National Highway 15)
At the El Fuerte Overpass
Los Mochis, Sinaloa, Mexico

Soldiers from Grupos Anfibios de Fuerzas Especiales, the Mexican Amphibious Special Forces Group, which patrolled the coastal area of Sinaloa State and Los Mochis in particular, lounged around the graffiti painted footbridge that spanned both the highway and a railway while they waited for permission to take down the hanging corpse.

Melendez's neck had stretched to about double its normal length while they waited. The Mexican Amphibious Special Forces Group had the decency to throw a blanket over the hanging body.

A freight train tore through while they waited, buffeting the hanging body and causing it to swing. Scooter, veteran of large and small wars and insurgencies thought he was about to be sick as a long pink mucus stringer grew and flowed from under the covered body to the ground, pooling below its feet.

Scooter averted his gaze from the body, looking into the deserted neighborhood on one side of the highway with its burnt out cars, and human detritus. Sheepishly, he turned and walked back to the car where Granger stood, sipping tepid coffee and eating a burrito.

"Where did the chow come from?"

Gary whistled to a soldier. "Uno mas, por favor, Cabo Garcia!"

Scooter saw a corporal turn and bring another burrito. Scooter thanked him in Spanish and then asked Gary, "What's in 'em?"

"Don't ask," Gary advised sagely, "just eat. They're good."

48

There were several coffee rings on the hood of the Volkswagen before an entourage of American and Mexican officials finally arrived hours later and agreed that the human remains of José Melendez could be photographed in place, pulled down, remanded to the custody of the US Government. Official transportation of the body had been arranged to the decedent's home in California.

"I bet they pump the poor bastard full of formaldehyde and lay him out on the Capitol Rotunda," Scooter said.

"There will be some outrage, but the President doesn't want this to impact trade or his amnesty initiative," Gary replied, more in tune with the moods of Washington than his pal Scooter. "There are thirty-million illegal Mexican nationals in the US. If they become legal, that's thirty million potential Democratic voters. He won't screw up that sort of coup for the sake of an Assistant US Attorney in California."

"So you don't think they'll do anything?"

"The US is involved in fighting homicidal maniacs in the Asian Subcontinent at the moment. We aren't able to fully concentrate on more than one thing—or one homicidal maniac at a time."

"What if this isn't the last one? What if they kidnap more of us?"

Gary looked at a bed sheet that had hung from the overpass. Crudely drawn in a black marker it read that there would be revenge for anyone who stood in the way of the Sinaloa Federation. He read it verbatim to Mike Sirrine when he spoke to him on the satellite phone earlier.

Sirrine said they were heroes. Gary said that he and Scooter were driving down Highway 15 and saw a body hanging from a plastic rope tied to the overpass railing. They stopped, read the message on the sheet and since it mentioned the US Attorney by name, they figured that the dead body belonged to the missing man. While they may have been lucky, they hardly qualified as sleuths.

"All the greater accomplishment because you're not real detectives!" Sirrine heaped praises on him until Gary hung up the phone and turned it off.

The US Consul General arrived in an armored Chevrolet Tahoe, accompanied by a Diplomatic Security Service detail from the Embassy in Mexico City. She walked over to where Scooter and Gary stood, next to their Volkswagen drinking the last of the coffee from their thermos. Gary wondered if OBI told her that their people found the dead man officially. As soon as the Consul opened her mouth, he learned that she wasn't in the loop.

Gary could tell that she had a very high drift factor—and seemed to be less than on her game. Heavy make-up caked on her deep black skin, her hair was buzz-cut short and she wore what Gary had come to think of as men's clothing: a preppy button down shirt, gray slacks and penny loafers. "I'm Debora Pearce, the American Consul General in Guadalajara." They all shook hands. "The Mexican Army said that you discovered the body of my poor unfortunate countryman."

"Yes," Gary said, "we were driving down the highway and there he was. Next to him they hung a sheet with a message on it."

Pearce asked, "Can I have your names?"

"I'm Emmanuel Romano," Gary said. "And this is my American cousin, Samuel Spade, of the Wisconsin Spades."

"Is that a racial comment?"

"Huh?"

"What you just said?"

"About what?"

"Spades."

Gary spoke to one of the diplomatic security people who looked to be a Filipino. Gary spoke Tagalog without accent. The DSS Agent replied in passable Filipino.

Pearce looked confused and the DSS Agent said that Gary/Emmanuel Romano didn't speak English well, but he tried to communicate as best he could. If it would help, he'd speak Filipino and the agent could translate for him.

"You don't look Filipino, Mr. Romano," Debra Pearce said flatly and without emotion.

Gary replied in English, "Is that a racial comment?" His eyes narrowed in suspicious outrage while he laughed inside.

Scooter snorted his coffee and began a coughing fit.

Pearce, unhappy and completely unfamiliar with Dashiell Hammett's character from *The Maltese Falcon*, took down their names. The DSS Agents got the joke and enjoyed it without telegraphing their understanding to Consul General Pearce.

Gary gave her a bogus telephone number in case somebody from the US State Department needed to speak with him further. Then they both got in the loaned Volkswagen and Scooter drove them back toward the loaned apartment in Mexico City.

As they drove south toward Culiacan, Scooter asked, "Don't you think that it's odd that the Consul didn't ask what we were doing driving down the highway in Los Mochis?"

"She works for the State Department."

"What does that have to do with anything? What we were doing is damned suspicious. How many Americans drive through that part of Sinaloa."

"She's a career Foreign Service Officer, and the last thing she wants is to make waves. She'll file a report on the heels of the one that the Office of Bilateral whatever sends out. Everybody will be slapping each other on the back because we found the guy's body. DEA will be unhappy because their brass will have expected their people to have made the find, but otherwise, there will be general jubilation.

"She'll mention that the body was found by a Filipino national named Emmanuel Romano and his sidekick, Sam Spade. That won't square up. She'll look like an idiot. This thing will go all the way to SecState."

Gary smiled a Mona Lisa smile.

"But what does it all mean? Really mean? The kidnapping, the hanging, the message?"

Gary popped the top on an energy drink so he could stay awake. Before he downed it, he told Scooter, "I have no idea—but it means something to somebody."

Cervecería de Oro
Hacienda de Tlaquepaque District
Guadalajara, Jalisco, Mexico

(El León) Iglesias-Aznar and his entourage reached Guadalajara, in mid-afternoon with time to have a drink and to lay-up for the rest of the day. Lingering in Sinaloa, deep inside enemy territory, didn't make any sense to them, so they pushed on to Guadalajara in Jalisco

State. Even though the Federation exercised some control in Jalisco, it was not an area of total control the way Sinaloa had become.

As they all walked into the bar, El León took El Indio aside. "You have the rifles here in town?"

"Yes, two Barrett Model 82A1A rifles in fifty caliber. The scopes are Schmitt and Bender Marksman scopes, the very finest in the world. I left them in the shrine room at Marta's house."

"And the ammunition we discussed?"

"The Raufoss rounds, yes. I'll show them to you tonight."

"But first a drink?"

El Indio nodded his head. It had been a long and successful day and he needed a drink.

They hid in plain site in the dive bar owned by a tall, plump, prune-faced narco captain with badly dyed hair and green contact lenses, who went by the moniker, El Machito. They doubted that he'd be present in the bar. If he showed up while they were having a drink, they planned to kill him.

An hour after arriving, and drinking, they left in the stolen Toyota and the van, driving east with El León and El Indio in the lead. Forty-five minutes later they arrived at Tepatitlán de Morelos, a small town on (Highway) Carretera Federal 80. El León's fifty-one year old cousin, Marta, kept a safe house for him in a rabbit warren of homes in the Cerrito de La Cruz district.

The garage held both the van and the stolen Toyota, now fitted with 'clean' Jalisco State license plates.

Outside, the house looked remarkably like the other homes in the area: faded plaster construction, peeling paint on wood framing and a wall surrounding the house tagged with graffiti and topped with broken glass set in concrete. Inside, a large basement had been excavated under the house and two adjacent homes to provide an expansive suite.

As soon as Julio Belon, the van owner, walked into the home, El Indio pulled a strong nylon cord from his trousers pocket and looped it over the driver's head, pulling the ligature tight around his neck. The two brothers, los Güeros Diablo, Pablo and Francisco held him while El Indio finished him. The doctor looked on, concerned, as Julio kicked and bucked, eyes bulging in terror.

The doctor from Chihuahua backed toward the wall, looking for a way out as El León took in the scene.

"Don't worry, doctor," El León said comfortingly, "Julio Belon does not worship Señora de las Sombras, so he had to die. His oath of life and death to me, while well intentioned, holds no weight."

Turning to the two brothers, he said, "Pablo, take his head and Francisco, his heels, and carry him into the shrine room. Follow me."

Señora de las Sombras, a human skeleton wearing a white wedding dress and a golden crown, stood in the corner of a high ceilinged chapel dedicated to the Santa Muerte. "Put the carcass there in front of the altar," El León directed.

El Indio helped arrange the body in a posture pleasing to la Señora. The brothers stood back and let El Indio make the final adjustments. Julio released his bowels in death, and though the stench bothered the brothers, there was nothing that could be done.

"Doctor Hernandez, would you like to conduct the service and the dedication of this sacrifice to the blessed saint?" El León asked sincerely, showing deference and humility that the doctor had not seen coming from El León in the brief span of their acquaintance.

The doctor took a small atomizer of perfume and sprayed it on the skeleton in the white wedding dress, as the other adherents to the faith looked on reverently. Then he poured a shot of Herradura Seleccion Suprema tequila into each of seven small, thick glasses, for Señora de las Sombras, the dead body of Juilio Belon, the two brothers, El Indio, El León and his cousin, Marta.

They each took a glass and drank them together.

"The Holy Death will be there for us when we are in need of a special favor as we sacrifice this man for her."

Doctor Hernandez lighted a tall candle with an embossed skeleton on the side.

He took a white cloth embroidered with the image of Señora de las Sombras, laid it on the altar and smoothed it. Then he took a clay incenser and lighted a stick of incense.

Lifting three small images of Señora de las Sombras in three colors, from the altar, he placed them in a triangular shape around the clay incenser. White at the head of the triangle, black at her right, red at her left.

"White Lady, Black Lady! We come before you to ask, to implore that you make your strength, power and your omnipresence against those who intend to destroy us. My Lady, I ask you to be our shield and our defender against everyone who sets their hand against us, that you, our protector, sever all obstacles that intervene, open doors that have closed before us and show us the right path. My Lady, there is nothing bad that you cannot conquer, or that you can't double it under your will. To you we give ourselves and await your kindness. Amen."

El León turned to the two long Barrett rifles, propped in a corner of the room and lifted one, surprised at its weight. "It's heavy."

"About fourteen kilograms," El Indio said. "They will fire an aimed shot about two thousand meters. The bullet itself can travel the length of seventy soccer fields laid end to end."

El Indio picked up a large cartridge from a box. "This is the Raufoss bullet. It's identified by the green paint over silver on its tip. It's an armor piercing, incendiary, high explosive round."

"This will do the job. Place them on the altar that Señora de las Sombras, our holy death, will bless their flight when that day comes."

El Indio shuddered, but he lifted the box of fifty caliber Browning machine gun cartridges and placed it on the altar.

"Do you have a flower, Marta, to seal our offering and close our service?"

Marta left, returning quickly with a red rose. She handed it to El León and he in turn, placed it on the altar on top of the ammunition.

They all crossed themselves in the Catholic fashion. The sacrifice complete, the service ended, the body of Julio Belon could be disposed of.

"What do you suggest we do with the sacrifice, Marta?"

"We can bury him here in the basement in the section where there is a dirt floor. I'll show you where. It's rather full down there so we have to be careful where we dig these days. Give me a moment. I need to find a place where the earth has not been disturbed yet."

8

Restaurante Elegance
Near the Basilica
Guadalajara, Jalisco, Mexico

El Tigre Grande, El Chapitô and El Ingeniero were concerned that they might not leave the gaudy banquet room behind the restaurant where the meeting took place around a large square table. In any cartel there was one person who called the shots both literally and figuratively. In Sinaloa, Ruben (El Macho) Gonzales claimed the title and ruled as the undisputed emperor of both the cartel and the state. He arrived in Jalisco to speak to his men there eye to eye, to lens them and scrutinize their reactions. Somebody kidnapped a US Attorney and then murdered him on Ruben Gonzales' doorstep, throwing the blame on him.

"We have discussed this many times," Ruben growled, "and I will not tolerate anyone who antagonizes the Norte Americanos needlessly. Today they leave us alone, sending token efforts against us to satisfy the masses. If we kidnap their leaders and kill them, they will no longer be tolerant and *that is bad for business.*"

El Tigre Grande, El Chapitô and El Ingeniero swallowed collectively. Ruben Gonzales did not tolerate anything that he judged as being bad for business. It didn't take Ruben more than a few minutes to satisfy himself that none of the three captains he looked at over his hooked nose were responsible for the act. They weren't sure what he was talking about, even though they put up a good front.

"If you find out who kidnapped and killed this American lawyer, I'll pay two million dollars."

El Ingeniero glanced slyly at his friends.

"Payment on proof. I don't want you to shoot someone, accuse the corpse and bring them to me for payment!"

The sly glance vanished.

55

"And while we speak about things that are bad for business, I have heard that the turd nephew of Rey del Cielo took delivery of one ton of Colombian from Cartel Norte Valle, stored it somewhere in Guadalajara and then moved it north across the border into Texas. The pimp did it without paying me tax," Ruben ranted. "Our authority is flaunted and if it is not dealt with swiftly and certainly, others will get the idea that they can sell without paying tax."

The three captains at the table looked solicitous and sorrowful as the boss required.

"That human lice, Santiago Iglesias-Aznar stored his load here in Guadalajara, El Ingeniero, and you didn't make an effort to collect it."

El Ingeniero hung his head, cursing the punk nephew of the King of the Sky.

"Therefore, you can pay the tax yourself, from your own wallet, or you can bring me that bastard's head."

He dealt with the numbers every single day and the tax of 20% or two million dollars was not a sum he'd give up willingly if there was any alternative.

"I'll deliver his head on a plate with his balls in his mouth," El Ingeniero said, pouring a shot of tequila and knocking it back forcefully as a type of vow.

"Our contact from Cartel Norte Valle said that the bastard has ordered another four thousand kilos and he plans to take delivery and ship it north in two months. That leads me to wonder who is distributing it for him in the States? When his uncle, who we all loved, left us, we absorbed dear uncle's wholesalers." He crossed himself in honor of the King of the Sky. "They've been ours ever since. So where does this pubescent punk come up with the means to distribute almost nine thousand pounds of product?"

El Tigre Grande, the oldest of the captains present at the meeting, said, "He's not a child anymore. We all remember him that way, but he's grown up and is as ambitious as Lucifer. I have heard that El Indio is on his payroll these days. I knew him back when we both worked for the Cubans. We called him El Loco Selva back then. He is a man of many talents."

Ruben Gonzales poured a glass of tequila, lifted it to El Ingeniero, and said, "I hope you have more talents than El Indio and his new master, Santiago Iglesias-Aznar.

9

Office of the Secretary of State
Washington, D. C.

In his office, on the top floor of the Eisenhower Executive Office Building, just west of the White House, the Secretary had been joined by the Deputy Secretary of State, the Director of US Foreign Assistance, the Undersecretary for Political Affairs and the Assistant Secretary for International Narcotics and Law Enforcement.

Nathan Wasliewski had been Secretary of State for just over a year and there had been crisis after crisis in the Administration, but he couldn't recall a single act that outraged him as much as the brazen kidnapping and murder of Assistant United States Attorney José Melendez. José graduated a year ahead of him from Yale Law and he had introduced him to Bethany Woods, the woman who became his wife and mother of his children.

He tossed a photo of José Melendez on the conference table. "I have the director of the FBI and the Assistant Director-in-Charge from Los Angeles waiting in the other room and when I'm done, they're going to come in here and bullshit us about how much they've been doing on the case."

He looked pointedly at Jane Hillary, Assistant Secretary of State for Narcotics and Law Enforcement. "Well done Jane, your people found him, but they were a bit too late." The Secretary looked down at an open file. "Gary Granger, one of our contract people, and Chief Warrant Officer Scott Olsen deserve a mountain of credit. The cable says that General Barton and Cheryl Osborne-Clarridge directed them to find Mr. Melendez and without further instruction, they went to the heart of darkness and found—José, hanging by the neck from a freeway overpass."

The Secretary's eyes became moist. "This is a depraved and vicious act and when we add it to so many others perpetrated by

58

these drug gangs, it rises to the level of being intolerable. I have a meeting with the President on the matter tonight after dinner. He's going to ask me for options, precedents and recommendations. I'll promise something within forty-eight hours. That means each of you have forty hours to provide me with a set of recommendations. Don't collaborate with each other. Don't cheat off each other's efforts. I know that you instinctively think this is a pissing contest and it's not. I want the widest and most creative set of options possible. I'll distill them, add my own thoughts and will take it to the President."

He looked around the table. They all looked very uncomfortable.

"Now let's bring in Director Sanz and his protégé, Associate Director Grey." The Secretary punched a button on the telephone at his left, bent toward it and said, "Send in the FBI please."

While they waited, he rang for the mess steward to refresh the coffee, directing him to pour two cups for the FBI.

Kyle Sanz and Chaia Grey sat in the two remaining chairs at the table. They brought files with them, presumably briefing aids for the State Department people present.

"Before you go through a dog and pony show and insult my intelligence, do you have any idea who actually kidnapped José Melendez from Corona, California and murdered him in Mexico?"

Kyle Sanz shrugged to Chaia Grey, who spoke, "We suspect that it was ordered by Ruben Gonzales, head of the Sinaloa Federation, but we have no idea who actually carried it out."

"Do we have telephone intercepts from Mexico, any intelligence that directly ties Gonzales to anything?"

"I've been in contact with the National Security Agency. They're checking but, as of now, we don't have anything."

Secretary Wasliewski stood and directed his comments to his executive staff. "I don't want your recommendations to include what is substantially a witch hunt. Likely as it is that this drug kingpin murdered my friend and a representative of this government. We operate on proof, not conjecture. I'll leave you to consult with Kyle and Ms. Grey, whose people are handling the investigation."

As an afterthought, he added, "And write up Granger and Olsen for some sort of appropriate award."

Harried and sleep deprived, Dana Hunter, Secretary of Homeland

Security walked into the meeting, very late and very angry, followed by six staffers. She carried over a hundred extra pounds on her short body and had the reputation for being belligerent. Nathan Wasliewski didn't care whether she was a bitch or not as she had not been either invited or needed at the meeting. The President blamed her and it looked as if she had just come from an ass chewing. The FBI Director and his cohort groveled to her and they made nice with her staff of apple polishers.

Nathan didn't want to pass pleasantries. He stood, offering Secretary Hunter his chair. "I've given my staff marching orders, Dana. Maybe your people can supply them with raw data or something. I need to talk to the President." He turned and left them abruptly and unceremoniously. It bordered on being impolite—unless he did indeed have to make an urgent phone call to the Oval Office.

The Secretary of State walked back to his office and closed the door. Jane Hillary would brief him on what everyone discussed in his absence and would cut out all the superfluous bullshit when she presented him with the bare bones.

Dana Hunter had been a lodestone for anti-administration criticism. First, her office issued a report recommending that all military veterans and retired police officers be put on a watch list as potential domestic terrorists, and later she mismanaged border security to epic proportions that may have led to José Melendez's death. Sitting with her in a meeting would be interpreted by some as approving of whatever harebrain scheme she came up with. He put a Winslow pipe in his mouth and sucked on the stem while he thought. He slipped on his reading glasses, opened a leather bound journal on his desk and consulted a telephone list. Tapping out the keys, he wondered if he was making a mistake by calling Jim Warren, the Deputy Director (Operations) of the Central Intelligence Agency on his personal line. Protocol called for a call to the Director who would filter any request down to whoever the Director wanted to give the task to. Nathan Wasliewski didn't want to do that, so he didn't.

Warren picked up on the third ring and went secure immediately. The caller, SecState, would appear on the screen as the telephones synchronized and created a secure link.

60

"Jim, this is Nathan Wasliewski, do you recognize my voice?"

"Yes, Mr. Secretary, and I confirm that your key is in the STU."

"I need a favor, off the books."

Warren paused. Nathan Wasliewski made his career by paying back favors. When Nathan asked for anything in Washington, he did so with the certain understanding that reciprocation would be forthcoming in the future. He'd built a reputation on that foundation.

"I'm listening," Warren said cautiously.

"It's about Mexico, that situation where one of those kingpins down there kidnapped and executed that US Attorney prosecuting a case against their friends."

"My condolences to Mrs. Melendez," Warren said flatly. "I know you and her husband were close."

"I went to school with both of them." Wazliewski chewed on his pipe stem. "Do you think this is a trend?"

"Nothing indicates that. Organized crime retaliates from time to time against a prosecutor."

"Is there anyone you can send to ferret out whether Melendez was dirty or why they chose him? This isn't a pattern we've seen but maybe they're changing their game."

"I'll do what I can. Usually that's something that the FBI does."

"I know. They'll tell me what they tell me and you can tell me what you found out. I want two opinions on this one. Don't ask me how I know, but I've been around this town a long time and I smell trouble in Mexico. If you or your people find anything, let me know personally and then you can report your findings officially through channels to your sister agencies. As I said, he was a friend of mine from law school. I'd consider this a big favor."

"Will do, Mr. Secretary."

Secretary Nathan Wasliewski tapped the button that ended the call and broke the security link.

Jim Warren thought about it for all of five minutes and then called Track Ryder. Ryder didn't answer so he left a coded, 'call me back' message with a phrase he'd set up with Track earlier. He'd sent Track to Mexico to arrange for the rendition of General Brigadier

Jorge Villanueva Sanchez a senior Mexican army officer who ordered the death of a CIA officer who had been operating under official cover in Tapachula. The murder had been investigated jointly by the Agency, FBI and DEA and the resulting proof rose to the level of being beyond any doubt at all. General Villanueva boasted his deeds. The CIA station had given the general the cryptonym DMGATOR.

The Mexicans balked at extraditing the murderer because of his army rank, but President Hinajosa hinted that if the general ended up in the US on vacation, they had no problem with him being held to answer. Warren personally sent Track to arrange the details of the kidnapping for DMGATOR (Villanueva) sanctioned by a Presidential Finding. Because of the public disclosures of extraordinary renditions of terrorists, Warren oversaw all current programs of that sort for the sake of security and management.

Track spent three weeks in-country and then outlined a plan for Jim Warren in which DMGATOR would take an involuntary trip to the Dominican Republic. Once there, they'd take notice of the US warrant for his arrest and remand him to US authorities. The general could sputter and complain all he wanted. He'd end up in a cell next to General Manuel Noriega, the Panamanian President who was prosecuted the same way.

Now, Warren reasoned, the general's trip to the US could wait until after they did what they had to do regarding the abduction of the US Attorney. Track Ryder was the only man they had in Mexico who might be able to get to the bottom of the matter quietly and quickly.

Ruben (El Macho) Gonzales and eleven of his closest lieutenants and advisors had recently been added to the Executive Intercept Transcript Summary that the National Security Agency distributed to the National Security Council and the CIA. Warren looked at the summary page for Gonzales with dismay and a little concern. There were no intercepts to be transcribed. That meant that El Macho and his inner circle used telephones that the NSA had not yet identified, or that he'd found another means of command and control over his narcotics empire.

So far, GOLFCART, the rotating codename for the Agency's all-knowing, all-seeing electronic monitoring program fell short of expectations where El Macho was concerned.

10

Sheraton Hotel
Av. Juarez 70
06010 Mexico City, DF, Mexico

Gary met Mike Sirrine in the lobby of the Sheraton in the Reforma and they had breakfast at The Cardinal Restaurant, inside the hotel.

Gary ordered coffee, Mike selected grapefruit juice.

"You're a hero," Mike said.

"If that's true it means that I'm about to be fucked. I worked hard at not being a hero for a long time because I've seen how they're treated. The CIA eats its own heroes with disturbing regularity."

"The last time I heard you talking like that, you were drunk."

"Drunken wisdom is still wisdom," Gary defended.

Mike smiled, "Being a hero is not so bad, you might even get laid behind it."

Gary fired a missile mischievously; "I hear that a lady named Oz, who we both apparently work for has it bad for you, brother. You are the hero in *her eyes.*"

"How did you—Scooter Olsen. He's been talking."

"Cheryl Osborne-Clarridge, a lawyer, highly placed, old Georgetown family, only married once before—annulled from what I hear. She'd be the right woman on your arm as you go for admiral."

The waiter hovered. Gary ordered machaca, Mike picked a frittata made with egg whites.

"She's on me like a cheap suit," Mike Sirrine said miserably.

"Give in."

"There's a fine line between cuddling and holding someone down so they can't get away. Oz doesn't get it."

Gary laughed. He liked the line about holding someone down and filed it away for future use. "Maybe the General can assign you somewhere far from her reach?"

"It's possible," Sirrine said, and sipped his grapefruit juice thoughtfully.

"A bird told me that Track Ryder is in-country."

Sirrine didn't recognize the name. "Should that mean something to me?"

"Is he working for OBI," Gary asked?

"No, I know everyone on the roster."

Gary pursed his lips. "I thought he might be seconded over here at OBI because he's *not* working for the CIA Station. I had drinks with the Chief last night at midnight."

"Don't you ever sleep, Gary?"

"I sleep, but I don't spend four hours a day working out in the gym so I get more done than you do." Gary jabbed playfully. "Isn't that why I'm here? I thought you brought me down here to work hard and make the State Department look good."

"I work out to keep in shape. And I'm not in the gym four hours a day." Mike knew that he lied to Gary but he went with the defense.

"It works when you're on the hunt for women and love. You need to stay in shape. BUT behind every successful man is his woman. Behind the fall of a successful man is usually another woman. Which reminds me, how's that married lady with the angry husband?"

"She's given birth twice since I left Mexico."

"Either one of them yours?"

"She named the oldest one Miguel. I don't know what she calls the younger one," Mike confided.

"Ah, that's sweet. Does he look like you?"

Mike nodded, 'yes,' with a hint of pride. "He's a good looking boy."

The food arrived and Gary seemed inclined to continue to probe. He had an annoyingly inquisitive streak that Mike forgot about in the intervening years. Mike shifted the conversation back, "So who is Track Ryder?"

"Who?"

"The guy you just asked me about. The one that's not on our payroll or on the roster for the Station."

"Hmm," Gary asked the waiter in rapid, fluent Spanish if they'd bring him a side order of blue corn tortillas.

"That Spanish sounds close to perfect to me," Sirrine said. "As I recall your Spanish was so rusty that you barely passed the test at level 3 when you were here last time."

"I didn't want to be called in to translate all the time. If I can barely get by ordering from a menu they cut me slack and don't give me mope work. If you'll recall, I wasn't all that popular when I was here before."

"You saved my ass."

"That was but one thing they held against me."

Lima Sierra 2
The Yucatan Peninsula, Mexico

Track Ryder cooled his heels for another evening, drinking beer and playing penny ante poker with Fish and two of the retired cops who protected Lima Sierra 2. He'd lost forty-six cents and turned in for the night when Fish started weeping as Willie Nelson sang, *An Angel Flying Too Close to the Ground*, over an i-Pod hooked up to a speaker.

Morning came a little later than was his custom. He looked at his watch face and slid out of the uncomfortable bed, staggering to the shower and turning on the hot faucet.

Scalded, showered and dressed, he walked out of the containerized housing unit wearing a clean short sleeve shirt, levis and the same Oakley special warfare boots as he'd worn for the past couple of weeks. Track turned right toward the galley. He could have followed his nose if he didn't know where it was. "I feel like Pavlov's dog," he told himself as he began to salivate.

Arturo, the ground crew gaffer was the only one eating breakfast, so Track asked him, "Mind if I join you?"

"I don't mind, sir. You're welcome."

The galley steward filled a mug with bitter Mexican hot chocolate and handed it to him. A moment later, he also brought him a glass of chilled orange.

"Today we're serving bacon, sausage, egg and pepper burritos," the steward said.

"Can I have two?"

"Yes." The steward said.

"You are the mystery man," Arturo said, matter-of-factly.

"I'd expect that there are a lot of mystery men who pass through here."

Arturo shrugged, "No, most of them are self-important bureaucrats who convince themselves that what they are doing will make a difference."

"But not me."

"No, not you. I've seen it the eyes of others. I was a narco when I was young. You have the same look in your eyes as they do."

Track ignored Arturo's comparison. "You were a trafficker before you found God?"

"Yes, I learned that you don't have to live a life of violence."

"Yet you work here, where violence will one day be used against those who are violent?"

"The cycle must be broken if Mexico is to survive. In my country the young are recruited with the lure of quick money, women and power. As they enter the dark world of the narcos, they are sadistically traumatized to become sadistic themselves. They feel helpless and those feelings translate into the pain they inflict on others as they create more narcos. Sometimes an abused child will go on to be an abuser as he grows into an adult?"

"And you think God is the answer."

The steward brought Track his breakfast and he took a large bite of his first burrito.

"There is no other answer. The narcos all worship Señora de las Sombras, the Holy Death. It is Satan, the serpent who tempted our first parents. God will work through those who oppose the great deceiver."

"Those are deep concepts," Track observed. "You think that God will triumph?"

"Ultimately yes, but his kingdom is not of this world. The world we live in is the Devil's dominion."

"No shit," Track said, as he took another bite of the burrito. "But this is a very tasty breakfast, so there is good in the world."

Arturo continued, serious as a heart attack, "Light eclipses darkness, but somebody has to light the candle."

"And that's why you're here with your flock?"

"That's why we are here. We are doing very little, however we're doing the right thing as best we can. Why are you here, mystery man?"

"Everyone has to be somewhere."

Arturo looked at him with compassion and Track decided to share a bit of himself without giving up too much. "At first I became who I am to deal with anxiety and dread. When I was a kid, I had panic attacks. To cope, I became tougher and harder than anyone else around me. It led to a career that some might consider to be somewhat like that of a narco."

"But you fight for a good cause," Arturo countered.

"One would hope, but certainly not always. I serve the government but government is not inherently moral."

"Then how do you live with yourself?"

Track thought, ate, drained his juice glass, "I don't betray my fundamental values. If I didn't have them, I wouldn't be me, would I? That's how I survive and remain sane—providing I'm not crazy. How would you really know?"

He started on his second burrito when Fish walked into the galley.

"I've been looking all over for you," Fish said.

"I'm here talking with Arturo."

"Hi Arturo," Fish said as an afterthought. "We can leave here whenever you're ready."

Track nodded to Arturo. "Nice to meet you." He grabbed his burrito, wrapped it in a napkin, polished off the last of the hot chocolate and said, "Kick the tires, light the fires and I'll get my stuff."

Arturo waved as Track walked out the door, followed by Fish.

Fish walked toward the runway and Track went to grab his backpack.

Fish had both engines running and warm by the time he saw Track walk clear of the buildings, talking animatedly on a satellite telephone and pacing. Track hung up, dialed another number from memory, talked for a few moments and then wrote something down. He called another number and talked for a few minutes. Fish just began to consider shutting the aircraft down when Track turned toward him and gave him a thumbs-up.

Track slid into the co-pilot's chair and adjusted the headset.

"Everything ok," Fish asked?

"Change of plans."

11

Office of Bilateral Implementation (OBI)
Mexico City, District Federal, Mexico

"What's the government going to do about this kidnapping," Scooter Olsen asked General Barton?

"I don't think they're going to do a damned thing. I've had two or three pencil pushers from Washington call me this morning asking me what I thought we should do. Neither State, Homeland Security or the FBI really has a handle on any part of this."

Scooter waited to see what the general suggested. Reading his mind, Barton told him, "If I tell those piranhas anything, they'll end up calling it Barton's plan and when it fails, I'll be on the spit. I told them we were studying the landscape and would get back to them. Let the political hacks find another scapegoat."

The truth may have been a bit harsher because Barton didn't know what to do. The US government pumped money to the Mexican Army through a fire hose and the Mexicans seemed unable to do much to curb the cartels beyond the odd high profile arrest or retribution killing.

"T. E. Lawrence said of the Arabs in the First World War, 'Do not try to do too much with your own hands. Better the Arabs do it tolerably than that you do it perfectly. It is their war, and you are to help them, not to win it for them.' If it was me, I'd quote Lawrence to the politicians and leave it at that," Scooter advised.

"Sage counsel, Scooter."

"We shouldn't reinvent the wheel, but we can learn from the past."

"The news media is throwing this kidnap-murder around this week, but it will die off and everyone will forget it in a month. Mrs. José Melendez will receive a hardy pension with perks, her children will be the beneficiaries of scholarships, she'll go on to find new love and the body of her husband will molder in the grave." General Barton looked hard at Scooter.

On the drive back from Sinaloa, Gary quoted Lawrence of Arabia to Scooter and it struck a cord. Now he'd reused it with some effect with the General. He expected Barton to pass the wisdom up the chain of command.

As Gary saw it, America sat on Mexico's northern border and stirring up a hornet's nest further would only create more of a political problem than the country had on their hands at the moment. He'd predicted that the FBI would launch an investigation, find what they found and it wouldn't go any further than that. At the same time, he lamented that being famous was like tying a can to your tail that clanked and made people notice who you were. Scooter noted that for a man who made a career of not drawing notice to himself, the present situation would be uncomfortable.

"If you insist on giving Granger an award, he'll quit."

Barton sat up in his chair and looked like a bull that had just been hit in the head by a baseball bat and stunned slightly. "He'll quit?"

"That's what he said."

"It would be an insult to my command," Barton blustered, realizing that Granger, a man he'd never met, who pulled a full retirement might not need the job. How could anyone deal with a man who didn't bask in the limelight accorded by a grateful government? Moreover, how could he *trust* such a man?

"He would rather not have any kudos awarded to him, sir."

If Granger didn't accept the award, it might jeopardize Barton's own proposed award, the State Department's award of Meritorious Honor, for sending Scooter and the sheep-dipped spy, Gary Granger, out to find the kidnapped lawyer.

Upon authorization, members of the U.S. military may wear the medal and ribbon in the appropriate order of precedence as a U.S. non-military personal decoration. Barton, a notorious medal hunter planned to carve another notch on his career and add to the ladder of colored ribbons he wore on his uniform. He didn't share his specific feelings with Scooter.

"There's glory in this for all of us. José Melendez went to law school with the Secretary of State. They're old friends—and he's ecstatic that I recovered and repatriated José's remains."

Scooter noted the slip and that Barton had taken full credit for the find. Scooter didn't care. That's what general officers and people intent on wearing stars did. That seemed to be the pay-back for all the brown-nosing.

Barton picked up a piece of paper from his desk. "This is a cable from Nathan himself. You and Granger will be receiving the State Department Award for Heroism."

He read from the citation, "In recognition of courage and outstanding performance under extraordinarily difficult and dangerous circumstances, Gary Granger did, without considerations for his own safety, attempt the rescue of a kidnapped person in the State of Sinaloa, Mexico from the Sinaloa Federation Narcotics Cartel." The general looked up. "Yours reads the same. This is one of the highest awards that the Secretary of State can bestow. From what I've learned, nominations are usually handled through channels but the Secretary pushed this through personally so it will happen, and you'd better get that bastard Granger on the bus. Am I being too subtle, Scooter?"

"Clear, sir."

"Where is he, Scooter?"

"Sir?"

"Where is Granger? He's supposed to report here for duty."

"I haven't seen him since he dropped me off, when we returned, sir," Scooter lied with a straight face. He was in the process of moving into the penthouse apartment with Gary Granger. He correctly thought that the less others knew of his living arrangements, the better.

"Go find him and gently explain the facts of life to him."

Scooter stood, but didn't salute since both he and the general wore civilian clothes. "Yes sir."

Scooter joined Commander Mike Sirrine and Gary for breakfast at The Cardinal in the lobby of the Sheraton Hotel just as they were finishing. Weaving between diners at tables as he walked toward them in the elite dining room, Scooter smiled at them both.

Scooter sat and a thin waiter in immaculate livery brought coffee in a silver service for him.

"Barton really wants you to accept your award, Gary."

"That's only because the old son-of-a-bitch is getting a ribbon that no other general officer has. He'd sell his children to get it."

"And he didn't have to lift a finger to earn it," Sirrine added. "All the greater honor."

"He ordered us into action," Scooter said, sanctimoniously, "at great risk to tarnishing his career if we'd failed. That risk alone is worth an award."

"Cheryl Osborne-Clarridge will be receiving the Superior Honor Award for doing nothing but taking credit for the cable I wrote," Sirrine said with mirth.

"Which means that she won't screw with me if I don't show up to work for a while?" Gary smiled mischievously.

"Gary, you could walk in there, take a shit on her desk and she'd pronounce it rose petals," Sirrine said emphatically. "She's never received an award for all her years at State. This is a very big deal for her. And her award is higher on the glory scale than General Barton's, so that adds to her sense of personal prestige.

"What are you gonna do, Gary," Scooter asked, "if you're not coming in to work?"

"I plan to lay about in the ambassador's apartment, drink, fornicate and eat, in that order."

Scooter, who was eligible for retirement at more or less of a moment's notice, thought that Gary had a splendid plan.

12

United States Courthouse
Southern District of Indiana
New Albany, Indiana

Judge Hoang Thoai Nguyen sat on the federal bench in Indiana but he lived in Kentucky, across the Ohio River from the courthouse in New Albany. His prized home on Elmwood Circle, located in one of the most desirable neighborhoods in the Green Spring district of Louisville, reminded him of the mansion where his family lived in Saigon before the war forced his evacuation as a child.

His name meant the 'King's Voice' in Vietnamese and his wife Thu Van Nguyen's meant 'Autumn Cloud'. The culture of his homeland remained important to him, even though he lived in a place where personal names had no particular poetry attached to them. In Kentucky, William Robert became Billy Bob and an odd mix of biblical names were attached to infants at birth without a clear sense of purpose. Though it struck him as being strange, there remained much of American culture that he understood at a surface level but not at a gut level after living in his adopted country for thirty-five years.

The Judge's twin boys, Dinh Khanh Nguyen and Dinh Bich Nguyen were both very different personalities. Dinh Khanh began his plebe year at the United States Military Academy at West Point and his brother Dinh Bich followed a different star, blowing glass and painting in oil. The poetry in Bich's soul struck his father as a reflection of his Asian heart. Khanh, the warrior defined the duality of the character of Vietnamese people and Judge Nguyen found real joy through his devotion to his sons.

In 2008, three criminal associates of Leopoldo (El Buitre) Caro-Madrid went on trial in Judge Nguyen's courtroom, charged with thirty-seven counts of narcotics trafficking, money laundering, racketeering and interstate transportation of stolen property. El Buitre dodged the bullet by jumping a million dollar bail and fleeing to Sinaloa in what had become a nearly traditional unlawful flight to avoid justice.

Following a three-week trial, a Southern Indiana jury found all three co-conspirators guilty on all counts as charged. Judge Nguyen sentenced them each to 520 consecutive years in federal prison. One defendant complained bitterly to Judge Nguyen that he couldn't do 520 years.

The judge leaned down over the bench peering over the half-moon shaped reading glasses resting on the bridge of his nose and said, "That's ok son. I don't think you'll last long enough to do the whole sentence."

A provisional US arrest warrant had been processed through the Mexican courts for El Buitre, but in Sinaloa State, neither the Army nor the Federal Police would dare to serve it. They were all family men with an interest in seeing old age.

In a move that his friends tagged as reckless, El Buitre, the vulture, came north to settle disputes between his own people years later. While traveling along Highway 89, near where it intersects with State Route 116 in Mt. Pleasant, Utah, he and his two bodyguards stopped for gasoline and a snack at the QuikMart. They purposely avoided the well-scrutinized Interstate 15 corridor because it received attention from the coordinated efforts of federal, state and local authorities working together in a High Intensity Drug Trafficking Area (HIDTA) Task Force. The somnolent Highway 89 that wound through one tiny farming community after another seemed to be a safer route.

Unfortunately for El Buitre, what once might have been true no longer was and the task force paid cash for tips that led to arrests. Every fuel and food stop looked for people who fit the profile and El Buitre looked like precisely who he was, a drug kingpin.

The traffic stop by city and state highway patrol officers took place north of Mt. Pleasant in the city of Fairview and solid investigation revealed his identity. The rest was history and the case went back to Judge Nguyen in the small federal courthouse in New

Albany for sentencing since El Buitre had been convicted in absentia in 2008.

The case didn't make any news in the US, but the arrest's ripples in Mexico were large enough to bring them to the attention of Felix Ochoa, who promptly discussed the matter with El León.

The next day, Felix boarded an airplane to Louisville, Kentucky.

It didn't take much effort at all to find out a great deal about Judge Nguyen. As a Vietnamese family, they stood out in the community where very few Southeast Asians lived.

Felix Ochoa did not look for God within himself. Felix felt sure that he existed within Niña Negra Santa, herself in a sense not the least bit metaphorical. The Holy Death surrounded him, and he drew sustenance from her to his very marrow. He found homeliness, an everyday-ness in his dramatic saint, who provided him with companionship in his eating, fighting, lusting, and devotion. She shared his most common thoughts and provided a spiritual resource with her companionship. The decorum of her formal worship did not translate into any necessity to Felix for formal prayers for he existed within her, as part of her.

She did not commune with him as an outside influence as Her will justified all of his actions. As a result, he felt completely at ease with El León's direction to put a bullet into the head of Dinh Bich Nguyen on the same day that his father sentenced El Buitre.

El Indio stalked the Louisville's river front streets, looking for a young man. He had a photo of what he called 'the little Chinaman' and didn't find an occasion to compare it to anyone because there were no Asians in the area. If they were there, they kept indoors or he just missed them.

Hunger began to gnaw at him and he stopped at two old train cars laid end to end that served as the dining room of Hannah's Meat-U-There food emporium.

Without a real grasp of American cooking or what might be the better menu choice, he opted for the special, chalked on a blackboard. Meatloaf, mashed potatoes, mixed veg and roll—$8.95. Anything to do with meat suited him.

The waitress took his order and brought him a Budweiser tall boy bottle while he waited for the food to be plated.

It didn't take long for the cook to peel a slap of meatloaf onto a plate, slap on a dollop of mashed, and spoon vegetables with most of the color steamed out of them. To disguise the mess, the cook ladled gravy over most of it and added one of yesterday's nearly stale rolls and a rock hard slice of butter attached to a piece of paper for the diner's convenience.

The waitress watched the ugly man for a reaction to the food that she wouldn't eat on a bet. He dug into the meat loaf immediately, eating huge bites wolfishly. He set the fork aside and began to use his fingers.

"I can get you another side of meatloaf if you want," she offered, angling for a better tip.

He had the whole meatloaf slab down before his throat began to close.

"You have onions in meat?" His voice slurred and rasped.

"In the meatloaf? God knows what the cook puts in it, but I'm positive they have onions in it.

The big, caveman-looking Mexican, shoved two fingers down his throat and vomited the meatloaf back up on the plate with five or six retching heaves.

"Oh-my-God," the waitress exclaimed.

Then the strange man pulled his levis down, revealing filthy skivvies. A pistol that had been in his waistband skittered to the floor and slid along the dirty black and white linoleum squares.

El Indio tugged an epi-pen auto-injector from his pocket. He put the tip of the injector to his thigh and fired it. The epinephrine went to work and slowly, he returned to normal as the waitress brought out a mop and towels to clean up his mess. She picked up the handgun by the grips and handed it to him.

"Sorry about the meatloaf, mister."

Dinh Bich adopted the American name, Sam, but he never told his father that in the American community, people called him Sam Winn. The judge had an old school attitude that his twin brother mirrored.

While he respected both of them, Sam's approach to life could best be described as Bohemian. He thought of himself as an American vagabond, pursuing the unconventional lifestyle of an artist, musician and poet. Sam moved out of his father's house the day that his brother left for West Point. He loved the Central Avenue five-story walk-up apartment for its shoddy appearance and for the bisexual free love that the people who lived there practiced together. His father would have swallowed his tongue if he'd known how his younger twin son decided to roll, but Sam reasoned that what he didn't know wouldn't hurt him.

The glass furnace had to be kept hot so that it would remain molten, but the reheating oven, called a glory hole, was not heated 24/7. To maximize his studio time, he arrived early and lighted the gas burners. Then he set out his shaping tools, waxed the long tongs called jacks and set out the long steel pipes he'd use to gather the red hot glass and form the shapeless globs into art.

Once everything had its place, he took a break and rolled a joint, then fired it and took a deep drag to calm his nerves. Blowing and shaping hot glass required a steady hand.

Sam had just poured granules of colored glass, called frit, onto a metal table when a large, round-shouldered man who had a face like a caveman walked into the studio. He didn't look well, and smelled like piss and vomit.

"Are you supposed to be here," Sam challenged.

"Are you the son of Judge Nguyen?"

"Yeah, so what?"

The big man pulled a pistol from inside his shirt and Sam turned to run.

The pistol bullet punched through the back of his skull, pulped his brain and when he twisted and fell on his back, the silver projectile protruded from the center of his forehead like a third eye.

El Indio took a white bed sheet he'd tucked inside of his belt and flicked it open, laying it gracefully over the body, still pumping blood.

The written message was clear. *'Those who fuck with the Sinaloa Federation will die.'*

13

Cheryl Osborne's Apartment
300 Lomas de Chapultepec,
Miguel Hidalgo, 11010 Ciudad de Mexico,
Distrito Federal, Mexico

Cheryl Osborne-Clarridge lived in a luxury apartment on Lomas de Chapultepec, about three kilometers from the Office of Bilateral Implementation, located near the Embassy. She liked to drink and party in the Colonia Condessa in Cuauhtémoc, located on the other side of the office, but not far. It made a short drive home when she'd been drinking.

Pablo and Francisco, the two brothers, los Güeros Diablo, set up on Cheryl's apartment, noting her departure, following her to and from the office where she worked. They'd wait, watch and note when she walked somewhere to eat her lunch. Cheryl ate salads when she dined with men and slightly heavier fare when she went out with other ladies from her office.

Sometimes they sat close enough to listen in on conversations but they never made much of it because though they spoke English, the language of officialdom had terms of its own that escaped them. One continually used was CONUS. From the banter of the Americans, people were continually going there or coming from there. The brothers did Internet searches but could never find that it meant CONtinental US, so they gave up.

The wily Felix Ochoa, El Indio himself, first identified her as a person they needed to pay attention to. She employed Abrille Fuentes, a maid who happened to be one of El Indio's bastard daughters. As a love child of the former revolutionary fighter, she didn't rise to anyone's attention as being other than a particularly unattractive woman in need of work. Cleared by the US Embassy, Abrille had been paid by two masters for years, working for the US

Diplomatic community, picking up tidbits of information and passing them onto her father.

El León felt as if they got lucky with Cheryl Osborne-Clarridge. She was precisely the sort of rod-up-the-ass, epicene, sallow-faced, functionary-bitch who would beat their drum against the Sinaloa Federation if handled properly.

Sometimes, Cheryl Osborne-Clarridge walked to the Condessa neighborhood alone. To los Güeros Diablo, she looked like a lonely heart. They patiently confirmed her vulnerability by documenting one-night stands that never repeated and solo drinking bouts.

Reports reached El León from Abrille through El Indio that Cheryl seemed to be depressed about a naval officer who kept spurning her advances. She also reported that Cheryl was at 'the right time of the month'.

Los Güeros Diablo said that Cheryl started drinking more, and alone. Combined together, it spelled 'vulnerable' to El León.

Other parts of the campaign moved smoothly and El León wanted to begin the process of disinformation directly to the Americans as soon as possible. From documents that Abrille scanned in Cheryl's apartment and delivered to him, she clearly had involvement in the counternarcotics effort, and worked at the Office of Bilateral Implementation, a notorious nest of American spies. He doubted that she would personally handle his 'defection', but their placement of the maid made her the best possible first contact.

Santiago Iglesias-Aznar followed Cheryl from her office on an evening stroll into the Colonia Contessa into Mexico City's answer to New York's East Village. He watched her window shop in the classic, leafy neighborhood.

When he went out for the evening on his own, El León joined the uber-cool in the avant-garde bars in the Reforma, but he had to admit that this place retained a definite feel that spoke to comfort and familiarity.

She ended up at Club Gorrión, an ideal spot for idle chatter and slinking a few frozen martinis. Comfortable chairs spread around inside offering intimate, dim lighting. El León had taken a girl there years before and recalled that his date loved the mango ice cream dessert they served. He decided to open with that.

Sitting in an overstuffed chair near Cheryl, he said, "May I keep you company?"

Cheryl scrutinized him in the sultry darkness and said, "Sure."

He stood under six feet, had a trim body, was impeccably dressed and spoke faintly accented English. She thought that he might be a diplomat she'd met at a function in the rubber-chicken circuit.

"Have we met?"

"No, not before now. My name is Santiago."

"Cheryl."

"You are a Canadian?"

"American."

"It's a pleasure."

The waitress strutted up to take their order and Santiago asked, "May I order an appetizer for you?"

"Uh, ok."

"Two mango ice creams."

"So what brings you here? Are you waiting for friends," Cheryl probed?

"No, I finished work late and thought I'd have a drink and unwind before I went home."

"Me too."

He sank back into the chair and slipped off his loafers. Cheryl took the cue from Santiago and took her shoes off as well.

"There is a war coming for America," El León commented. "The Sinaloa Federation wants to be able to sell their narcotics anywhere in America and they won't tolerate interference anymore. The Americans will be forced to go along with the Federation or they'll keep killing."

"What?" Cheryl came up onto high alert, though she remained supine in the stuffed comfort of the chair.

"The news, "El León directed her attention to an English language newspaper on the coffee table in front of them. He picked it up, turned back a few pages and paraphrased. "Nogales, Arizona: A U.S. Border Patrol spokesman said that no arrests have yet been made. Two people are sought in connection with the shooting death of a border agent Thursday night near Rio Rico. Border Patrol spokesman Barry Borenstein confirmed the death of agent Terrance Moore." He looked up at her. "The body had been covered by a bed sheet with a warning from the Sinaloa Federation written on it."

"I hadn't heard that."

"There is no reason that you should," El León said. "It is not the business for women. It's bloody and horrible."

"What do you think will happen?"

"I have family who are narcos and the talk is that the Federation will continue to kidnap and murder and the Americans are afraid to do anything to stop them. Maybe the Americans will open the border so that all of their cocaine can come into the US unmolested? The alternative will be more violence."

"That's insulting."

"I meant no offense to your country. It's just that the Sinaloa Federation is very powerful."

"As powerful as the United States of America?" Cheryl snorted lightly. "We have the most powerful military in the world."

"Yes, and yet a United States Attorney can be abducted from his home and hung by his neck in Sinaloa and a Border Patrol Agent can be murdered without consequences."

Cheryl didn't mention the death of a Judge's son in Louisville, Kentucky.

The mango ice cream arrived and El León nudged a bowl in Cheryl's direction. She picked it up and took a bite. "Oh, my God, this is great."

"Yes, they make very good ice cream here."

"You say that your family is in the narcotics business?"

"In Mexico everyone knows somebody in the business."

She spooned two more bites of mango ice cream.

El León subtly disclosed, "Rey del Cielo was my uncle. He was the head of all the narcotics cartels twenty years ago when I was a small boy. Now he's dead, of course. Since then everyone in my family has gone into legitimate business but you could say that the financial pump was primed by narcotics money."

Cheryl took a large bite of ice cream.

"And here I am, eating mango ice cream with the nephew of Rey del Cielo."

"Just a man drawn to a pretty woman."

"What else do they say?"

"The Sinaloa Federation will continue to find retribution for every act that the Americans commit against them until your countrymen give up."

"Does the Sinaloa Federation really think that they can win a war with the United States of America?"

"Sure, they've been winning for a long time. Thousands of tons a year, billions of pesos in profit."

El León ordered triple shot margaritas. And then when they were finished, he motioned for another round.

Los Güeros Diablo followed her home and watched carefully to insure that she made it safely into her apartment.

The following morning, Cheryl didn't arrive at the Office of Bilateral Implementation until after 10:00. It took four cups of coffee and half of a hand full of aspirin to get her head from spinning and painful thumping. The combination of insider information, margaritas and mango ice cream put a real twist on her. She by-passed her floor and walked directly to Scooter Olsen's office. She'd give Scooter the task of personally checking out Santiago Iglesias-Aznar, knowing that he'd give General Barton the information before he passed it on to her.

After she tasked Scooter, she walked across the hall and past General Barton's secretary, knocked once and entered the great man's office.

He had a newspaper open.

"A Border Patrol agent was shot to death near Nogales and they found a sheet over him with a message, the same as the kid in Louisville."

"Yeah, I know." He motioned to cables stacked on his desk., "And so does the President, the State Department, NORAD and everyone else. The shit is running downhill and it's running downhill to you,

Oz. Which brings me to ask where in the good Christ you were this morning?"

"I have a source."

"*You* have a source."

"Santiago Iglesias-Aznar, a nephew of the former head of all the cartels, Rey del Cielo."

Barton folded his newspaper once and then once again, and set it on his desktop. "When did you meet this, Santiago Iglesias?"

"At a bar last night in Colonia Contessa."

"Is it your job to manage money we're dolling out to the Mexican Army or is it your job to find informers?"

"I just met him. He told me that the Sinaloa Federation has declared war on the United States."

"He said that, did he?"

"Yes he did."

"And have you checked him out?"

"Scooter Olsen is doing that."

"MASTER OLSEN!"

A few moment's later, Scooter knocked on the General's door, stuck his head in and said, "Yes sir?"

"Santiago Iglesias?"

"Apparently he is the nephew of the late, great, Rey del Cielo. We're doing a full work-up, association matrix, the whole nine yards. I should have something for your desk in an hour or so."

"Keep me in the loop, Scooter."

"Yessir!"

Scooter closed the door.

"Now, Cheryl, run this whole thing past me once more. You met Rey del Cielo's nephew in a bar and had a few drinks with him. Did you fuck him, Cheryl?"

"I don't see that as—"

Barton bellowed, "That is precisely my business."

She began to tear up, and it angered her that she'd react that way. "I met him, we talked, he shared what he'd heard."

"Does he know where you work?"

"Absolutely not. He simply shared his concerns with an American. He speaks fluent English and seems fond of America."

84

"You met a narco in a bar—"

"—He's not a narco," Cheryl interrupted. "He admitted that his uncle's narcotics money funded his business interests. He owns land and exports produce to the US, Canada and South America."

"And he exports coke and meth in the produce trucks that cross the border into the States," Barton opined.

"I don't know what he does. I simply know that I spoke with him and that he was candid with me. He seems to be tapped into the narco's world."

The general took a deep breath. "You may be right." He picked up his secure phone and dialed a number by heart. When the steady light showed that the conversation would be secure, he spoke. When he finished, he hung up the handset.

"Was that Frank Dunnion?"

"That's right, and we're going to take a drive and meet the Chief of Station, in Iztacalco."

Nine kilometers and thirty minutes later they met CIA Station Chief, Frank Dunnion, in an apartment where the only furniture was a plastic table with metal legs and four old wooden US Government issue office chairs.

Dunnion poured coffee. "This is my own personal blend, Colombian roast. Let me know if you like it. It comes directly from Colombia to me in the pouch."

"This mud is delicious," General Barton pronounced appreciatively."

"I'll send you a five pound bag of beans. The secret is the fresh grind."

"We've come in contact with Santiago Iglesias-Aznar. Maybe I should say that Cheryl here has. We need to know how to treat the information he's given us and how to exploit future contacts if we decide to go that route."

"I know Iglesias by reputation. The guy is in a position to hear things," Dunnion confirmed.

"We'd like to hand him off to your people," Barton said without consulting Cheryl. "Oz here isn't ready to deal with this sort of thing. She's an administrator."

Dunnion raised a bushy eyebrow in Cheryl's direction. "Iglesias came to her directly."

"We met in a bar."

"Irrespective, if he spoke to you, he did so because he was comfortable with you. The last thing we need to do is to ruffle his feathers. Can you speak with him again?"

"I have his phone number. I passed it through channels."

"Ok, let's let the number crunchers figure out who he's calling and who he's connected to. The Agency has been highly reluctant to get into fighting illegal drugs, and that really is what the violence here is all about. We, meaning the Agency, just never believed it should be involved in any kind of police action. We provide assistance to DEA as more of token good will—to show some sort of effort, effort that is demanded from the White House. Of course things have changed with these kidnappings and killings on American soil. It's not simply a jurisdictional issue with DEA. It's dangerous, and it is decidedly unappreciated by our host country, especially our host intelligence service.

"One of our people was running an informant here in country, but it got the druggies all hot and bothered and they threatened to kill him. So, he's hunkering down in a hotel in Mexico City that we have specially guarded. He's going to stay there for another month or so, until the end of his tour. If he leaves the hotel, there's a high probability that he'll be killed. If I send him home short of his tour it puts me in an awkward situation."

"Should we go to DEA," Barton asked?

Dunnion sipped his coffee without comment

"I'd like to have Gary Granger help me if it's ok with you," Cheryl asked humbly.

"I heard that Granger is in town," Dunnion said.

Barton asked, "Do you know him?"

"More by reputation than anything. He's one of those guys who gets the job done, knows everyone from Bangkok to Beruit and flies under the radar, had a reputation as a species of cowboy in Asia. He works for you these days, does he?"

"Yes, he's one of my people. He's on contract to State."

"Have you ever actually met him," Dunnion asked? "I'm not making fun of you. Gary will always exceed expectations—he simply has an aversion for walking into a US Government facility in a foreign country. The man is an eccentric. He's one of the real ghosts in the business. He collects favors the way a rock star collects social diseases, and he rarely uses them. Do you know what that means?"

Cheryl shrugged.

"It means that Granger is one serious motherfucker. If he'd showed up at your office and introduced himself with the expectation that he'd be working office hours, I would have told you that he did it because he's off his rocker."

General Barton leaned close to Cheryl and spoke soto voce, "You've never *MET* him yet?"

Cheryl shook her head faintly.

"If Granger works with you, I won't have a horse in the race and it's fine by me. He'll throw the spaghetti against the wall and see if it sticks. It could be a dangle by the Sinaloa Federation or somebody else working a false flag. You have to be careful with this sort of acquisition," Dunnion cautioned.

"And DEA?"

"You can hand him off to DEA once you, meaning Gary, has drained him. That way my hands are clean of the stain that DEA will accuse me of being painted with."

"So you think Granger is competent," Barton asked?

"He's brilliant but he's an independent actor, a civilian contractor working for OBI and he's out of *my* orbit."

As Cheryl walked down the hallway to her apartment, her senses were assaulted by garlic, spices and cooking smells that cause her to salivate. She'd considered going back to Colonia Contessa to a trendy restaurant and then drinks at Club Gorrión, but she was alone and even though the only thing she had at home was shredded wheat and milk, it had been a long day.

The delicious cooking smells increased and as she opened her apartment door, they flooded over her. A slightly overweight gray haired man wearing a beige guayabera style shirt, levis and cowboy boots stood behind her stove working a skillet.

"Close the door."

She pulled it closed behind her and reached for a can of chemical mace in her purse.

"I hope you're ok with shrimp scampi, fresh made pane di segale, a mixed salad and a nice pinot grigio from Campania."

Cheryl looked at Gary as if he walked out of a spacecraft from Mars that landed on the street in front of her house and asked to have her take him to her leader.

"The larder was bare so I took the liberty of laying in some stores. I thought Italian was a good pick because most people like it. I risked a shellfish allergy." He paused and looked at her pointedly.

"I'm fine with shellfish," She said as if she was in a dream and had a hard time waking up. Cheryl fingered the cap of the can of mace inside her purse.

"I'm Gary Granger. I guess you're my boss, right? Be a dear and take the linguini off the stove, toss it into the colander and run a bit of cold water on it. Linguini is much better if it's served slightly al dente."

"How did you find out where I live? I rented the apartment under an assumed name."

Gary laughed warmly, "Under the name of your best friend in law school, Harriet Timmons. Don't feel bad about it. You used the Embassy for a reference for a domestic and listed the address in your paperwork."

"You got into my file in the Embassy Security Office?"

"I didn't do it personally, no. Really—no need. I used to work here in Mexico City and called in a favor."

"Of course you did," Cheryl said, recalling what Frank Dunnion told her. "No need to soil your own hands. The king of the ghosts, King Rat of the intelligence service."

"Yeah," Gary blushed slightly, accepting the compliment, "I had a busy day today and barely made it here in time to whip up dinner so we can get to know each other."

"I usually don't entertain my staff in my home," Cheryl's voice took on a touch of ice.

"But I'm your favorite helper these days," Gary said in good humor. "You're a hero and I hear you're getting a big award."

Gary saw the change in Cheryl immediately. The hand came out of the purse. He doubted that she'd carry a pistol. She seemed to be the sort who would tote mace with her to ward off unwanted attention.

"That scampi smells delicious, Gary. I may keep you around. You're a great helper. To be honest, it smells like something my grandmother would have made. She passed five years ago and I still miss her."

"Why do you think that grandparents and grandchildren get along so well? They have the same enemy, the mother."

She looked at him closely, pondering on what he said so blandly as he plated dinner.

"That makes sense," Cheryl conceded, "in a twisted sort of way."

"It's better to eat privately here at the house than at La Casa de las Sirenas, Templo Mayor or God forbid, the Los Angeles Pizza Kitchen."

"How do you know where I eat?"

"Doesn't everyone eat there? Dinner's ready."

Abrille reported to her father, El Indio, that Cheryl Osborne must have hired a cook and based on the condition of the sheets, she also had a boyfriend. She neglected to report that the parsimonious Ms. Osborne-Clarridge also tipped her an additional two hundred pesos, a clear sign that she was out of her mind or in love.

Cheryl mentioned that she had been looking for a cat but didn't think she needed it anymore. That seemed to clinch the boyfriend suspicion.

14

The Los Angeles Pizza Kitchen Restaurant
Near the Office of Bilateral Implementation
Mexico City, Mexico

Gary Granger held out knuckles and Mike Sirrine tapped them gently.

"I don't know how you got Oz off my back, but per your instructions, I asked her out."

"And what happened?"

"She said that she had plans to see a movie with somebody else and gave me an unenthusiastic rain check."

"Whose your daddy?"

"Gary, you are the man."

"I have to follow you around like an elephant turd scooper for the circus parade."

"Yeah. That's a fact. I'm glad we crossed paths in the can at the Old Dominion Club."

Gary ordered a single malt scotch. Mike asked for soda water with lime.

Mike said, "I owe you a big one for getting that snobbish, sexless bitch off my six. You're my wingman for life."

"You're going to need to keep everyone off my ass for a few days."

"That may be difficult. The general keeps asking to meet you and we're running out of excuses."

Gary dropped his scotch in one throw and ordered another one while he thought.

"I'm going to be on the road for a few days doing God's work, so I'm not going to be available by phone or in person to anyone. I'll work on General Barton but do what you can to keep the heat off for a few days."

"It's not Barton's fault. The SecState is going nuts over the Judge's son being executed. You've seen the photos, they're grizzly."

"What do they think that a fucking headshot looks like? It messes up the head, mushes the brain, makes the eyes blow out sometimes. The Judge's kid looked better than some I've seen. No matter how you slice it, the closed casket is better than putting all that's left – some goo and a foot or something like that in the box and calling it a body." Gary reflected for a moment, killing his second scotch and scratching the bar for a third. "This thing will get worse. I feel it in my bones. And I can widen my ass in a chair at the Office of Bilateral whatever or I can do something about it."

"Alone?"

"Me and the angels."

Presidente Gabriel Hinojosa-Garcia sat in the back of his Armored Chevrolet Suburban limousine and reflected on events that led to the ride where he smiled at splendidly uniformed Brigadier General Darrell Barton, US Army.

The general shared small talk with the Mexican President and his staff. While the General's aid, Master Chief Warrant Officer Scott Olsen politely looked out the window, General Barton couldn't keep his eyes off the legs of the President's commercial aid, a former Miss Mexico, and that's why she had joined them. Eye candy. Gabriel Hinojosa thought that if Barton flirted with his aid, Barton wouldn't be nearly as inclined to speak to him.

El Presidente Hinojosa had been trying to convince the Brazilian trade delegation to agree to a compact that would bring jobs to Mexico and increase their mutual commerce but the Brazilians held off because it was a one-way deal. Mexico had nothing to put on the table that amounted to anything significant. He had not been popular in his first four years of his six-year term as Mexico's chief executive and with the narco wars heating up and crossing the US Border, he needed something positive to take to the legislature and to the voting public if his party was to remain in power.

Suddenly and unexpectedly, the Brazilians caved in. The only thing he had to do was to take a limo ride with an American general;

he'd met when they cut the blue ribbon to open the Office of Bilateral Implementation, three years earlier. He rationalized that it wasn't even a long limo ride. The three-and-a-half kilometer trip from the Office of Bilateral Implementation to the Military Academy only took a few minutes with the siren screaming overhead and his out-riders on their motorcycles stopping the heavy traffic. The Brazilian Chief-of-Mission for the economic advancement of Brazil caved only if their specifications where the American officer were met.

The Brazilians laid out their specifications precisely. On the ride they'd take to inspect something of Hinojosa's choosing, he would sing the praises of Gary Granger, a man he'd never met. In conjunction with the inspection, he'd also suggest that Granger recommended that the general deserved the Condecoración por Mérito en Campaña contra el Narcotráfico, de segunda categoría (Mexican Anti-Narcotics Campaign Medal of Merit, Second Class).

While it stuck in El Presidente's throat, there was nothing out-of-the ordinary with pinning an award on the chest of the head of the Office of Bilateral Implementation. The only thing that the Brazilians stressed was that it had to happen very quickly and that the name Gary Granger be spread on it like mortar on a block wall you were building.

Darrell Barton thought that Isadora Fuentes, a former Miss Mexico, wearing five inch spike heels and a black dress short enough and low enough to leave very little to the imagination, had to be the most beautiful woman he'd ever set eyes on.

"General Barton, Gary Granger speaks very highly of you," President Hinojosa said, in an off-handed way.

Not much could force his eyes from Isadora, but that did it.

"Granger?"

Nobody noticed that Chief Master Warrant Officer Olsen, General's aid, involuntarily smiled broadly.

"Yes, and it was he who suggested that my government was less than attentive in recognizing your profound achievements in Mexico, assisting our battle against narcotraffickers."

"I'm simply a public servant doing my part for our mutual interests."

"Don't be silly, General," Hinojosa spread it on thick, "Mr. Granger explained in the clearest terms that almost every advance we've made is because of your personal work, your tireless effort."

Barton blushed slightly.

"How do you know Granger?"

"He's a man of many talents," President Hinojosa said cryptically.

General Barton kept his game face on, but wondered what the fuck Gary Granger was up to.

"When we arrive at Heróico Colegio Militar to inspect the corps of cadets, I will award you with the Condecoración por Mérito en Campaña contra el Narcotráfico." He handed General Barton a large black enamel box.

General Barton opened it and looked down on the gaudy medal. A red-enameled gilt cross, with an 8-pointed star of multiple blunt rays gleamed back at him. The green central medallion, a gilt map of Mexico, surrounded by a white band inscribed, *Merito en Campana* above and *Narcotrafico* below was suspended by a small replica of a Mexican eagle from a wide ribbon with five equal green-black-green-black-green stripes with a gilt bar at the top inscribed *Mexico*.

"What about that Granger?" General Barton commented under his breath.

"That's one impressive gong," Scooter Olsen said admiringly. "I doubt there's another general officer with one of those."

15

Cheryl Osborne's Apartment
300 Lomas de Chapultepec,
Miguel Hidalgo, 11010 Ciudad de Mexico,
Distrito Federal, Mexico

Gary stayed in bed when Cheryl left for the office and he went back to sleep until he heard the doorknob turn. He slid off the far side of the bed, and pulled a Glock Model 21, .45 caliber handgun, accredited and licensed to the Italian Embassy's chief of security, from his well worn computer case. The Glock had no safety. When a round had been put in battery, finger pressure alone would fire the pistol.

Abrille Fuentes, the maid, poked her head in the bedroom and then began rifling paperwork that Oz left on her desk in a corner of the living room.

She withdrew a cell phone and called a number, "Father, it's Abrille, I'm here in the lady's house. There is a ledger showing that the Americans are giving another five million dollars and three helicopters because of the pressure brought by the Sinaloa Federation—No, it's just documents on money—Yes, I'll look more carefully and I'll call you back."

Gary walked into the room with a towel around his shoulders wearing pajama bottoms. When he saw her, he feigned surprise.

"Are you the maid," He asked in English?

Abrille spoke in rapid fire Spanish and looked closely at him to determine whether or not he understood what she might have been saying. The man with the towel seemed very plain, slightly overweight and much older than her employer.

"I don't speak Spanish, Mrs. Osborne is my hermana," Gary said, trying to explain that he was Oz's brother, using a broad Texas accent. "I'm visiting here but I'll be gone soon. I'll pasado." He drew

94

out the word Texas style, in the hope that she'd buy his lack of understanding.

Abrille nodded briefly and then beat a hasty retreat out of the apartment. Gary didn't follow her.

He felt certain that the maid was on a hunt for some sort of operational intelligence. He'd looked over the documents that Cheryl brought home with her to work on earlier, out of idle curiosity. Most were of the For Official Use Only variety and weren't classified. Some of what she had in her briefcase fit in the who-gives-a-shit sort of clutter like news clippings. Putting the hammer on the nail to figure out precisely what the maid was after in situations such as this wasn't nearly as easy as it sounded.

He went back into the bedroom and called Oz. "Cheryl, I'm sorry to bother you but I think I may have scared your maid away. What is her name?"

"Abrille Fuentes."

"Can you give me her cell number? Maybe I can call her and tell her it's ok to come back. I need to leave town this morning for a few days and she can come back and clean as soon as I'm gone."

Oz gave Gary the number. He jotted it down in a notebook.

"Has she been cleared by the Embassy?"

"Yes, sweetheart, of course *you know* she has."

"Right, I'm sure she has been."

Langosta José Luis Restaurant
Cabo San Lucas,
Baha California Sur, Mexico

Gary had a table in a corner of the greasy spoon lobster shack where he sat, nursing a bottle of Negro Modelo with a shot of tequila to keep the beer company. Track found him and their conversation revolved around Gary's ex-wives and Vivian, who had recently hired an attorney to dissolve the current marriage contract.

"How much of your pension will she take?"

"She's going to share it with the other ex-wives. They'll each take a cut."

"Will you be ok, Gary?"

"I'll make do."

"How did you know I was in Mexico, Gary?"

"Are you in Mexico? If you were here, it would be a secret. Everything you do is a secret, right?"

"*You* trained me, Gary."

"Did I? I think I trained an Air Force pararescue type named Llewellyn who had the misfortune to attend the Military Operational Training Course—a 'flashlight repair school' if I recall the parlance."

"Yeah, my fucking life took a hard right turn after that, and drawing you in Malaysia finished the job."

"They wanted somebody to show you the ropes."

"As I recall, we spent the first month or two in whorehouses. It's all still a blur."

"—And bars. I had to loosen you up," Gary clarified with a sense of righteous justification. "You're not going to complain about the quality of the Malaysian tail are you?"

Track blushed slightly, remembering. Then he changed the subject, "What can be done about this narcotics problem—with the Sinaloa Federation?"

"You mean the murder and kidnap of our people. It's not about dope. Nobody really cares about narcotics." Gary waved his bottle of beer pointing the mouth around the bar. "Narcotics accounts for about a quarter of their gross national product." He waved a hand, indicating that even the run down restaurant benefited from the drug trade. "Cut one leg off a chair and what happens?"

Track Ryder said, "I don't know if I'm with you on this, Gary."

"Nobody at the Agency ever cared about narcotics. That's why they kept the Office of Narcotics at headquarters in the basement, literally and figuratively. Only the lame, sick or lazy were assigned there for one prime reason. It's a consumption problem inside our great country. Everybody knows that. Cut off external opiate and cocaine imports and they cook meth in trailers in the woods in Arkansas and Colorado. It reminds me of the stills churning out moonshine during prohibition.

"The world's economy essentially crumbled in '08 and the narcos found themselves sitting on a pile of cash with thousands of respectable, legitimate businesses in Mexico distressed and unable to borrow from banks. The narcos were there with hard money loans. Several years later, who owns legitimate businesses in Mexico?"

"But the violence?"

A platter of lobster tails arrived with tortillas and other fixings.

"I'm not an old Mexico hand, Track, but in the old days there was manageable violence in Mexico because the army managed the drug business. If anyone got out of control, they showed the narco how it was done downtown. Today it's different and I don't think it will change back. The Institutional Revolutionary Party ran the country for a long time and gained credibility because they turned the army loose on everyone. Orderly regime change brought the National Action Party and they decided to reform the system, which dragged the narco genie out of the bottle and it's not going back in."

Track replied, "People well above my pay grade, and I won't mention Jim Warren's name, are being squeezed and it will get worse. They want an easy solution to the violence in the US. They could give a shit how many Mexicans are murdered in Mexico. The kidnapping in California, the Judge's kid shot in the head in Kentucky, a Border Patrol agent killed with that sheet thrown over the body—same as Kentucky and the kidnapped guy they hung, indicate a pattern."

Gary Granger rolled his eyes. He didn't say what he thought. There was a time when Track wouldn't be asking his opinion nor would Gary be sharing the obvious.

"So what's changed?" Track asked, "It makes no sense for the Sinaloa Federation to provoke the US."

"Do you want to know what I think?"

"Yes, Gary, that's why I'm plying you with booze and feeding you lobster."

"My GOD," Gary shouted, "are *you* really buying?"

Track whispered mischievously, "The 'trust fund' is buying."

"Ok, I have a hunch but that's all it is. Somebody wants the US to kick the Sinaloa Federation's ass and they're doing this to provoke the US."

"A rival cartel?"

"That's my guess, and the provocation will continue until the public pressure on the Administration and Congress reaches the

97

point where they won't have any choice but direct military action against the Sinaloa Federation."

Track carved out a hunk of lobster, dipped it in butter and then took a bite.

"I don't know, Gary. That seems farfetched."

"I said it was a hunch. I don't have a shred of evidence."

"How could we find out if it's true," Track asked?

"As counterintuitive as it sounds, I say we cut to the chase and have a meeting with Ruben Gonzales. He's the head of the Federation, the CEO of CEO's in Mexico."

"You mean, just drive up to the front door of the most wanted man on the continent and say, 'howzit hanging?'"

Gary replied, "Yeah. Something like that. Start a dialog with the bastard and let him know that whoever is doing what they're doing, even if it's him, will end up badly for him—and good for his competitors."

"I hate it when you make sense, Gary, but I don't like it."

Gary opened his mouth and spoke as Track said the same phrase simultaneously, "You don't have to like it. You just have to do it."

"Normally I can predict what some asshole like El Macho will say but in this case, I have no idea."

Track said, "That's a problem?"

Gary's hard stare said, *think it through.*

Track ate lobster and spoke as he thought and ate, "If he tells us that he has nothing to do with it, (a) nobody in Washington will believe the word of a narcotics kingpin, (b) whoever is doing it will up the ante until we do something spectacular to calm the sensibilities of the voting public (c) and we'll be back at square one."

"That's my boy. And come to think of it, there are kids across the planet that might be mine—for all I know, you're one of 'em."

"I was taken off task to do this bullshit," Track groused as he created a burrito with the lobster and a dab of guacamole covering the mess with tomatillo salsa before he rolled the makings in a fresh, hot tortilla.

"You usually have an airplane."

"Fish is flying me around. I stole him from the Office of Bilateral Implementation."

"Does General Barton know that?"

Track bit the burrito in an aggressive manner that let Gary know that nobody told the General that he lost an airplane.

"I had to fly up here commercial," Gary said dryly.

"Thanks for coming, I think."

Gary smiled, "How is Fish?"

"He never changes—So you think that whoever is doing this will keep whacking people in the States until we do something?"

"Yes," Gary said, "and I think what we've seen is the tip of the iceberg. There's no way that these people will let us know who they really are. We can speculate that it might be the Beltrans or the Zetas, but they've never done this before because it could backfire on them and they have a vested stake in keeping détente with the US. I think it's a small player. Maybe it's a new narco, or one that we haven't identified so far? The Valencia Cartel in Colima was a mystery for a very long time before anyone knew they were there and they turned out to be a very big player."

"What happened to them?"

"The Sinaloa Federation owns the politicians. They turned the Mexican Army out after them and more or less wiped them out?"

Track asked, "So could it be the Valencia Cartel out for revenge?"

"Could be."

"But you don't think so?"

"I don't know."

Track gnawed on his burrito. Gary sipped his tequila and then washed it down with a long draught of Negro Modelo.

"Are you stepping on Frank Dunnion's toes," Gary asked, concerned only slightly with protocol and the Chief of Station's feelings.

"Warren is screaming at him personally through the Division Chief's mouth. The Director wants some sort of hard intelligence on this. So far all Frank can do is to tell them that the Sinaloa Federation is behind it. I chatted with him the other day on secure and he gave an unofficial green light to find out what we can."

Track looked through a film of grime that covered the window. Pointing he said, "Sinaloa is there, right across the Sea of Cortez."

Gary suggested, "Then tell Fish to kick the tires and light the fires."

Track picked up his cell phone.

"Are you going to tell your buddy, the Deputy Director, what we're up to?"

As the call to Fish rang in his cell phone, Track replied, "He'd have to tell me no. That's his job. When I was a kid, I asked God for a bike, but I know God doesn't work that way. So I stole a bike and asked for forgiveness."

Gary began to roll a lobster burrito for the road, smiling. Track Ryder was his kind of case officer. But—he reasoned with himself, Track had been well trained.

"Fish is running with that airborne telephone surveillance group managed by OBI?"

Track ended the call. Fish hadn't answered. "Yeah."

"Would you do me a giant favor and give him this cell phone number and have them get on it? Tell him there will be an action order from General Barton today or tomorrow and it has priority over all other tasking."

Gary scribed Abrile Fuentes' cell phone number on a bar napkin and handed it to Track.

"If you tell me this, you're also telling me that you will send the black surveillance group the tasking cable?"

"Yeah," Gary said vaguely, "Somebody will. I need them up on it. I want them to follow the phone and give me the numbers of every phone that comes within ten feet of that cell phone whether or not it's transponding."

"They can do that," Track confirmed. "How long do you need them to stay on it?"

"For at least a week."

"You're going to suck up three aircraft for a week?"

"No, General Barton is."

"May I ask why?"

"May I ask what your real mission was here before it was preempted by this blood and guts stuff?"

Track's sense of operational security gagged in his throat, he got it, and replied, "I get your point. Ok, I'll get it to Fish."

100

Track called Fish again.

Gary called Scooter Olsen and had him re-task the Army's RC-12Q surveillance aircraft based at Lima Sierra 2.

"Can I ask why," Scooter said, "because if Barton finds out that I have re-tasked his beloved RC12's, he's going to be well beyond pissed."

"If I'm right, you can take the credit, if I'm wrong, you can lay it on me. These State Department types are going to fire me eventually. Don't I have any credit with that bastard for his medal?"

Gary knew that the aircraft could detect any cellular telephone whether or not it was in use and pinpoint its location. By following that phone, any phones that came near it could also be identified by number and tracked back to a nominal user. It was a valuable and powerful tool in the Army's arsenal. The instruments were so powerful that if they could get close enough, they could also detect a cell phone that had been turned off so long as the battery carried a charge.

"Ok, Gary, run with it, man. I have your back," Scooter said.

"I'll be gone for a few days. Oz will cover for me if anyone is looking for me."

Gary got off the cell phone about the same time that Track did.

"Fish is on it. He's going to run interference for us and he'll also get what we need for the next phase of this boondoggle."

Dirt Road north of Alamos, Sonora, Mexico

Fish called ahead. He had a friend in Alamos he'd known for a long time who parked a green late model Ford F-150 by the side of a long, straight dirt road without power lines running near it. Aircraft landed on the road before and they would again. The City of Alamos boasted a paved runway, but landing there invited scrutiny.

Track walked around and looked at the tires, and the truck in general. It seemed to be in good shape. Gary pulled the interior hood release. Track peered inside, "It's like new," he reported. He hefted two strapped down jerry cans in the bed of the pick-up. They seemed to be full. He replaced the strapping and sat behind the wheel. Gary moved to the shotgun seat. Track twisted the key and the engine turned over immediately.

Gary opened the glove box and found a well-used Colt Model 1911 handgun with two extra clips. He scrutinized the ammunition. .45 ACP hardball wasn't the best option but it would do if they shot through the arsenal that they brought from Fish's airplane.

Track drove south as directed to a rock with graffiti on it. Behind the rock, an old metal box had been buried in a shallow hole. He took a stack of hundred dollar bills, stuffed the money inside and then put it back into the hole. Gary helped him kick dirt over it.

They got back into the truck and drove southbound toward Sinaloa.

Track drove about twenty kilometers through agricultural country when he approached a small makeshift shack to the side of the road. It appeared to have been cobbled together from the remnants of a tumbledown shed.

"Pull over," Gary suggested.

"Why?"

"*Los halcones*, the hawks. It's a cartel lookout post."

As they drove, Gary pulled two clerical collars from his computer case and handed one of them to Track. He attached his and then helped Track fasten one around his neck.

"Let me do the talking."

Track watched Gary transform. He'd heard through the rumor mill that Gary could change his face slightly when in mufti, to match the role he decided to play. Gary never did it for him when they worked together in the old days.

As the Ford pulled to the side of the road, crunching on gravel, Gary stepped out of the truck, speaking loudly to the surprised halcone in rapid fire Spanish, "We have been sent by God to perform an exorcism and to *cast Satan out!*"

The halcone crossed himself and backed into the shack, "Satan is here in Sonora and south in Sinaloa," he confessed, crossing himself one more time for good measure!

"That is why God sent us here, my friend, and we seek those who have been possessed by demons so that we may cast them out by the power of Jesus Christ!" Gary thrust a crucifix, with a tortured and

LARRY B. LAMBERT

bleeding image of Christ in agony on the cross, affixed, into the face of the lookout.

Gary switched into high gear to deliver a sermonette in rapid-fire Spanish, "God not only creates all things visible and invisible, but governs and protects his creatures as well. The devil and his demons chose to be estranged from God. Likewise, *man*, created in the image of God, abused the gift of his liberty, having been *persuaded to sin by the devil*. Thus a terrible struggle against the powers of darkness has pervaded the whole of human history. It was the very Lord Jesus' who first gained victories over Satan. Recall the exorcisms he performed and his healing of those who were under the devil's power. Sent by his merciful Father, Christ destroyed death by his own death and reconstituted human nature by rising triumphant from the grave. Finally, Christ gave this power to expel spirits to the Apostles so that in his name, the Church might carry on the work of her Lord. We are here to perform that work. The bishop of this diocese has given us *specific faculty to Cast out Satan* under the authority granted by Cardinal Jorge Medina Rojas, Prefect of the Congregation for Divine Worship and the Discipline of the Sacraments in response to article 79 of Sacrosanctum Concilium, and I charge YOU," Gary pointed an accusing finger at the shrinking lookout, "to direct us to the home or abode of a person possessed of Satan."

"The only person I can think of is my mother-in-law, but she lives in Mazatlan."

"Give me your telephone number and I will call you when we reach Mazatlan."

The halcone provided his cell number to Gary and watched as the angry old priest jumped into the pick-up truck.

Track floored the gas and they thundered south.

Thereafter, as they approached roadside lookout posts, they could see the halcones walk away without looking back. The word had been past that two mad priests seeking to cast out Satan were driving south in a Green Ford 150 pick-up truck. They reported the passing truck but none of them, who technically sold their soul to their narcotrafficker masters, wanted to deal with a priest on a mission to exorcise. Under normal circumstances, strangers would be followed, but nobody wanted anything to do with priests calling the wicked to God's justice.

The halcone from Sonora commented to others on his cell phone that the truck should be cleared all the way to Mazatlan, where the priests would cast Satan from the body of his mother-in-law, who was clearly possessed. He cautioned that they would stop wherever moved upon during their journey to do so to perform the Rite of Exorcism.

16

Office of the Secretary of State
Washington, DC

Nathan Wasliewski's executive assistant ushered Jane Hillary, Assistant Secretary of State for Narcotics and Law Enforcement, into his expansive office.

Nathan read from a stack of reports on his desk. He waved her toward him with a hand he worked like a flipper. "Come, sit."

Jane asked, "Did you read the one from Debora Pearce?"

"I'm re-reading it with a slow deliberate carelessness. I can't believe anyone of her station would author such a goofy piece of crap."

"Cal-Berkeley."

"Ah."

Nathan set the cables aside and looked up at Jane Hillary for a moment. "The Mexican government sent personal envoys to Judge Nguyen, Grace Moore, Border Patrol Agent Terrance Moore's wife, and to Bethany Melendez to express condolences, as though they had some responsibility."

"They do," Jane replied, "they haven't brought Ruben Gonzales to justice."

"And we're sitting here waiting for El Macho's thugs to strike again. The president doesn't want to alienate Hispanic voters with a response that could be construed as overly aggressive and there's no need to make entreaties with the Mexican government. They know what's going on here, but I don't think they realize what's at stake politically. We can only sustain so much of this without being forced by the public to take unilateral action, irrespective of the president's concern for the tender feelings of Hispanic voters."

Jane said, "The problem with taking action against the Sinaloa Federation directly is that there's no honor in success. They're just murderers. However, if we suffer some sort of setback or defeat, we'll suffer a loss of prestige and the president will suffer politically and it will roll down hill to us.

"He's lost two-and-a-half percent favorability in the polls over this so far and there is no telling when something else will happen."

Jane asked, "Will we send the Mexican government more money?"

"It's like pouring perfume on a pig. We're already giving them millions in direct aid and more millions in equipment and soft money."

"The FBI doesn't talk to me," Jane groused.

"Kyle Sanz would, but they don't know precisely why the Sinaloa Federation has declared war on the United States. I have back channel inquiries underway through the CIA but that has yet to yield anything. Sometimes these things take time."

"What does the president say?"

"He wants everyone to come up with a solution but, frankly, I read over what you all gave me and none of it seems to address the problem. We're faced with these modern day bandits in Mexico and I think back to historical precedent and context and can only come up José Doroteo Arango-Arámbula."

"Who?"

"Pancho Villa. His real name was José Arango-Arámbula and he's a hero in Mexico. The US sent General Blackjack Pershing into Mexico looking for him after he raided the US Army fort at Columbus, New Mexico. Some troopers from the US 13th Cavalry died in the attack. Then Villa attacked two towns in Texas in his war on America. Pershing chased Pancho Villa through Mexico for nine months until the US entered World War One. The President recalled Pershing to lead the expedition against Germany in Belgium and France."

"So you think it's going to be a war?"

"Against the cartel, certainly. Not against Mexico. If the attacks on Americans on American soil continue, the president won't have any choice. Hispanic votes or not, he'll order the military to take the war to the cartel directly."

"What happened to Pancho Villa?"

"Pershing didn't catch him, but somebody assassinated him after the First World War ended."

"Did we do it?"

"I don't think so, but it's difficult to know who was behind it." Nathan Wasliewski took his pipe from his desk, the way he did when he needed to think and tapped the stem on his teeth. "There are unintended consequences to going down and taking the war to the cartels directly, ignoring the Mexicans and violating their national sovereignty is not going to happen. Besides really ticking off the Mexicans, there is the issue of martyrdom. They name streets and elementary schools after Pancho Villa down there. I've seen his statue in Chihuahua. There's a festival in his honor in Durango every year."

"So what are we going to do, sir?"

"Whatever we do, we need to proceed carefully."

Mexico City, Mexico

El León prayed supine, stretched out on the cold marble floor of the clock gallery. He called loudly and fervently to the Holy Death with tears in his eyes. "These demons are like reflections in a mirror—my enemies are but deluded apparitions, remove them. Their chatter is like a discontinuous echo—remove it. Their riches and possessions are like violent poison, choke them with it. Their appearances of grandeur are like dog turds wrapped in brocade, allow them to experience the stink of their own corruption!"

He didn't know precisely what to do next, but he needed to proceed carefully. The Holy Death required humility and he felt comfortable giving it fully.

El Indio entered respectfully, taking his shoes off by the door and waited. When his boss finished his prayers, he walked forward respectfully. "What are the Americans doing?"

"I don't think that they're doing anything."

"I have heard that the pressure is increasing on all the wholesalers from all cartels in America."

El León said, "That's temporary. It's meaningless. I've ordered a very large quantity of coca from Colombia. I also have a ship with precursors for five thousand pounds of meth coming from India that will be docking at Manzanillo within three weeks."

107

"Señora de las Sombras will have the answer, Jefe."

"I need to move it once it's cooked. But you are right. The dark saint will have the answer for us. But the best thing would be for the Americans to kill El Macho and his people."

El León stood, walked to the altar and poured tequila for himself and for El Indio. "Let us pray together, then we'll get everyone together and drive to Guadalajara and pick up the big rifles for the brothers. I am afraid that they'll need them.

El Indio bowed his head, *"Divina Trinidad en el Padre Eterno puso para cegar la vida de totos los mortals, a la que a todos llegamas tarde o mas tenprano y que no le important las riquezas o juventudes, pues es pareja con viegos, jovenes o ninos, a los que Habra de llevar a sus dominios..."*

17

Kent County Superior Court,
Warwick, Rhode Island

After the long hard court battle, Judge Julius R Höglund, sitting in Kent County for the Superior Court of the State of Rhode Island, stopped for gasoline on the edge of town, just past eight in the evening on a Wednesday. The jury came back late, convicting Carlos Jiminez on two of four counts. They'd move to the sentencing phase next week.

Two years previously, undercover narcotics officers from Providence made one of the largest cocaine arrests in state history, seizing over a thousand pounds of narcotics, three handguns and, unfortunately, only Jiminez. His two companions successfully fled.

The biggest guns on the defense bar showed up to defend him, but the overwhelming evidence combined with the jury's distaste for Mexican drug traffickers swayed the conviction on half of the counts. Jiminez faced twenty-five years in prison. Even though he was only a mule, transporting the narcotics, Judge Höglund expected to see him do his time at the High Security Prison in Cranston.

As large as the quantity of narcotics seized was, the reality remained that Jiminez was at most a symbol of jurisprudence and his incarceration wouldn't mean anything except that Carlos himself wouldn't be hauling anymore dope.

Wearing a lightweight jacket to fend off the evening breeze, Doctor Juan Hernandez, the doctor from Chihuahua, said a prayer of fervent faith to Señora de las Sombras, the Holy Death, to accept this sacrifice into her bosom, to help him escape capture after he did what he'd come to do.

The Judge set the automatic lever on the gasoline flow and looked around. He looked down at the short man who had pulled up next to the opposite pump.

Judge Höglund stood over six feet five inches. Doctor Hernandez had to lift his heels to reach five feet nine inches.

One of his last thoughts before the pain hit was that the man looked like a doctor. As he bent and reached to withdraw the gas pump handle, the doctor from Chihuahua plunged a hypodermic needle into his neck and sent 40 cc's of potassium chloride into his bloodstream.

The Judge turned, confused and Juan Hernandez stepped into the passenger door of the car and sped away from the gas station.

As he looked, another man, he'd never seen before, draped a white bed sheet with writing on it over the windshield of his car. The first pain hit like a sledgehammer as he pulled the sheet off the car, pain radiating up his left arm, paralyzing it. Then a weight and unimaginable pain hit his chest as his heart stopped and began to die.

Judge Julius R. Höglund never connected the incident with his work in and for the State of Rhode Island, but then again, that was only speculation on the part of the Rhode Island State Police and the Federal Bureau of Investigation. The surveillance cameras in Greg's Discount Gas recorded license plates from two stolen cars and the faces of men nobody could connect with a name. It had been an anonymous, dispassionate attack, *a hit*, in the police lexicon. The message on the sheet had been clear and it was released on the evening news. "When you imprison or interfere with the Sinaloa Federation, your fate is death."

Both stolen cars, identified at the murder scene, had been torched together in a ravine. The police found them two days later.

Office of Bilateral Implementation (OBI)
Mexico City, District Federal, Mexico

General Barton, his aid, WO5 Scooter Olsen, Oz, and the senior representatives from each of the six agencies of the federal government assigned to OBI, found padded faux leather chairs around the large simulated mahogany conference table on the 24th Floor. The windows had been sealed and covered with a laminate of copper mesh and dense foam plate to provide security against eavesdroppers. All of the electrical plugs had been replaced with tempest-approved plugs and the secure telephones had specially shielded cable so as not to release any electronic signatures into the airwaves. The room was short of being an accredited sensitive compartmented information facility as prescribed in DCID 6/9, but it had been deemed secure.

"Is everyone aware of the latest assassination in Rhode Island?"

They all looked at General Barton for some sort of additional disclosure. The FBI Supervisory Special Agent poised to write so as not to miss any of what the General would say.

"I watched the report on Wolf News and it was a lot more comprehensive than what I'm getting through classified channels." He shifted uncomfortably in his chair, "From here on, I need the on-duty watch officer to call me whenever something like this breaks. I'm sure your respective agencies have all been asking you for back-channel updates."

None of them said anything but Barton knew how it worked. They all reported back to staff irrespective of the nominal command he had over them.

"What are you telling your masters back in DC?"

Oz leapt to everyone's defense, "I don't think anyone here would back-door you, General Barton. I think it's unwise to assume."

General Barton replied evenly, "What can you assume when you find a lawyer buried up to his neck in cement?"

Scooter answered "Someone ran out of cement."

Everyone fidgeted uncomfortably in his or her chairs. Oz always flaunted her law degree even though half of the people in the room also had law degrees.

"What is the difference between erotic and kinky, Oz? Erotic is using a feather. Kinky is using the whole chicken."

Oz looked thoroughly confused.

Barton looked around the room and asked Scooter Olsen, "Where's Gary Granger?"

Krause, a smart ass from DEA asked, "Who? Oh, yeah, I think he's meeting with President Hinajosa, right Oz? I mean, he answers to you."

First cement and chickens and now the missing Gary Granger. Oz didn't know how to handle the situation so she said, "I sent him out to find out what's going on. The last time you did it, he found the kidnapped US Attorney."

Barton opened his mouth to respond, thought twice, closed it and then he said, "If that matter of the man you spoke to the other night comes up, make sure you have Granger there with you."

Oz nodded and looked down.

"Let's hear from DEA. Andrew Krause, you seem to want to be my helper, what do you have for us?"

"The price of cocaine in the States is skyrocketing with all the publicity, increased enforcement, and so forth and meth is following coke up in cost."

The General smiled, "Does this mean that they'll price themselves out of the market and the demand for dope will vanish?"

"No," Krause said seriously, "but the people who get loads through are going to make a fortune."

"Maybe this is a ploy by the Sinaloa Federation to make more profits? Has anyone considered that is why all of these people have been kidnapped, stabbed, shot, drugged and otherwise eliminated?"

Nobody had thought of that, but based on their facial expressions, most of them thought it might be worth sending out on a cable by way of factual speculation. If they could attribute it to anyone other than General Barton or Andrew Krause from DEA, they could get credit for generating an intelligence information report. Once DEA confirmed it, they'd get a check mark in the good column that was taken into account along with all the other check marks (good and bad) they received during the reporting cycle and counted toward the measure of their overall effectiveness.

Their superiors who evaluated the reports never took into account that they merely took the information they reported from a co-worker in another agency and passed it on as something novel. In practice it had a lot in common with the 18th Century practice of selling the same horse to more than one buyer. Information reported by the more obscure newspapers provided the bulk of their stock in trade.

The fact that the price of street narcotics (as documented by DEA) had gone up made it plausible that the Sinaloa Federation was using death and public opinion to jack up the price, even though none of them had anything harder than the speculation that General Barton threw out to them in the meeting. As a result, they all felt a bit cheated and let down by the content of the General's conclave.

"Call your new source and ask him what *HE* thinks," General Barton directed Oz, as they walked out of the conference room.

After the meeting, Oz called Santiago Iglesias-Aznar and one of El León's seven cell phones rang.

She called at an awkward time, because El León and a significant portion of his entourage, including El Indio, were preparing to depart to San Isidro Mazatepec, about fifteen kilometers outside Guadalajara to pray to a shrine that an old crone there constructed as a tribute to the Holy Death. The Jalisco State Judicial Police favored the shrine of San Isidro since its inception and prayed there often.

The woman of the altar hailed from the Tepito neighborhood in Mexico City. Four years previously when she moved home to help her aging mother, she took collections and built the shrine, patterned after the shrine many favored in Tepito.

"I'm busy now, call me later," El León said and hung up the telephone.

His mind drifted to the double life size fiberglass skeleton inside the half-acre compound secured behind an adobe wall. Rusted iron gates topped with spikes, with human skulls skewered on the spikes helped ward off unbelievers who might be tempted to plunder the holy place. The shrine occupied a lot that still smelled of the hide tannery that was there before the ground had been consecrated. A bar sat on one side of the shrine and a tire repair shop on the other.

Then he thought of the woman, of the pilgrimage of sorts his men would make to visit Señora de las Sombras and he pulled a deck of tarot cards from his pocket. Tapping them from the box, he took the deck in his hand and motioned El Indio to his side.

"I will read the cards, because they speak the truth and can deliver the message I need from Señora de las Sombras. A telephone call from a woman you didn't expect to hear from is not a good omen when you begin a journey of faith," he spat sourly, thinking of the

American woman who bothered him on the cusp of such an important trip.

El Indio nodded his head vigorously. Women were notoriously bad luck.

El León shuffled the deck according to the ritual and laid five cards on the hood of his armored Mercedes, face down.

The first two represented the past, the next the present, the fourth, the immediate future and the fifth, a slightly more distant event or portent of events.

He turned them over carefully, one at a time.

One – *The World* – "The end of a long term project is in sight"

Two – *The Five of Pentacles*– "Stealth, representing our stealthy approach to our problem leading to ultimate victory?"

Three – *The Queen of Swords* – "Perhaps the woman who just called. A woman who brings danger, but with danger comes the prospect of opportunity."

Four – *The Chariot* – "A journey filled with peril. Our journey to the shrine? Make sure the men have extra ammunition and wear body armor."

Five – *The Nine of Wands* – "If we are faithful to the Holy Death, we will be victorious in the end."

El Indio said, "The cards advise caution on our journey."

El León added, "And possible opportunity through using the woman. Have your daughter spend extra time cleaning. Take an extra two thousand dollars and give her a bonus."

Mariano Otero Road between Guadalajara and San Isidro Mazatepec Jalisco, Mexico

The seven car caravan of Santiago Iglesias-Aznar, also known as El León, wound through a river bottom along a two-lane paved road flanked by shrubs and trees.

The Sinaloa Federation caught them in a classic ambush. Somewhere between forty and fifty gunslingers were throwing rounds down range at the caravan from the front and both sides.

El León and El Indio sat in the back seat of the third car back, an armored Mercedes S500. AK-47 slugs pounded the bulletproof windshield, making it pop and spider web, but not to the point of defeating the armor.

"They'll hit us with an RPG," El Indio shouted, making a tactical decision. An RPG rocket hit the Ford Expedition in front of them, incinerating the men inside. "We'll go out on this side!"

El Indio pulled an object from a pouch in the seat back in front of him, roughly the size of a soup can, with a spoon and pin on the top. "Smoke, Jefe!"

He pulled the pin, released the spoon, opened the door and rolled it out. Red smoke began to envelop the car. He rolled out low, followed by El León. A rocket propelled grenade streaked into the car and exploded as El León crawled away and shrapnel tore into the back of the bulletproof vest he wore, but none of it seared or tore flesh.

The smoke obscured them and they ran back to the rear of the caravan where the tail of their convoy had turned their vehicles broadside to the attack in a protective barricade. El Indio dragged an M-16 from the grip of one of their men who had been killed, as he ran. The bullets chased them as the smoke from the grenade curled and thinned. El Indio seemed to be shoved sideways by an invisible force and El León lifted and carried him forward, bleeding. He'd been hit, but the bullet tore through the interior of the Kevlar vest from left to right, expending its force in a grazing path without hurting El Indio seriously.

A ditch ran parallel to the road and El León swerved for it, dropping over a meter into water a few inches deep in the bottom. It provided a temporary defilade as shots popped and snapped on the dirt over them.

The canal must have been used for sewage from some up-stream farm because it stank of corruption and that smell masked any trace of sweet loam. El León grunted and then he accepted it. The smell was better than the alternative.

Nine-tenths of tactics available are taught in books but there exists an irrational tenth that flows from situational instincts that are as natural as a reflex.

"Get into the trees on the left side of the road," El León shouted to his men, while crouching in a ditch on the right side. "Move forward and roll up that flank. I'll cover you from where I am. El Indio handed his boss the M-16 that he'd picked up from the dead man and El León fired a few quick bursts into the brush, ducking afterward as a fusillade responded to his impudence.

El Indio, who seemed to have been stunned by the bullet that bisected his vest, started to come back and looked up at El León. "I took one in the bulletproof vest and I think it tore the skin off my back. You saved my life."

"Only temporarily," He responded, lifted over the lip of the ditch and fired two rounds." The magazine was empty. El León had a handgun, as did El Indio, and when they were empty, their enemies would walk right up and execute them in the ditch.

"The cards told us about this," El Indio said. "Our Holy Death cautioned us to bring more ammunition and we disobeyed her by not bringing enough.

El León's men seemed to be advancing along the other side of the road. He peered up over the ditch. Nobody shot at him. They were all either defending themselves or maybe running?

"We must trust Señora de las Sombras." El León began to fire his handgun at the retreating enemy blindly, punching brush as did El Indio. Then they were both empty.

El Indio said a silent prayer that stopped suddenly as a shadow cast over them. El Ingeniero, himself, stood over them holding his AK-47 to his shoulder targeting them, a wide smile with white teeth bracketed by gold fillings that gleamed in the light. From the bottom of the ditch where both El Indio and El León sat, muddy and bloody they couldn't see much more than a the dark shape of a man and the smile, but they knew who held the rifle.

"You thought you were too important to pay the tax."

"To you?"

"To Ruben—to El Macho, through me. If you want to move product through our territory, you'll pay or you'll die," El Ingeniero said simply.

"The Americans will kill you and everyone in your cartel," El León prophesied.

116

"So it was you who caused all this trouble? You ant, you piojos humanos!" He cheeked the rifle's stock, pulled the trigger and a round splashed into the water next to El León's head. The second shot blew up in the chamber, sending the rifle bolt back through El Ingeniero's eye, pulping it, and continuing into his brain, killing him instantly. A fine mist of blood, bone fragments and gore projected in a delicate radial pattern from his shattered skull.

He dropped over backward, with the AK-47 bolt protruding from his head. Two men behind him turned and ran into the trees.

El Indio heard them crashing through the brush beyond as they ran panicked. "It's a miracle."

"It's the will of Señora de las Sombras, a reward to the faithful as She promises."

El Indio shook his shaggy head in ascent. "It is a true miracle. The rifle could not shoot a bullet that would hit you, Jeffe!"

El León said, "Take a machete from one of the cars, Felix, and remove his head. It will be a token of our devotion to the Holy Death. We will take it back with us and give it to her."

"Maybe it would be better if we left it as a message?"

"Now is the moment where faith and following Her will is important. Leaving the head would be vanity, not devotion."

El Indio apologized, "Sorry, El León," he offered, "I thought of the honors of men, not of my duty to Holy Death." And he went to find a machete.

18

Enedina Palma-Gonzales home
Juan Pablo Sainz A, 201
Centro, 80000 Culiacan, Sinaloa, Mexico

Ruben Gonzales had just begun to eat a steak in his suite, located in his sister's basement in Culiacan, when the word came.

He marveled that the carefully planned ambush El Ingeniero executed on Santiago Iglesias-Aznar not only failed to deliver the head of the man who called himself El León, but El Ingeniero had, himself, been beheaded in the process.

Initial reports said that the men with El León stood steadfast and though he lost half of his soldiers, they turned the tide against a superior number of men from the Sinaloa Federation who had every possible advantage in the engagement.

"First the problems with the Americans and now this! Perhaps I should train some rabbits to do the work. They'd do it better than my men can."

Those who shared the meal with him didn't speak further as he stood at the table, knocking his chair over backwards and drawing a gold inlaid .45 Colt semi-auto. He waved the pistol at all of them. Then, without saying another word, he stalked away angrily.

The command post in the basement suite was one of several that he owned. This one served as a principal headquarters for Culiacan and featured flat screen televisions, computers and a separate conference room where he could plan with his captains. Staff manned it twenty-four hours a day and coordinated the reports of look-outs and others on a long white board that allowed El Macho to view security related matters at a glance.

A Guadalajara news station walked through the battle scene of burned out cars and bodies. He watched the report with his hands on his hips. They usually walked softly when *his* losses were news, but this time they talked about his men running in the presence of "a rival cartel". Since when did anyone have the balls to elevate Santiago Iglesias to the status of rival, and his band of misfits to the position of a cartel?

This would end as soon as he convened a war council and put the punk Iglesias-Aznar on his own personal most-wanted list.

Royal Viper Casino
Boulevard Niños Héroes
Centro, 80000 Culiacan, Sinaloa, Mexico

They rolled past the Royal Viper Casino in the green Ford pick-up and the brief view didn't give Gary much of a chance to scope the place properly. It looked to be a flat-roofed building constructed of cinder blocks, plastered and painted yellow and red. The garish combination fit with the drug money that built modern Culiacan.

"Ok, where to now?"

Gary directed Track, "Head up to the church on the hill, the Templo de Nuestra Señora de Guadalupe." Gary pointed and Track turned, driving in that direction.

"I wouldn't have picked the name, Royal Viper, for my casino," Track said.

"The name Culiacan comes from the word *colhuacan*—a kingdom of snakes. Ancient Indians worshiped the snake god here, or maybe it refers to the Culiacan river that winds through the valley like a snake."

"We shouldn't roll past the casino again any time soon," Track cautioned. Once past the casino, he reached into his backpack with his right hand while they drove.

"I'll get whatever you want out of the pack" Gary offered.

Track pulled out a tan cap and snugged it over his light tan hair, pulling the brim low. Gary scrutinized the embroidery on the face. The slogan, 'embrace the hate' had been stitched above the image of a demon and 'three echo' below.

"I like the cap. What does it mean?"

"SEAL Team Three, Echo Platoon—from Afghanistan."

"Given what we're about, that's fitting."

"We who are about to die salute you," Track said, quoting countless gladiators who bled out their last drops on the sandy battlefield of Rome's Coliseum.

"Ok, to hell with the church. Let's get this thing going, turn the truck around." Then he thought again, "Before I start saluting people on my way into the Coliseum, I need a beer or something to steady myself."

Track dropped him at Asadero El Chochi, on Highway 15. The Asadero wasn't a quarter of a mile from the Municipal Palace, where Gary could hail a taxi that would take him a little less than a kilometer to the casino.

Gary came up with the scheme to get a message to Ruben Gonzales. He reasoned that then, the ball would be in the Kingpin's court and they might find out what was really going on. El Macho could respond or not but it seamed reasonable that he would.

Though Gary had never set foot inside of the Royal Viper Casino, the Drug Enforcement Administration said that it was common knowledge that Gonzales owned it. Furthermore, since every casino had cameras covering the action because the management wanted to know if players or employees were stealing from them, Gary's request would be taped for posterity.

When Gary explained it to Track, all Track could say was, "It would take a massive sack to walk into a gaming house that belonged to the head of the Sinaloa Federation in the drug lord's own town, and rip him off."

"Exactly. And to protect against somebody who thought his balls were big enough, Gonzales will have the place wired six ways from Sunday."

"What if you don't come back?"

"I have a will. It's on file at the Agency. See that it's executed. The three ex-wives will be fighting it like feral dogs over a bone. I set it up that way. Do all you can to help Oz if I don't make it. She's fragile despite her Ice Bitch exterior."

"You don't have to do this, Gary."

"There isn't a better person than me. You can't break cover and I'm a nobody. I'm a contract mope for the State Department. You can't get any less important than that. It's even less important than being an FBI Agent—and I never thought a station that low in life existed."

Gary smiled at the FBI jab. So did Track.

"I can't rescue you."

"Listen in on the radio." Gary tapped the transmitter attached to his chest, "so you have a sense of how it went and I'll meet you in Mexico City tomorrow if it all goes well."

"I've got a thirteen hour drive and you have a three hour flight. Somehow I feel like I may have drawn the short straw. I might just drive to Mazatlan, dump the truck and fly back."

Gary said, "Whatever. I'll meet you at Pancho's in Pachuca de Soto for menudo in the morning if I make it."

The taxi dropped him off in front under a painted aluminum awning. Gary walked into the Royal Viper Casino, passing two very large doormen carrying mini-Uzi submachine guns slung under their arms.

The security men looked at Gary as if he just hopped off a space ship. He didn't fit the demographic. They nodded at a floor manager who took one look at Gary and came to the same conclusion.

The floor manager tried to get a grip on the situation before he confronted Gary with two even better-armed thugs.

The gringo, obviously not from Culiacan looked as if he'd be more comfortable wearing garish shorts, black socks and sandals and an 'I (heart) Mexico' tourist t-shirt. He had to be in his late fifties, and appeared to be an overweight bean counter, who took a wrong turn down the coast at a resort.

"May I help you, senior?" The floor manager asked with panache. He wore a new black tuxedo and was paid to be the soul of courtesy. If that failed, the hard option stood immediately behind him like two Rottweilers waiting to take someone apart.

"I'm here to deliver a message to Ruben Gonzales."

"I'm afraid that I don't know anyone by that name. Maybe you should leave and go somewhere else?"

"He owns the place and I want to stand in front of one of your cameras and say what I came here to say. Then I'll go."

"You may go, or maybe you won't," The manager cautioned. "Maybe it's best that you leave now while you can. People here can be very sensitive."

"He'll want to hear what I have to say. If you can't set this up, get somebody who can and let's get this going. I don't have all day."

Sergio Garcia-Garcia, general manager of The Royal Viper Casino had been auditioning new cocktail waitresses and even though he left strict instructions that nobody should disturb him, the worthless floor manager set a messenger who banged on his door until he answered.

"I'll stuff your balls in your throat if this is frivolous," Sergio Garcia-Garcia said with menace.

"I'm just doing what I was told to do."

"I'll choke you with your own balls just the same. Give me a moment." The door slammed in the messenger's face and he spent the next five minutes standing outside of Mr. Garcia's office, contemplating a return to the farm. Money at the Viper Casino beat the farm, but he felt far more likely he'd grow old with his testicles intact, working long back-breaking days on the farm.

Sergio Garcia stormed out of his office, past the messenger, who caught a glimpse of a naked woman, throwing a gossamer robe around her shoulders.

The floor manager stood next to a very ordinary looking gringo, sweating in the air-conditioned casino.

"I didn't want to bother you, but he insisted."

Gary reached into his pocket and withdrew a black credential case. He showed it to Sergio Garcia, "I'm Special Agent Smith with the U. S. Federal Bureau of Investigation and I have a message for Ruben Gonzales that I want to record on your equipment here."

The credentials looked real. Sergio handed them to one of the thugs, who'd been born in Plano, Texas, graduated from Plano East High School and could both read and write English.

"They look genuine to me."

Sergio thought about it for all of three minutes without saying a word. The floor manager was right to call him. The situation was completely unprecedented, very complicated and hazardous for

122

anyone who didn't handle it precisely the way Mr. Gonzales would want it dealt with.

"I don't know any Ruben Gonzales, but if you have a message for somebody, you can record it here. If somebody by that name comes by or sends someone, maybe they'll receive the message. Maybe not."

Gary smiled, "That sounds great. Thanks. And could I have a beer to wet things down? My mouth is dry."

Sergio snapped his fingers and the messenger, intrigued at the turn of events, ran to fetch a beer as requested.

Sergio ordered that a counting room no longer in use be cleared so that the FBI man could deliver his message to the Lord of Lords himself. To Sergio, it was almost like praying to God on video.

"My name is Special Agent Smith with the Federal Bureau of Investigation," Gary said, and then he laughed. "But that's not my name and these credentials are false. I carried them to open the door. I don't work for the FBI. I knew who my father was and he claimed me as his son."

Yes, Gary reasoned, it was a cheap shot at the FBI, but it would serve to break the ice with the King of Narcos.

"I work at the Office of Bilateral Implementation in Mexico City and represent the government of the United States. My government is concerned with the unprovoked violence that you've shown toward its citizens on our native soil."

Gary didn't know how he came across. He thought that he might be acting a bit too imperious; however, he played the role of government bureaucrat and factotum and wanted to play it correctly.

"Further acts of aggression will result in unilateral action, as opposed to bilateral cooperation," Gary threatened with the stick. Now he pushed a carrot onto the spike. "But we can talk first if you're willing."

Gary turned to white-faced Sergio Garcia-Garcia. "That's all I have to say, sir. I can wait for an hour if he wants to respond, then I'll take a taxi to the airport and board the 5:25 AeroMexico flight to Mexico City. You can send the message to him now or whenever you'd like.

Life is strange and Ruben Gonzales had been on his way to the casino when Gary showed. Phone calls that offered a confused and mixed message resulted in Gonzales returning to his bunker.

Events had taken a turn for the surreal. He watched the video of the message and ultimatum the American delivered in the basement of his sister's residence two blocks from the casino, not an hour after he received the news that the ambush planned on El León had gone horribly wrong.

His closest advisors were with him in the basement home as they played the video of Gary sitting in the room, speaking matter-of-factly, for the fifth time. They did not arrive at a consensus, but he had a role to play as the CEO of the Sinaloa Federation.

"Should we kill the American?"

El Macho said, "No, he's simply a messenger and it would only reinforce what they think now. It would make matters worse. Kill a pig, and then write this on a bed sheet with the pig's blood. 'Fuck You'. Hand it to the American as he boards his flight to Mexico City.

All of Ruben's advisors liked that idea.

Ruben didn't, but as the boss, he needed to establish a sense of confidence and bravado. Failure to respond in some boorish way would reflect badly on him with his people and he couldn't allow that loss of face to take place. He ruled by machismo, moral terror and fear.

19

Three hours later

Gary's flight arrived in Mexico City at 8:30 pm. As he walked through the terminal, a little girl selling kittens in a basket, caught his eye. They seemed to be ordinary cats, but he shelled out two US dollars and bought one of the kittens for Oz, who had mentioned that she would like to have a cat in the apartment to catch mice.

He took a taxi to Cheryl's apartment and arrived as she walked out the door to a late-night party at the Greek Embassy. Gary presented the gray kitten with pride.

"Gary! You brought me a kitten? How did you know that I wanted a cat?"

"You mentioned the mouse problem and said you were thinking about it. I've named him tin man because he's gray and he'll be living in the house of Oz."

She seemed thrilled and Gary blushed with pride at having pulled off a gift that she genuinely liked. "Tinny will keep me company while you're away!" Oz made a up a basket with a pillow in it, "I've never had a cat. I don't know if he'll sleep in it."

"I'm not a cat person," Gary confided. "So I don't know but maybe Tin Man will appreciate the effort?"

They left Tin Man in the apartment with a saucer of milk and drove to the party in Cheryl's Volvo. 9:30 pm worked out to be fashionably early to the Greeks.

Gary agreed to go with her because he needed the down time after the sphincter-pinching afternoon. A torn sheet with the words, "fuck you," written in some type of blood seemed to be less than ambiguous, but he thought a lot about the universe of possible responses to his video message and that one would have seemed to be the least likely.

Cheryl had never actually been out with Gary and he seemed to be very distracted and distant. All they had done so far was to eat a

125

really good dinner and breakfast that Gary prepared and have sex for three straight hours. She'd never had sex for three straight hours and the food was world class, so getting to know Gary better seemed to make sense. He'd been glib personally when they first met but now in the rollicking company of the Greeks, all of that had faded.

"Don't you like the party, Gary?" *Is it me? He just gave me a kitten, does that mean something special? Does he plan to leave me? Maybe he is and gave me Tin Man as company?*

How many times is it appropriate to say 'What?' before you just nod and smile because you still didn't hear or understand a word they said? Gary tried to be funny but he felt eighty years old. He really didn't know why he went to Cheryl's apartment instead of going to the penthouse. Maybe the human connection finally meant more now than it had in his past three marriages?

Gary asked, "How long do you want to stay?"

"We just got here, we can't go yet." *What is he really saying? I wonder if he's bored with me? Maybe I didn't please him? I told him that I liked the cooking. He came back to visit and instead of inviting him in, I brought him here.*

"That's Okay."

Cheryl's instincts came up on high alert. Not being a man, she didn't know quite how to interpret what he was trying to tell her. 'That's Okay' was a statement she used when she needed a moment to think on how to make a man pay for his mistake. Gary seemed a bit more innocent when he said it, as if he really meant he'd stay to keep her company at the reception.

She decided to test him and see what he might have really meant. So she excused herself to the ladies room.

When she returned, Gary had a drink the color of watered-down milk in the crystal tumbler and he chatted with an older Chinese woman in Chinese. She walked up and slipped a possessive hand onto his elbow.

Gary introduced, "Cheryl Osborne, allow me to introduce Her Excellency, Weena Zhang, the Ambassador from the People's Republic of China."

The Chinese Ambassador said something to Gary in Chinese and Gary immediately switched back to English to respond. "Cheryl is

126

both my boss and the Deputy Chief of Mission in the US State Department's effort to assist the Mexican people to defeat the narcotics cartels. She is key in our country's effort to do this, and is a personal friend of the Secretary of State. In fact, he just recently honored her with a medal for her efforts."

Ambassador Zhang smiled and said, "Gary is revered in China. We know he's a spy but he is a remarkable man. You're lucky to be working with him." And then she turned to make small talk with a squat swarthy man, who Cheryl had seen at a party before, perhaps Armenian?

"Can I get you an ouzo," Gary asked, steering Cheryl toward the bar?

"Maybe, do you have a suggestion?"

"I think that you would enjoy Greek brandy more than ouzo." Gary looked at the bartender and said, "Metaxa Grand Olympian Reserve."

The Bartender hesitated and then pulled a Baccarat crystal bottle from the shelf and poured into a small desert glass.

Gary handed the glass to Cheryl, "Metaxa is a Greek brandy invented by a silk trader named Spyros Metaxas in 1888. The Greeks call it, The Elixir of Life. This particular brand of Metaxa is quite expensive, but I like it the best."

Cheryl tasted it. It felt like a waterfall of scents and flavors in her mouth. "It's quite remarkable."

He abruptly said, "I'm not feeling well, Cheryl, can we go?"

She looked at him more closely in the dim light. He *had* become pale.

"Sure, Gary."

During the night he began to shiver and Cheryl thought he might have the flu. He put on a warm coat and covered himself with extra blankets, but Gary couldn't stop shaking.

"What's wrong?"

"Malaria."

"The first time I thought I had it, I was off on a trip in the literal middle of nowhere in the Pamir Mountains in Western China. By the time I returned to civilization, I had a nurse take a blood sample and it showed I was fine. Maybe the virus retreated back into the liver. It does that with Malaria.

"Maybe six months later I had another episode and the doctor confirmed I have vivax malaria. The symptoms come on slowly. I thought I was coming down with the flu. Joint aches, lethargy, and the blahs. Then tonight at the party, I felt the photophobia. My eyes were becoming very sensitive to light and that's a sure sign that it's going to be bad."

Cheryl asked, "What do you need me to do?"

"Nothing, sweetheart. I'll take metaquinine and it will go away in a couple of days."

"How did you contract malaria?"

Gary said, "A fucking mosquito bit me somewhere between Sumatra and Laos."

"Can't they cure it?"

"No, but stress can bring it on and I've been under a lot of pressure these last few days."

"Doing what?"

"Bird watching."

"Which means I shouldn't ask."

Gary winked and then sent Cheryl to the meeting place to tell Track that he couldn't meet him there. "Tell Track that the guy told me to fuck off."

"That's what you want me to tell this guy, named Track?"

"Yeah, make sure you tell him word for word, and tell him that I'll leave a message on his satellite number when I'm sane and healthy."

Gary felt younger. He ran through a tangled jungle with other men. Some were in front of him and others behind him. His muscles ached with an unrelenting pain that throbbed and shot through his legs up into his torso.

"Oh fuck!" The man in front of him jogged left and Gary saw an alligator that looked impossibly prehistoric.

"I'm dreaming," he told himself as he followed the other poor sweat-soaked bastard.

They broke through a tree line and he recalled that he'd been doing this every day. They had to run up a steep embankment to plywood sheds. The graying wood had USN stenciled in faded letters on each slab. Sometimes the letters 'USN' were upright, sometimes they were upside down. Whoever built the sheds didn't give a shit and it bothered him. He knew before he reached the sheds that they contained combat rubber raiding craft that were used in training that he did not participate in. His objective was one of six dip tanks where they tested and ran up the outboard motors that bolted onto the rear of the raiding craft when they were operational.

He saw the eastern most tank's oil-slicked filth with a navy petty officer holding a cane in his hand standing next to it and raced for it.

His muscles hurt too much to do a flying leap into that particular dip tank so he stopped and dropped into it.

The training objective was to hold your breath as long as possible after running ten kilometers. If you broke the surface before three minutes, the petty officer hit you in the face with a cane and you could take two deep breaths before submerging again.

Gary didn't make twenty seconds before he broke the surface but nobody hit him in the face. Change of plan?

He tried to clear the oil from his eyes and there, standing next to each dip tank was a heavily muscled man wearing boxing shorts. He stood at least six foot four and had roughly eighty pounds on Gary.

The instructor's hoarse voice screamed, as much as the guy could scream after having done it for eight weeks for them to get up because the close quarters battle portion of their course just began.

"Get up you white motherfucker," the huge black man standing next to him said. "I'm going to break your fucking cracker ass."

Standing forlorn, dripping in slime and goo, Gary had been conditioned to follow orders and did it now. The big guy began to use his head for a speed bag. He had large gloves on and wasn't hitting him hard, but each blow landed no matter how Gary dodged or attempted to block them.

In the faux reality of the dream, he still recalled the black blur that was the man's bald head. The beating wasn't. He felt more like a mouse being taunted by a cat and it enraged him. He could see the man smiled and he wasn't wearing a mouth protector. He didn't expect the shrimpy man they told him to beat on to hit him back. The big man won the championship in the ring. His confidence surged as he continued to slap and tap at Gary.

Gary saw red in the dream just as he had in life so long ago and reached for the only thing he could think of. The black boxer was one of those men who had a long scrotum and Gary didn't know that until he grabbed through the thin gray cotton fabric of the boxer's loose fitting work-out shorts. He pulled with all his might.

The punches stopped as the big boxer went to his knees in pain. Gary wanted to beat the big man's head soft but somebody grabbed him and held him fast from behind.

His eyes opened and his face was stuffed into a sweat soaked pillow. Cheryl held him, speaking soft words to him.

"It's ok, Gary, I have you. You're safe here with me."

Gary disengaged from her weakly.

"You were dreaming."

"About thirty years ago the Agency sent me to a course the Navy taught to teach their people to escape and evade from jungle situations. There were Navy guys with us. I nearly crippled the heavyweight-boxing champion of the Atlantic Fleet. We were in some cesspool near Panama City Florida and the boxers were going to some sort of match in town when the training staff asked them if they wanted to have some fun. I dropped the champ by grabbing his balls and Lombardo, a SEAL who'd been in the tank next to me, wrestled this welterweight and beat the shit out of him on the ground. We weren't as easy as they thought we'd be."

"That sounds horrible, Gary."

"The training was but I got close to Lombardo, an Italian kid from Philadelphia. After training I kept tabs on him. The Irish Republican Army killed him in Ulster after he'd been seconded to 42 Royal Marine Commando in '75. They told his parents that he died in a training accident at Little Creek, Virginia."

"It's past, Gary."

"Not really. I still dream. I can't escape the dreams unless I drink. When I pass out, drunk, I don't dream, but I wake up with one hell of a hangover. Sadly, booze doesn't do anything to soften the effects of Malaria, unless I drink beer with ice cubes in it."

Cheryl spent the next three days with Gary, doting on him, washing sweat soaked linen and blankets.

She'd hold him and they talked. He was too weak to go fetch groceries with her so she took his list and filled the order.

"I brought you a couple of newspapers," Oz said as she unpacked the groceries.

"I don't engage in the unhealthy habit of wallowing in the troubles of five billion strangers." Gary picked up the *Wall Street Journal* and began to thumb through it. "The *Journal* is different because it concerns itself with greed, and that is the moving force of humanity. As a spy, I concern myself with critical bullshit like that."

"At the party—the one where you got sick, the Bishop of Mexico saw us together. He said that he knew you and that if I was with you, I was lucky. He told me that you were his favorite atheist."

"Does that mean we're going to talk religion?"

Cheryl said gently, "Only if you want to."

Gary considered a smartass answer to her question but he couldn't bring himself to be a prickly, jerk to the lady who had been nursing him back to health. "Let's say you're a text book member of any religious order and claim to believe in God. You ask for forgiveness when you sin and you try very hard to live your life according to that religious code you adhere to. No matter how hard you try to stare into the void and mutter your prayers, they go unanswered.

"I spent a lot of time being put down, underestimated, stereotyped and forgotten. It has nothing to do with atheism; it is the mark of a good case officer. It is the kiss of death if you want to have a meteoric career in the clandestine service. Then again, being an atheist, the purpose in life is to continue and to serve your inner voice, not the strident ranting of a preacher.

"Those that I fight I do not hate, those that I guard I do not love."

"That sounds sad and prosaic, Gary."

"It's not me, it's William Butler Yeats. You need to turn to a real poet when you have to define your purpose in life. Maybe to the extent that the Bible is poetic, I can get onboard."

"So that's all there is?"

"A lonely impulse of delight."

131

"That's it?"

"That's the purpose of life—why I wake up in the morning and put one foot in front of the other."

Cheryl's eyes grew heavy, "That's so sad, Gary."

"Not to me. I don't do what I do for a heavenly reward; I don't do it for honor or for praise. I don't fight destiny or wrestle with divining the higher moral purpose. There is no dread, no bitterness, no footprints on the sandy beach that you claim aren't yours, no karma, no strains of 'Swing Low Sweet Chariot'."

"But God loves you, Gary."

"No, Cheryl, you love me."

She kissed him.

"I taste like fever."

Cheryl kissed him again. "I still think God loves you, Gary."

"There is no mystical force that surrounds us and I'm too old for the Jedi Mind trick."

"Do you mind if I believe enough for both of us?"

"No, I don't mind. And I have no problem with you praying for my soul because if you do, you'll be the only one who does. There are three former Mrs. Gary Grangers and together they form the 'I hate Gary Club'. Maybe you need to call them one at a time and get the full story on me before you start trying to pray me out of hell. They'd tell you that I deserve every ounce of torment that I get. There's a particularly dark place in a woman's heart for an ex-husband."

"So you are telling me that you hold out the possibility that you're wrong?"

"I don't think I said that but, yes, I could be completely wrong. I tend to believe those who are seeking the truth and doubt those who claim to have found it. But maybe somebody has. It would be nice if there were a foundation of evidence. If somebody wants to believe something hard enough, that belief system is usually indexed to his desires, not to empirical truth. If that same man is presented facts he'll work to prove them wrong—if he's presented the option to act on his instincts, he'll embrace any concept however scant the proof. So if you really want to be safe consider concepts only as valid as the proof they're built on."

Cheryl said, "I think the Bible is true."

"And I'm of the opinion that humanity is at war with itself because they're trying to make sense of a harmless enigma. The Bible is man's attempt to explain what can't be explained."

Track called first thing in the morning and suggested that Gary download his e-mail from secure. The process wasn't laborious but Gary's head wasn't in it and the effort of precisely linking passwords and the waiting time for the system to decrypt took roughly twice as long as it should have.

While he labored to link into reality after having been gone with malarial fevers, Oz started in on Abrille.

"Do you think she'd mind if I bought her some nice dresses?"

Oz liked her maid, Abrille, but Gary didn't know precisely why. Maybe it was her sheer ugliness? The lady did have a pathetic quality about her that he believed masked her true nature. The question was who employed her, and if somebody other than Cheryl paid her tab.

In the old days, Gary would have suspected the Russians. Back then it was always the principal adversary. These days, not so much, and there was nothing that Cheryl could provide the Chinese or the Russians. The cartels, on the other hand, might be able to benefit from files she brought home to work on. Cheryl didn't keep classified information in her apartment, but a skilled professional could piece together the bulk of unclassified data to fill specific knowledge gaps.

"I think I might set her up with one of the guys from the office."

"She's a gargoyle, Cheryl."

"She's sweet. She has a sweet spirit about her."

Gary turned his attention to his computer. The requested data came though and displayed on the monitor. He examined a link association matrix showing the cellular telephone numbers that the maid rubbed elbows with or called. She didn't have to dial or receive a call. Simply close proximity over a period of time with another telephone earned it a place on the association chart. None of the names meant anything to Gary. He looked at his watch and decided to play a little game.

Keying material for crypto access was audited and controlled, so what he proposed to do as he assembled a device and plugged it into the USB port on his computer, was most irregular. He pulled a headset from the computer case and snugged it down, adjusting the microphone.

Oz asked, "Are you calling someone?"

"Shhhh."

A screen came up with names of people whose crypto keys he'd placed in the memory. He scrolled down and selected Secretary Dana Hunter, Homeland Security and then had the computer dial CIA-Latin America Division-Counterintelligence Section Chief Bruno Chase. Chase would never have taken a call directly from Gary, who he owed a dozen favors, but he would answer the phone if the Secretary of Homeland Security called directly.

Without preamble, Gary went secure. So did Bruno Chase.

"Good morning, Madam Secretary. It's an honor."

"I have always loved truth so passionately that I have often resorted to lying as a way of introducing it into the minds which were ignorant of its charms."

Silence on the line.

"Giacomo Casanova," Bruno correctly identified the author.

"As for myself, I always willingly acknowledge my own self as the principal cause of every good and every evil which may befall me; therefore I have always found myself capable of being my own pupil, and ready to love my teacher."

"Gary?"

"Hey Bruno."

"I thought you retired."

Bruno seemed about to say something unkind so Gary cut him off, "—I thought so myself."

"I see you lifted Dana Hunter's crypto key."

"Just cloned it."

"That's twenty to life in prison, sitting in a cell next to Aldridge Ames in Marion, Illinois."

"Rick Ames sold secrets. I merely use them, Bruno, and I need a favor."

"A favor?" Bruno sounded reluctant. Most people held Bruno to be a favor-asker, not a favor giver.

"For the sake of the widow's son, Bruno." Gary invoked a Masonic mandate even though he wasn't a mason. He knew that Bruno was.

"Not for that but for saving my ass in Tokyo."

"As you will, Bruno. I'm going to send you an association matrix and need deep analysis on it pronto."

"Dare I ask where the fuck you are?"

"Mexico – working on stuff you might be interested in."

"I heard something about you driving down Highway 15 in Los Mochis and finding something dangling from an overpass."

"Someone – yeah, that was me."

"Send it and call me on your own key in four hours. Then maybe I can give you a guess as to how long it will take."

"Thanks."

Gary hit the end button, closed the notebook computer, removed his device and went into the kitchen to make a breakfast soufflé for Cheryl.

Once she left for the office, he got back on the computer, set things up and called Bruno one more time on secure, this time using a crypto key from the Department of Energy. As with the last call, he went secure without a salutation.

"This must be you, Gary."

"I couldn't wait the full four hours."

"Turns out you don't have to. I shot it to the Fort and they jumped right on it. As it happens, they already had the raw material. Did you know that?"

Gary didn't, but wasn't surprised that Track or the pilots themselves forwarded the information directly to the National Security Agency in Maryland.

"No, but that's good if they've already worked it over."

"Abrille Fuentes met several times with one very interesting guy who had seven active cell phones on him. They did an intercept and think it's her father because of the context of the conversation."

"Anything interesting?"

"Not in what was said, but two of the alias names come back to Felix Ochoa, El Loco Selva, a ninety caliber heavy hitter for Castro back in the day. He had a long pedigree, but today he's working for the Sinaloa Federation under the moniker El Indio. While the NSA was cranking on this, I took the liberty of pulling the ID photo of

Abrille Fuentes. She's not quite as homely as the old man, but they look a lot alike. I didn't think anyone that ugly could breed, but I'm constantly surprised."

"Maybe it was a rape?"

"Does that help you out?"

"Tons."

"Are you going to report this or leave her in place?"

"What do you think?"

Gary called Track Ryder and let him know what he planned to do and Track approved. He also agreed to run the tasking out of headquarters to keep tabs on Felix Ochoa through the surveillance protocols they had in place. That meant that CIA would dedicate assets to the problem and Gary could coast on the matter of Felix Ochoa instead of manipulating his way into getting the data that he needed.

He called Bruno Chase again and Bruno signed off on it, intrigued at what Gary dredged up.

20

Special Meeting of the
National Security Council Deputies Committee
The Pentagon, Washington, DC

The NSC Deputies Committee served as the principal interagency forum for consideration of policy issues affecting national security. Pursuant to its charter, it had been convened to put all of the analytical products prepared by the component agencies of the government on the table so that the completed report to the National Security Council would be comprehensive.

"This briefing is classified TOP SECRET-NOFORN-WNINTEL." The Deputy National Security Advisor to the President convened the meeting that included Deputy Secretary of State Jane Hillary, the Under Secretary of Defense for Policy, the Deputy Attorney General, the Deputy Director of the Office of Management and Budget, the Deputy Director of the Department of Homeland Security, Deputy Director Jim Warren from Central Intelligence, the Vice Chairman of the Joint Chiefs of Staff, the Deputy Chief of Staff to the President for Policy, the Chief of Staff and National Security Adviser to the Vice President, the Deputy Assistant to the President for International Economic Affairs, the Deputy Director of National Intelligence and the Assistant to the President. Each deputy department head brought an assistant and a few select analysts, who collaborated to bring their particular department's recommendation to the floor.

Assistant Director-in-Charge, Chaia Grey, Federal Bureau of Investigation, had been invited as a guest even though the FBI wasn't part of the National Security Council. She brought half a dozen staff members, each of whom were prepared to address a particular aspect of the situation.

Jim Warren did not want to attend the meeting, but he had no choice. The gathering of politicians and factotums of the bureaucracy demanded his presence and most of them secretly wanted CIA—and somebody specific at CIA, in this case it was Warren himself—as a scapegoat of last resort if whatever course of action they were to suggest, failed.

The Policy and Coordination Committee meeting on the subject presaged the general meeting of the committee and Warren didn't like what they seemed to be trying to sell.

Warren stood third in procession and addressed the committee, "The internal struggle between drug cartels and with the Mexican government has been for economic control of lucrative narcotics trade routes into the United States. Because this has not been a political struggle in the traditional sense, we have not spent the resources that we might have. There is no war of national liberation or specific interest by these cartels to replace the constituted government, though they control six states in the country almost absolutely.

"The Mexican military's response to the problem has generated a near textbook guerilla war. The Mexican government is perforated with corrupt officials and cronies. They have been unable or unwilling to capture Ruben Gonzales, the head of the Sinaloa Federation. Our response to this situation with the Merida Initiative was appropriate and remains so at present. The murders, which have taken place on American soil, remain within the perview of American law enforcement and the Department of Homeland Security. They are not and cannot be attributed to any particular failure within the Mexican nation's ability to govern. We have seen this sort of organized crime behavior before and are likely to again.

"President Hinajosa's government has not invited us into Mexico to do other than advise, and while contingency plans to intervene directly have been formulated, this Agency does not feel that their execution is well advised. There are consequences to any unilateral action that are unacceptable in our opinion. Outside of the diplomatic disaster that will result, we run the risks normally associated with any guerilla war as we have seen in Iraq and Afghanistan.

"If we send in too few people, we risk annihilation. If we send in too many we end up shadow boxing. The first rule of guerillas, and in this case, we're talking about a narcotics cartel that doesn't have a particular political objective at present, is only to fight when you are absolutely certain you will win. This is how they've been engaging the Mexican military effectively.

"Our military and intelligence community is accustomed to fighting those with a political agenda, not those with a commercial agenda—supplying the Untied States with narcotics that the public demands. In essence, the American public will be directly funding the opposition.

"The local populace will view our soldiers as invaders, the narco-traffickers are embedded and the economy depends on their continued success..."

He sat down, having stated a case and made recommendations that were more or less ignored by Jane Hillary from State, who began by reading off the names of dead US Government officials to date, "Julius R. Höglund, Rhode Island Superior Court Judge, injected with poison and murdered at a gas station near his home; Judge Hoang Thoai Nguyen's, son Dinh Bich, shot in the head; Assistant United States Attorney José Melendez, Central District of California, abducted near his home, taken across the Mexican border and hung publically; Border Patrol Agent Terrance Moore, murdered near Nogales, Arizona.

"Now today, we learn of a Lead Border Patrol Agent, Bernard Sanchez the BORTAC acting supervisor and George Trautwein, an Assistant Patrol Agent in Charge, murdered in their homes in Phoenix. In each case we have similar totems and threats left behind in writing. The FBI doesn't believe that any of them have been copycat killings. There is a cadence to these murders and they all take place at the same time as a member of the Sinaloa Federation is convicted or sentenced. In the case of Melendez, they would have been convicted within a week or so of his kidnapping and subsequent murder..."

Even though Jane Hillary did not suggest any sort of military intervention, she hinted that an executive action of some sort—wet work directed at Ruben Gonzales—might be the appropriate response. The natural argument ran that he'd be replaced and the Sinaloa Federation would roll on, doing business as usual, and in this case, murdering government officials that hindered it's efforts to distribute narcotics.

Jane Hillary's rant ended with a quote from the Doolittle Report to the Hoover Commission, "We must learn to subvert, sabotage and destroy our enemies by more clear, more sophisticated and more effective methods than those used against us."

Assistant Director-in-Charge, Chaia Grey gave a dry, more or less forensic account of what had happened, designed to give the appearance that the FBI had a handle on it and as they moved forward, the FBI would work toward assuring security to federal and state officers and their families as they prosecuted drug kingpins. It sounded hollow to Warren and Jim Warren thought it probably sounded hollow to Chaia Grey.

Grey buttonholed Warren on their way out of the meeting, "So what do you think will happen, Jim?"

"Nothing."

"We're sealing the border."

"The President doesn't want it sealed. It's bad domestic politics and it increases the economic pressure on Mexico. If you haven't looked closely, it's not a pretty picture down there. A revolution inside Mexico is not in anyone's best interests. So you can blather on with fairy tales all you want, the border will remain as before and the Border Patrol will put on a show for the public while allowing business as usual," Warren said, handing his briefcase to an aid, turning and facing Grey more directly. "And he absolutely doesn't want to deal with concentrating and then deporting with the thirty million or so illegal alien Mexican nationals living here in the US—because *concentration camps* or their moral equivalent would have to be used during the process."

"Do you want those people to die in vain?"

"They're not worth a guerilla war in Mexico. Imagine the deportation nightmare that would be caused by the illegals living in the Lower Forty-Eight."

"And the executive option on Ruben Gonzales?"

"It's the President's call and while I think he might favor that, it's way above my pay grade. The dumber people think you are, the more surprised they're going to be when you kill them and El Macho is trying to chew off a war. While that sounds dumb, El Macho Gonzales seems to be comfortable in Mexico and getting to him is not going to be easy even if we have a lethal finding. The President has the War Powers Act and only needs to notify Congress. He'd have thirty days to do what he needed to do without getting them to approve, even though in this case we'd be going after a criminal, not waging war against Mexico."

Grey pushed, "And will you advocate that?"

"It's not my call. The Director will advise the President."

"What will you advise the Director to do, Jim?"

"That's between the Director and myself, good day, Ms. Grey."

Warren took his briefcase back from the aid, turned and walked away.

21

The Coffee Stop
Ave 1 de Mayo con Avenida Huixquilucan
Mexico DF, Distrito Federal 54738

Oz split hairs. General Barton and Frank Dunnion, the CIA Station Chief, told her not to meet El León without Gary being present and running things, but nobody said that they couldn't talk on the phone. So she called him twice. On both occasions he ranted on Ruben Gonzales and President Hinojosa, with emphasis on how El Macho Gonzales planned to keep on killing until the Americans allowed him to sell narcotics products, unmolested.

El León accused the head of state for creating the current cartel wars in Mexico and Oz took exception to what he told her. To Oz, President Gabriel Hinojosa-Garcia was just about the only thing going right in Mexico. His understanding, compassionate, yet assertive leadership presented a model of executive authority.

She waited twenty minutes for Santiago Iglesias-Aznar, becoming more anxious as the hands on the clock moved. Gary had left town without saying much; the dapper Iglesias called, and she drove to Luna Park as he requested. Meeting the informer excited her sense of intrigue, but also her foreboding at doing something incredibly stupid.

Santiago Iglesias showed up wearing a blue tracksuit, ordered a latte and sat down next to her, laying three cellular telephones on the small round table that separated them. They passed a moment chatting about the weather and then he took off his Gucci sunglasses and began a rant on her hero, President Gabriel Hinojosa.

"You don't understand how the situation got to where it is, where warfare between cartels became so acceptable," El León patiently explained to Cheryl. "For a moment, suspend disbelief and listen to me."

She crossed her arms but didn't say anything.

"When Partido Acción Nacional (PAN) snatched power from the Partido Revolucionario Institucional (PRI), there was a major shift that took time to adjust to. The PRI Party held all the political might in its hands for many years. They had a lot more money than the PAN and the new party had spent itself dry winning the election. So where to come up with a couple hundred million dollars—a billion pesos?"

He paused, waiting politely for a response.

"I don't know," Oz admitted, "raise taxes?"

"Taxes in Mexico work differently than they do in the US. The people with untraceable money in Mexico are the narcos. Presidente Hinojosa's men went to each of the cartels, selling states in Mexico. The Beltrans bought Gurrero, Morelos and the State of Mexico. The Sinaloa bought the State of Mexico too, and so did La Familia Michoacan. The Mexican government maximized their return by selling the right to control the narcotics territories to more than one cartel. The cartels then began a shooting war to keep what they paid for. The State of Mexico went for ten million US Dollars and by selling it three times, they made thirty million."

Cheryl said, "I can't believe that."

"You don't have to," El León said, patiently, "but the franchises began the wars at a level of intensity never before seen in Mexico and that's where we are now."

"Assuming I buy that, how does it explain the kidnapping and murder of people in the US Government?"

El León spread his hands defensively, "Don't ask me to explain what is going on in the mind of Ruben Gonzales. I think he's insane. Maybe he has Syphilis? They say in the later stages, it goes to the brain and drives men mad." He struggled to keep from laughing out loud but couldn't suppress a smile.

"Syphilis?"

"I don't know how to explain the acts of a madman like Ruben Gonzales. He thinks that he is God. People say that he's bribed his way into the highest offices in Mexico and that is the reason his people are seldom touched while the Army crushes the other cartels.

Now when the courts in America rule against his people, he reacts with vengeance. How do I know it's not syphilis?"

22

Between Gannett and Picabo, Idaho

Lance Parkyn's young family lived in a trailer, that he called a coach, on land he paid cash for. He'd hauled the fifty-foot single-wide up a winding dirt road to the top of a rocky bluff overlooking cultivated ground. His truck struggled to pull it over one ridge and then further to a windy knoll that had a 360-degree view of the surrounding countryside.

Lance didn't bother to make friends in town and his wife declined an invitation to join the local PTA. She told the busy-bodies that she'd be home schooling.

Carl Grant, the man who ran Grant's Hardware in Picabo, on US Highway 20, denounced Lance to the Blaine County Sheriff's Department in the hopes that Parkyn had been setting up a lab to cook methamphetamine. Small rewards were offered for such information and Carl Grant loved to inform almost more than he loved overcharging people at the cash register.

Bobby Lish and Marvin Oram, two deputies from the Sheriff's department drove up the hill, marveling that anyone could drag a trailer of that dimension up the hillside along the radical curves that snaked along the contour of the mountain to the ridge where it ended up. When they arrived at Lance Parkyn's place they found that the trailer had been dented from the endeavor of hauling and that Parkyn had little talent for sheet metal repair. Parkyn did know how to use rigger's tape to great effect, which led the more senior of the two deputies to suspect that Parkyn had served in the military.

A faded and dated Honda Accord with Idaho license plates was parked near the trailer. They ran the plate. It came back to Lance and Susan Parkyn at a P. O. Box in Gannett.

Children's toys were scattered along the rocky, uneven approach to the home. Two little boys, who had been playing, scampered inside at the deputies' approach.

Susan Parkyn came to the door wearing a plain housedress and invited the officers in. She was twenty-something, short, thin and plain looking with a sense of determined resignation about her.

"We're looking for Mr. Parkyn," Deputy Lish asked, looking at plaques on the wall attesting to Lance's military service in the United States Marine Corps.

"It's his shrine to himself," Susan said. "He was in the Marine Corps—*we* were in the Corps until he got into trouble in Badakhshan Province and he was discharged. Then we came here from Camp Pendleton.

"How long has he been out?"

"Ten months last April."

"Mrs. Parkyn, it's none of our business," Deputy Oram said, "but what does Mr. Parkyn do for a living."

"He works for International Dolomite. He's a traveling salesman."

"What does he sell?"

"Chalk. He works for a company that makes chalk."

"Chalk?"

"Everyone has to do something, Deputy Oram," Susan said, looking at Oram's nameplate on his uniformed chest.

Deputy Lish looked closely at the pictures hanging from the fake wood paneled walls, "Quite a comedown from a Marine Corps Scout Sniper."

One of the little boys handed Deputy Oram a glass of water and the deputy took it.

"Oh, my gosh, don't drink it deputy, Lemuel dipped it from the toilet. He does that to get a refreshment for guests."

The deputy handed the glass quickly to Mrs. Parkyn.

"If everything is ok, we'll be going. We are just checking to make sure everyone is safe and healthy here," Deputy Lish, the senior of the two, concluded.

"Lance should be back from his trip within a couple of weeks. Do you want me to have him look you up? He'll be sad that he missed you. He gets on well with marines and police officers."

On the trip down the hill, Deputy Lish said that he tried for scout sniper in the Marine Corps and couldn't make it.

146

"I'll bet he has some stories to tell," Deputy Oram replied, "and now he sells chalk. Go figure."

Susan Parkyn had over one hundred thousand dollars in cash packed into an air tight/water tight Pelican case buried under four feet of rocks and earth behind the trailer that Lance called a coach. Her husband earned that sum the six months since he had been discharged from the United States Marine Corps dishonorably for the unauthorized killing of an Afghan fighter in the process of surrendering on the Kakan-Fayzabad road. Lance's captain considered it a murder and wrote it up that way. Lance saw it as payback for a marine who he believed the haji killed with a remotely detonated Improvised Explosive Device. Upper echelons at 8th and I in Washington DC thought that a dishonorable discharge was far more than Staff Sergeant Parkyn deserved, but politics held sway and he separated from the Corps.

Lance Parkyn never earned a dishonest dollar in his life but he left the Corps with only one skill. He could shoot and he knew how to train people to shoot.

Wendell Schild grew up a dirt-poor mixed-race kid from the Atlanta slums. His mother raised him on her own since his father left before he had been born. He dropped out of high school to help support his two half-sisters and ailing mother.

Lance Parkyn, third of four boys, had been raised as an upper-middle class white kid from Spokane, Washington. His father, a surgeon, spent a lot of his time with his sons. His mother stayed at home. He had a year of community college under his belt when he decided that he needed to prove himself and serve his country more than he needed to sit through classes and turn hamburgers after school.

Schild and Parkyn came from two completely different planets— nearly in different galaxies. If they hadn't both joined the Marine Corps they would never have met each other. Neither man would have appreciated that multiple Americas exist simultaneously. For all the differences between them, they were both Marines and were as close as any two men born to the same mother.

Lance Parkyn stood five foot nine and handled the long, heavy Barrett Model 82A1A rifle as if it was a natural extension of his body. At about the same time on the same day as the Blaine County Sheriff's Deputies visited his home, he and his buddy, Wendell Schild began to instruct twin brothers who called themselves los Güeros Diablo to effectively operate the fifty caliber sniper rifle.

He and Wendell Schild, also a former Marine Corps Sniper had both been contacted through a third party, who contracted training with few questions asked. In this case, because the Mexican Army asked for specialized training outside of regular channels, nobody commented on the why, only on the cash they were paid in advance.

Capitán Segundo Gabriel Aznar, a Mexican army captain in uniform met them when they landed. Captain Aznar explained that he and the Sargento Primero served in the 25th Military Zone, as staff members, presently on detached service from the Fifth Independent Infantry Regiment.

Once outside of the passenger terminal, his assistant, Sargento Primero Otto Sanchez, handed Lance a loaded M16A1. The sergeant, who rode with them in their rented car, also passed a bandolier of loaded magazines to Wendell as they rolled over speed bumps on their way out of the airport terminal parking lot.
Two hours later, on their first day in Mexico, Parkyn shot a man who was trying to steal the car they rented at the Pueblo airport.

They followed their hosts on the highway out of town and drove toward a large semi-extinct volcano, presumably to see the sights. Everyone parked and left the captain's army staff car and their rental as they walked up a hill.

Not long after they started up the hill, two Mexican men drove up in an old blue Pontiac four-door sedan and started messing with the rented car.

"He's trying to steal your car," Captain Aznar told Lance. "You should stop him."

Lance thought that it looked fishy, but he rolled with it.

"Can you hit him from here?"

"Can a bear crap in the woods?" The single shot, a 100 meter ranged effort had to wait until the car wasn't in the line of fire. He didn't want the bullet to pass through the target and into the car. He had rented it with his own credit card and would have to pay for any damages. From experience, Parkyn knew that the 5.56 mm round sometimes passes through a human who is left wondering what hit him. If it doesn't hit bone, it often doesn't cause a lot of damage.

In this case the would-be robber dropped into leafy weeds and didn't twitch.

He handed the rifle to Wendell, who pulled off a headshot as the other man got into the Pontiac.

They all walked down and looked at the dead men. Both Lance and Wendell had shot hundreds of men in the head and while the two Mexican soldiers, handlers whose job it had been to pick up both Schild and Parkyn and deliver them to the training site were very impressed with the shots, there was nothing at all remarkable about them.

Lance suggested that they call somebody to pick up the bodies, but Captain Aznar said that they could remain where they died. Both former marines wondered about *that*, but—they rolled with it.

Lance thought, they'd been set-ups, leading Lance Parkyn to suspect that Captain Aznar and Senior Sergeant Sanchez hadn't done much shooting at any range at all. He wondered if the attempted 'theft' had been a test of sorts. If that was true, it made no sense because they hired both he and Wendell to train men to hit a target up to a mile away.

Since the Mexican army was there, Lance and Wendell presumed that they were sanctioned kills. Captain Aznar explained as much. Lance spoke Spanish. Schild didn't, so Lance translated.

The training site consisted of a handful of rusted metal trailers on desolate land, ten kilometers east of Izúcar de Matamoros. Lance translated for Wendell Schild that Izúcar de Matamoros, meant sugar of the dead negro. They discussed the possible origin of the name as they drove behind the olive drab Mexican Army 4x4 up into the foothills of Xochiltepec. Wendell Schild, the tall, mixed race man from

Atlanta, didn't feel comfortable that any town would be named, 'dead black man,' sugar or no sugar.

Neither of the former marines, both who had risen to the rank of staff sergeant before being cashiered for various reasons, could have known that the Mexican Army officers running the training course were both shirt-tail relatives of El León. Even if they'd known, the lure of cash would have held sway.

The second day they were there at the camp, Lance pulled out his satellite telephone, called a number and left a message for his old friend, Track Ryder. They'd met years before in Columbia, where Hezbollah agents decided to train Columbian insurgents. Ever since then, Lance let Track know where he was and more or less what he was up to. There wasn't any formal routine to the contact. Just a heads-up in case Track or his employer had an interest in what Lance saw or heard.

Lance didn't understand how things worked but he took it for granted that sometimes he saw or did something that would rise to the point of being interesting to somebody at CIA. The Central Intelligence Agency didn't care what he was doing. Track Ryder, on the other hand, usually did.

Captain Aznar explained that the Barrett rifles he handed out were new, taken from the army inventory for the limited purpose of training Pablo and Francisco Sauceda-Nuevo, who had been selected to participate in the program.

The Sauceda twins had very fair skin, sly, brutal coal black eyes and a hard set to their expressions. Even though they were not identical twins, they did look very much alike and Lance found it eerie that they seemed to think alike.

Capitán Segundo Gabriel Aznar had all of the earmarks of a young, handsome, energetic and ambitious officer, but time passed and they didn't do much for the first week. Francisco and Pablo did well shooting M-16 rifles from a prone position at 100 meters, but Lance expected a trained chimp to be able to hit a paper plate at 100 meters. Two trips to the range were all they had to show for the first seven days and it led to arguments between Lance and Wendell over the training schedule. Wendell argued that each of them received $25,000 in cash before they left and they had been booked for a month. If the clients wanted to drag this out, they should be allowed to do so. There was always the possibility that they'd need to pay for more training if things went slowly. While he and Lance shouldn't drag things, out, it was not their fault if the employer did.

Wendell worried about the wife, two sons, a mother and two sisters who lived with him and who he supported. With money he had earned with Lance since separating from the Corps, he bought a three-bedroom house in Beaufort County, South Carolina, not far from Marine Corps Recruit Depot, Parris Island.

Captain Aznar came into camp on the eighth day with fresh food for the cook and instructions from above.

It was the first dime that Lance heard him refer to the twins as los Güeros Diablo, the white devils.

"We need to meet together to discuss the training," Aznar told Lance. "But first we will eat steaks and drink some tequila."

"Maybe we can speak English for Wendell's benefit?"

"Certainly."

Lance managed to steer the dinner conversation in the direction of training. "I set out an 800-meter range across the ridge and down into the valley as a backdrop." He indicated the direction with his hand and Captain Aznar showed interest in the topic. "The breeze seems to be constant in the afternoon but the mornings have been very still. I haven't had to make many scope adjustments except to correct slightly for spin drift and Magnus drift. Those Schmidt and Bender 5—25 power scopes are excellent. They bring you right up on the target."

"Los Güeros Diablo will both shoot at the same target at between 800 and 1,000 meters. I have direction in the matter that should help the training."

"So we're not teaching them to be snipers, the way the Marine Corps would," Wendell asked for clarification?

"No, you only need to teach them to operate the weapons and make a shot at one target. Furthermore, the rifles will be fired from tripods, so los Güeros Diablo will be seated when they fire. They need to begin training in that way."

That must mean an urban environment. Lance thought that training them for a shot from a tripod, and that only, was a very strange request.

"Did you bring the tripods?"

Captain Aznar blushed, "I don't have them but will bring them mañana."

Lance pushed a bit as he recharged the captain's glass with another drink of the local, very coarse tequila. "Does mañana mean tomorrow, or sometime in the future?"

"When I get them, it will be the time to bring them."

"That's fine, Captain Aznar," Wendell said, kicking Lance under the table, "but we've only been paid for thirty days."

"If it takes longer, you will be compensated."

Wendell beamed with the hope of more earnings.

The next day both Pablo and Francisco turned out early along with Captain Aznar for orientation to the .50 caliber rifles. Both Lance and Wendell wore Marine Corps green camo fatigues and red baseball caps with the anchor, globe and eagle embroidered in yellow thread on the peak.

Since los Güeros Diablo and the captain spoke English, the training would be conducted in that language for Wendell's benefit.

Wendell began with that cant and cadence used by all Marine Corps instructors, "The .50 Browning Machine Gun cartridge or 12.7x99 NATO cartridge that we will be using in the Barrett Model 82A1A rifle officially entered service in 1921. Canadian Corporal Rob Furlong made the longest confirmed kill with *this* cartridge in Afghanistan. He killed an enemy soldier at 2,430 meters. Corporal Furlong used a McMillan Tac-50 rifle to execute this shot. There was a longer ranged kill made by a British sniper shooting the .338 Lapua Magnum cartridge, but we're going to be shooting the BMG 50 and it's a damned fine round."

"Do you know which particular round the twins will be using," Lance asked?

"The Raufoss bullet," Aznar said nonchalantly.

"Armor piercing, incendiary, high explosive round."

"They will fire at a target moving toward them with this bullet and will fire as many times as they are able."

"So we're talking a vehicle?"

"I don't know what they will be shooting at, Lance, but based on the specified bullet, I think that is correct."

Lance kept thinking about Track Ryder. He had to tell somebody about this. These two devil twins were training now under his instruction to take out a moving vehicle with Raufoss rounds at under 1,000 meters. The target would be much larger than a person and with the exploding Raufoss round, it would devastate anyone inside the moving vehicle. Who was the intended target? The President of Mexico? Worse still, the US President? Captain Aznar didn't seem to know who or what the intended target was and the twins wouldn't care.

Wendell continued his cant, "Carlos Hancock was one of the best snipers in history. He had 93 confirmed kills and many more unconfirmed kills. He was a United States Marine Corps scout sniper who had the distinction of being both an incredible marksman and a near perfect marine. Being good isn't necessarily measured by your shooting, but by executing your kills using the highest standards of stalking and waiting. Carlos Hancock pinned down an entire North Vietnamese company in a rice paddy. They stayed there for three days and Carlos took 'em one at a time, until they decided to break out. During that entire time, Sergeant Hancock never moved and the gooks never knew where he was. *THAT* is sniping."

"Can you teach us to do that," Francisco Sauceda asked? His brother, Pablo nodded his head vigorously in agreement.

"Yes, but not in the three weeks we have left here," Wendell stressed. That would take a great deal of time because it involves a number of specific skills including orienteering, stalking, shooting techniques, physical conditioning, and so forth. It would require much more time."

"Maybe when we finish this task," Pablo said, "you and Sergeant Lance could teach us?"

"Of course."

Lance hefted the heavy black rifle and set it on a table in front of them. "The rifle is near worthless without the scope. This is the Schmidt and Bender Police Marksman 2 LP riflescope. It is a 5—25 power by 56 wide field of view with parallax adjustment here in this

153

turret." He pointed at the parallax adjustment that could be used from ten meters to infinity.

"This scope provides you a very high degree of accuracy out to 2,000 meters. That means if the scope is sighted in and you account for variables including wind velocity, the curvature of the Earth, your own breathing and trigger pull characteristics, your point of aim will be your point of impact at an object, person, or body part at a mile and a quarter distant. The kinetic force of the bullet striking a human body is so great that it's common for the members to violently separate from the trunk, and a hit just about anywhere will be lethal.

"Wind will usually make a significant distance as you get out into the 1,000 meter range bracket. Your rifle bore has a right-hand twist so the bullet will spin clockwise. If the wind is coming from 9 o'clock, it will make the bullet strike low and to the right. A wind at 3 o'clock will make the round impact high and left as it tries to climb the wind pressure. How far the rounds deviate from the intended point of impact has to do with wind strength. That's why adjusting your scope to compensate for the wind is important. This model offers 93 minutes of angle in one-centimeter clicks. One click at 100 meters equates to a 1-centimeter adjustment. Applying the rule of subtension, one click at 1,000 meters means ten centimeters and two clicks means a twenty-centimeter change. This applies to both windage and elevation."

He looked at the twins. He'd lost them. He switched to Spanish and went over it carefully one more time.

Later as he and Wendell lay in adjacent cots, before they went to sleep they discussed the problem of teaching men to be snipers who had every bad habit in the book from trigger flinching to shooting at objects on the range that were not designated targets, such as rocks and birds.

"If they plan to hit anything at 1,000 meters, it's going to have to be something big," Wendell said definitively. "They said that it will be moving toward them so that will make things easier. I don't know if they're going to be on the plane with the target, above it or below it. That may make a difference in how we train them if they know. There are also velocity considerations."

"Let's do the best we can with these idiots and get out of here," Lance added and for the first time, Wendell agreed.

Track Ryder hung up with Lance Parkyn and called Jim Warren on his Sat Phone.

They waited for the call to go secure and Warren fired off his signature, "Whatchagot?" Warren had a habit of cutting to the chase, Track recalled. Maybe that is why Jim Warren was CIA's Deputy Director, Operations and Track remained a field man.

"Something came up that I'm going to pass along to you."

"Do I need to take notes?"

"Nah, but we talked to the head of the Sinaloa Federation, after a manner of speaking, and asked him why he was attacking people in the US."

"Ruben Gonzales—really? What did he say?"

"Fuck you – written in pigs blood on a piece of fabric."

"He's an eloquent bastard and it may be his undoing."

Track smiled, "Do you want me to keep on this narco thing down here?" He'd hoped to be released to continue with his previous mission. The narco thing felt seamy and less interesting.

Warren's voice lowered an octave, "There is a contingency plan on the table that the president refuses to act on, but there are wheels in motion anyway just in case he changes his mind. There is a finding on his desk—a lethal finding on Ruben Gonzales and the top people in the criminal organization calling itself the Sinaloa Federation. If he puts his chop on it, we can take Gonzales whenever we can find him. Nathan Wasliewski has spoken to his Mexican counterparts and they're considering a move to allow us to unilateral action on their soil but they haven't jumped yet either. That sort of thing is bad for politics in Mexico."

"You said, contingency—Who's driving the car from an operational sense down here?"

"Bruce Phinizy, a Marine Corps major general. The rest of us are along for the ride in a supporting role. They're calling it VALIANT COURSE at the president's suggestion. When and if it's real, I'll need you back in DC to brief various and sundry people."

155

"Who's in the loop down here?"

"Frank Dunnion will be adding to the list as he is moved to. You're part of our effort from headquarters and you *will not* be taking orders from anyone but me, so nothing has changed."

"Would you add Gary Granger?"

"State can do that, he's Nathan Wasliewski's man now."

"I need him on the list immediately so that we can talk about things. I am way behind Gary on the whys and wherefores here in Mexico."

"Granger—I thought we got rid of that dinosaur. Is he still playing William Tell, making and shooting those damned crossbows?"

"He's good."

"I take it that you worked with him before?"

"He broke me in back when I was a nugget, fresh from the farm."

"Then you know that he's not controllable under any imaginable universe. Nobody could catch him doing anything wrong back when he worked for us and he always passed his polygraph, but—Ok, I'll put him on the list. You can talk to him about VALIANT COURSE, stressing that for the moment it's only a contingency plan.

"Contingency or not, we're fully activating Lima Sierra Two, a landing strip in the middle of the Yucatan. Sea Bees will be pushing back the jungle with bulldozers today or tomorrow. The Joint Chiefs authorized preliminary infrastructure to take Ruben Gonzales out with extreme prejudice if the president approves it."

"Delta Force?"

"Two platoons from Delta will be transitioning to LS2 with supporting elements from the 160th Special Operations Aviation Regiment immediately. If the balloon goes up, we'll have two companies from the 3rd Battalion, 75th Infantry Regiment with support and augmentation from the Ranger Special Troops Battalion. Suitable air assets will be added to the Table of Organization and Equipment to support the 75th. The Marines will be moving down in ships and will stage off La Paz, over the horizon.

"It sounds complicated to me. A lot of people and hardware and one illusive target."

Warren didn't comment. He just moved on. "I need warnings and indications of future attacks here in the US."

"A cartel, and I'm not sure which cartel, is training snipers with .50 caliber rifles."

"It would stand to reason that it's the Sinaloa Federation," Warren said.

"There are a number of cartels down here and almost all of them are at war with all the other cartels. There are alliances of convenience, but there isn't much honor among thieves. We know that they have snipers. This may be nothing. The only additional information that I have is that they're practicing against a large target, not a person."

"Let me know if it gets more interesting than that."

Warren ended the call and the secure light on the telephone winked out.

23

Office of Bilateral Implementation (OBI)
Mexico City, District Federal, Mexico

General Barton sputtered, "Syphilis?"

"That's what Santiago told me."

"We can't report that some syphilitic drug lord is wasting our people because he has the clap. I won't sign off on a wild cable with that sort of unsubstantiated social disease speculation."

Oz said, "I'm not suggesting that you tell anyone or that what the informer said is true—simply that he told me that it might be some sort of crazed lunacy that had been induced by untreated syphilis."

"What did Granger say?"

Oz paused, reluctant to say more.

"Did you hear me, Ms. Osborne?"

"I didn't take him with me, I met the informer alone, in a public place."

The General took on a paternal tone, "There were almost two dozen kidnappings in Mexico City, and almost all of the abducted were taken in public. Doesn't that mean anything to you, Oz?

"I thought it was safe enough. We met in a bar last time and he didn't slip me a flunitrazepam."

"A what," Barton asked?

"A date rape drug," Oz clarified. "He could have drugged me and raped me but he didn't."

Even though that sounded like wishful thinking on her part from her tone of voice, Barton let it go.

"But the larger issue is that Iglesias thinks that Gonzales is behind all this mayhem, and our man is in a position to know, isn't he?"

"I'd think so. He comes from the royal lineage of drug smugglers, if anyone can dare to look at it that way. He's a pedigreed legacy narco."

Andrew Krause, the Supervisory Special Agent from DEA who had been assigned to OBI, walked into the general's office, tapping on the door.

"Sit down. We've been talking about Santiago Iglesias-Aznar."

Krause said, "El León."

"Is that his nickname?"

"He doesn't seem to have taken to his family's trade, but he lives like a pharaoh on the money that they left him."

Barton stressed the next question, "Is what he says likely to be accurate?"

"I'd think so, General. But that's like asking me if everything I say is accurate. It depends on my motivation. If my girlfriend were to ask me if I thought she was fat, I'd lie out of a sense of self-preservation."

General Barton handed a telephone number association matrix to Krause. "This is the number he gave Oz when he met her at the bar."

"These guys always carry a dozen cell phones with them," Krause said absently while he looked down the short list. "I don't see much on this. He's calling an Army captain?"

"Capitán Segundo Gabriel *Aznar*," Barton said, "Maybe he's a relative?"

Krause grunted thoughtfully. "Did you check out his pedigree?"

"He's a junior captain in the Fifth Independent Infantry Regiment. You never know about these things, but he sounds like a nobody."

Oz pointed out the obvious, "El León called him fifteen times and they talked for quite a while each time."

"What should we do with it, Krause?" Barton began thinking of golf on the upcoming weekend, having become totally bored with the discussion with the smart ass DEA supervisor and Oz, who he thought of as a wing nut.

"If he's a cousin, they could be discussing family business for all we know. We have a number association capture here, not a wiretap transcript."

Oz asked, "Should we task NSA to intercept, tap and transcribe? It may be important."

"NSA is on my ass now with all of the tasking we're handing out because of the cartels eliminating officials in CONUS. If I was a betting man, I'd guess that every alphabet agency is pushing to get a handle on this so that they can claim the credit."

Barton handed Oz the telephone association matrix. "Hang on to this. Maybe Capitán Segundo Gabriel Aznar will surface again and we can revisit this. For now, all his namesake, Santiago Iglesias-Aznar is doing is trolling. Maybe he thinks you're hot, Oz. Maybe he's telling us this just to get in your knickers."

Krause looked sharply at Barton, who rolled his eyes.

Oz, who had been looking down at the paperwork, said, "Maybe he does."

24

Ten kilometers east of Izúcar de Matamoros, Puebla, Mexico

Overcast, leaden skies covered the rolling hills and scrubland, but it had not rained yet. People in the distance heard what might have passed for thunder in a land where the listeners weren't used to hearing gunshots.

Los Güeros Diablo, Pablo and Francisco Sauceda, fired at two large wooden targets constructed on the range to specifications Capitán Segundo Gabriel Aznar provided.

Lance thought that the two 4'x8' plywood sheets, joined to make eight-foot-square target were just about what the twins needed to assure repeated hits at 1,000 meters.

The Sauceda brothers successfully kept the rounds smacking into the wood as Captain Aznar prodded them to use rapid fire on the plywood targets.

They were firing from tripods and Wendell stood near by, offering suggestions as they banged away.

When both shooters took a break, they talked to Wendell in broken English.

The captain walked to Lance, who had been observing from a distance. "You and Wendell have done well. You've earned your money." Then he handed Lance a brown manila envelope.

Lance pocketed it without counting.

"It's another fourteen thousand that you can split with Wendell or keep for yourself."

"Wendell loves money. I'll make sure that he gets his share."

"As you will."

"You said that the brothers will be shooting at a large target?"

Captain Aznar looked at Lance closely, "Best that you don't ask about such things, my friend. Spend the bonus and forget all about me, about los Güeros Diablo and go on with your life. Such knowledge or disclosure will only count against you. You can see the target size. Let it go at that."

Lance waited until he landed in Houston before he left a message for Track. Whenever and wherever the twins planned to shoot something, it would be big and they'd both be shooting at the same target with armor piercing high explosive ammunition.

When El León, leader of the recently formed Nuevo Millennium Cartel told Felix Ochoa proudly that he would go down in history as one of the world's great mass murderers, he thought the boss was kidding. The taciturn narco leader took offense at his smile and easy dismissal of the absurd notion. Felix laughed at the joke—but only until the fancy .45 automatic came out of the desk and he found himself looking down the business end of what seemed to him to be a very black tunnel. There wouldn't be a train coming out of the tunnel, but the bullet that would splatter him to eternity would be just as deadly for anyone in its path as a speeding locomotive.

El León said, "The Americans haven't done anything," and he set the pistol aside. "We need to let them know that the Sinaloa Federation is serious. The trial of Hector Vazquez will begin in San Diego within the next two weeks. The cards tell me that Señora de las Sombras demands a *large* blood sacrifice if she is to make us successful."

"We have been selling well in San Jose and the San Francisco Bay cities," El Indio said. "The networks in America are hungry for product and the price is high."

"Do you suggest that we do business without removing our competition?"

"Our efforts have been focused on those who have been part of the American government's efforts against the Federation. You suggest a vast departure from that plan."

"The plan has always been to goad the Americans to do something. If the Americans don't eliminate Ruben Gonzalez and the Sinaloa Federation, the Sinaloa Federation will come at us again.

Remember the ambush?" He pointed to the clean skull of El Ingeniero resting on his desk with the AK-47's bolt in the right eye socket. "The Holy Death saved us but how long will her condescension last if we don't take steps to remove the stone in our shoe? We need to get this over with so that we can get on with business. One does not establish a regime in order to safeguard a revolution; one makes a revolution in order to establish a new business. "

El León sent the skull to a man who owned an army of carrion beetles that polished all of the meat from the bones of a dead body that was to serve as an image of Señora de las Sombras or of a trophy, as with El Ingeniero. "It is a remarkably telling trophy, though the man with the carrion beetles bleached his skull it before he sent it back to me. I prefer the natural ivory patina of freshly cleaned bone."

El Indio said humbly, "I've heard of other similar incidents where the AK-47 failed in a similar way."

"Our blessed Holy Death is protecting the righteous, but all the same, we should transition to the American M-16 rifle since it seems to have fewer operating problems. Have our friends in Honduras loose a hundred or so from their arsenal at the earliest. And don't worry about deaths. It is Her will."

163

25

**Cheryl Osborne's Apartment
300 Lomas de Chapultepec,
Miguel Hidalgo, 11010 Ciudad de Mexico,
Distrito Federal, Mexico**

When Oz came back from the Office, she smelled the tangy scent of fragrant beef seared over mesquite chips.

Opening the door she walked in briskly as Gary doted over steaks on the patio bar-b-que.

"Medium-plus in four minutes," Gary said.

"How did you know when I was coming home?"

"I have spies at OBI. I've timed the drive before, so I put the steaks on plus or minus five minutes for traffic and traffic signals."

"Can I change?"

"Yeah, the meat needs to rest a bit once I pull it off the fire and before you eat it. I have scalloped potatoes with minced jalapeño peppers baking in the bottom oven, an apple cobbler cooling on the counter and two salads in the refrigerator. I'll have it on the table when you get comfy."

She came home with news and a head of steam. Oz rationalized that as his manager, she had to manage Gary, but the steaks and dinner changed her carefully planned push to bring him into line.

Gary uncorked a Mexican cabernet as she walked into the dining room wearing sweat pants and a loose blouse.

"Don't go braless if you don't want to be raped before dinner."

Nobody ever talked to her like that before and Oz loved it.

They made it through the salad, the steak and the main course before she brought up work.

"General Barton is about to skin me alive if I don't present you at the office."

Gary picked up his cell phone and punched in numbers.

"Who are you calling?"

"Barton, on his private line—Gary Granger, General. I'm headed to Oz's apartment and bringing desert. She's going to debrief me and wondered if you want to join us."

"Even *I* don't have his private number," Cheryl said in the background.

"Can't this wait for office hours, Granger?"

"Sure. I'll be in whenever-the-fuck."

"See here, you work for me, goddamnit."

"I keep my supervisor informed, this is a courtesy call."

"Listen here, Granger—"

Gary pushed the red button on the phone and canceled the call.

"That may be a bit less respectful and subordinate than he's used to," Oz said, dryly.

"Before he gets here, we need to clear something up."

Ice formed around Oz's heart and she began to panic. In her soul, she felt certain that Gary would dump her. It happened before and now he fixed her a five star meal and was going to lower the boom.

Gary continued, "I think I love you. There have been three previous Mrs. Grangers and I'm not an easy man to be married to. If you spoke to any one of them, they'd tell you that I'm possibly the worst husband on the planet. Worse still, they're right. I was.

"My work habits keep me out late, and sometimes I'm gone for days, but I almost always deliver the goods. Therein rests the onion because the previous Mrs. Grangers didn't get it and worked at punishing me, the way women do to men when they're not sufficiently attentive. I have been a heavy drinker at times, but usually only when I'm lonely. We have a twenty year difference in age—."

"—Gary."

"And we don't know each other that well—"

"—Gary, let me get a word in edgewise. I haven't had the best luck with men because I can be a prize bitch. I know I'm not that pretty and I'm really not that smart. I pretend, you know, smoke and mirrors, but I'm really lost here in Mexico. And—" She hesitated unsure of herself, faltering. "Gary, you're the most amazing and interesting man I've ever met and I'm falling in love with you too. I felt sure that you would use me or that you'd leave me for somebody else.

"At the party the other night, I worked to keep my composure. You knew everyone and everyone knew you. Nobody knows who I am. Usually when I am interested in a man, they run away. Not you."

Gary said, "A friend of mine told me the other day that there's a fine line between cuddling and holding someone down so they can't get away."

Oz smiled warmly, "Is there? Maybe that's my problem with you. I want to hold you down and keep you for myself."

"For the first time in my life, that's precisely what I want."

"Me too."

"I could be lying to you, Oz. After all you are my boss. At another time, in another place this would be precisely what I would be doing to manipulate you. After all, I'm a spy, an old whore, as they say."

"Not now?"

"At first I thought about lying to you, and I can't explain why, but I love you and I'll earn your trust and your faith. I don't want to grow old alone."

"You're not old, Gary."

"I'm going on 61. Paul McCartney wrote a song entitled, 'When I'm Sixty-Four'—*'Will you still need me? Will you still feed me? When I'm sixty-four?'* And at age 60, I have to admit that 64 does not sound nearly as old as it did when I was twenty. At some point you notice that your body is changing and faltering. Those you have loved and shared life with begin to fade and then die. Doing it alone is not a pleasant thought for me, Oz. I hope that doesn't sound selfish."

"I love you, Gary."

"The next time someone says, 'I love you,' take them to a warehouse where the old are discarded. Look directly into all the faces, look directly into all the eyes, and do not draw away if anyone of them still has the strength to take your hand."

"Don't be morbid."

"I only want you to think about what you're signing on for. There's about a twenty-year difference in age between us. Skin that once you loved to caress will become old cotton, and I will lose my own way at some point in this journey. Landmarks once familiar won't be anymore. There will be only a shell with the smallest of sparks left in it. But nobody, least of all me, wants to die old and alone."

He touched her eyelids gently and she closed them and thrilled at his caress. "The seemingly endless mischief in sky blue eyes will fade as cornflowers do, colorful for just one season."

"I love your eyes, Gary."

He stroked the fabric on her couch. "They'll dim just like a shining brocade that catches the light and quickens the pulse becomes nothing but worn wool. I'm a lot closer to that point than you are and if you sign on, I want you for the duration, not just for a day or a week, Oz. Today I can still run around and be a smart ass but the day will come when I can't."

She kissed him deeply and tenderly, then slowly broke it off. "I'm in it for the duration."

General Barton arrived half an hour later in a huff, but accepted a bowl of Gary's cobbler with vanilla ice cream gratefully. Three or four hearty bites later and he seemed to have reconciled himself to the after-hours meeting.

"The Army-Navy Game is coming up, I guess they'll be playing in Philadelphia again," Gary said.

"Army is on a serious losing streak and Mike Sirrine forced a bet on me that I know I'll lose."

"Did he give you points?"

"Straight up—a matter of honor."

"He'll take your money and will enjoy fleecing you."

Barton grumbled, Fuck Sirrine and the damned Navy—So why am I here at Oz's apartment eating this marvelous cobbler?"

"First, it's nice to meet you, General."

"You've done me some favors, Granger, but I don't want you to mistake my kindness for weakness."

"I'm not going into the office, I am not going to be a toady and I'll do the best I can to support Oz and her mission as well as to help you and Scooter Olsen."

"I appreciate your ardent feelings, Granger, but this is not a private operation that you've hired on to and it's not the Central Intelligence Agency."

"The US is going to war against the Sinaloa Federation. To possibly avert that and find out who is behind all the mayhem, I walked through the front door of the Royal Viper Casino, owned by Ruben Gonzales, last week, to deliver an ultimatum."

"Under whose orders?"

"Oz, since I work for her, but this is the first she's heard of it."

Oz gasped, wide eyed.

"Let's say that the people who needed to deliver a message from the National Command Authority couldn't break cover so I was the self-designated bullet sponge."

"Ok, what did the nefarious El Macho Gonzales say?"

"He told me to fuck off, after a manner of speaking. The details aren't important."

"Let me get this straight, Granger, you just waltzed in and told him what?"

"I told him we, meaning the American government, was going to declare war on him as a terrorist running a terrorist organization, threatening the national security of the good old USA. And I offered him a parlay, the opportunity to talk back before the worst happened."

"And he told you to get fucked? That's what he said?"

Granger opened his briefcase and handed him the torn sheet with the words 'fuck you' written on it. "That's pig's blood, general. I don't want it back, you can keep it."

"How did you get on with your superiors at the Agency, Granger? I'm just guessing that they kept you as far from The Campus as possible."

"I didn't spend much time at headquarters. And I didn't get on with them nearly as well as you and I are getting on, General. See, the rank and prestige never blew my skirt up and that's what all the preppy kids want out of the business. I didn't attend Yale, no school tie. The work pays a subsistence wage but I come from money so that didn't motivate me."

168

"I've known guys like you and I'm not impressed. You're in it to play the game and show everyone else you can do it better."

"That's precisely how I play the game, General—pay attention Oz. And that's why you need me out running around. The alternative would be to release me from my contract and I'll stay in Mexico playing on somebody else's card, and no, I'm not a turncoat. I'm an old bastard and know enough to keep my options open."

"You're a manipulative prick."

"I'm a fucking spy. I didn't end up as a brass star on the memorial wall of the foyer in Langley. In the Agency they call us old whores, and I wear that term like a medal. That's all I know how to do. I'm a rather good old whore."

"You're not a bad cook either," Oz added.

Gary gave Oz a fond glance, "Yeah, I can spy and cook. That's the limit of my talent."

"So what the fuck do you expect me to do, Granger," General Barton asked?

"Let me play this one out and see what I can find. I frankly have concerns about the direction that Uncle Sam is taking because there is nothing to indicate that the Sinaloa Cartel is the prime mover in all of the murders, sheets with magic marker writing on them notwithstanding."

"Who do you think is doing this?"

"Somebody we haven't noticed yet."

"Could it be Los Zetas," Barton asked? He harbored a suspicion that the Sinaloa Federation might have contracted the work out to the Zetas, a criminal organization comprised of Mexican Special Forces deserters, corrupt federal and state police officers and Guatemalan soldiers.

"Los Zetas are at war with the Federation. They're allied with what little is left of the Gulf Cartel and the Beltran Leyva Family."

"How can you prove your theory, Granger?"

"I don't have anything, yet. I just have to keep at it. The dead always tell a story. It's up to us to listen."

"The DEA is pissed off at you."

"Why?"

"You haven't included them."

Gary rubbed his chin, looking at Barton and then at Oz. "What do you both suggest that I do to calm them down?"

26

Rancho Ache-N-Back
San Buenaventura Tecaltsingo
Puebla, Mexico

Rancho Ache-N-Back wasn't a regular working ranch. A US Ambassador bought the property northwest of Heroica Puebla de Zaragoza, about an hour and a half's drive from the center of Mexico City, for himself, fifty years previously. He found the name while trying to improve the land, and then had a heart attack and died. Even though his personal improvements didn't remain, the name stuck. His widow deeded the estate in trust to the Embassy and it served as an off-site facility for official and unofficial business from that day on. The Embassy budget supported it and provided for a staff.

The great house and several outbuildings were linked by a stone wall that surrounded the central plaza where Commander Mike Sirrine, Military Attaché and CW5 Scott (Scooter) Olsen stood next to a black Ford Crown Victoria that belonged to the Embassy, waiting for Gary Granger and Oz to arrive.

"Oz and Gary. I never would have thought it would have gone down like that," Mike Sirrine thought out loud.

"You ought to see the place he gave up, just to move in with her— A full- blown penthouse with everything including hot and cold running nubile women." Scooter clarified his opinion as best he could. "I think that whatever is between them is real."

"Maybe Gary is playing an angle?"

"Doubtful," Scooter said. "He's a lonely guy with a lot of contacts and favors but nobody on the inside that he can feel under his flesh. That's what love is and without it, life gets parched as a desert."

"Christ, Scooter, you're getting poetic on me."

Scooter feigned hurt playfully, "It's all that high living in that penthouse, wine like sweet velvet, women like honey, and a chef who comes in three times a week and whips something up for dinner and leaves it in the refrigerator."

"That'll make you poetic," Sirrine said sagely.

"That and fishing. You know, I haven't been fishing since I've been here. There's too much petty running around to do and it seems to creep into every weekend. Fishing is for the soul."

"And eating the fish?"

"A pleasant bonus."

Gary drove up to the metal door and a moment later the gate slowly pushed open, driven by grinding gears that were operated by an old caretaker.

Gary pulled the car into the courtyard, past Scooter and Mike toward a rambling, ivy-clad building set back in the spacious grounds. Oz waved cheerfully. Scooter and Mike waved back, trying not to look incredulous.

They walked over to the shade of an old tree where Gary parked Oz's Volvo. Gary got out, walked around the car to the passenger door and let Oz out.

"Are the DEA people here?"

Scooter motioned absently toward two black GMC Yukons parked by the great house. "They beat us here. We wanted to have a word before we walked into the abattoir."

"They just want to flex some muscle because we've been running around in what they consider to be their turf without asking for their blessing."

Mike clarified, "They say we're shitting on their investigation."

"As I understand it, the murders and kidnapping are within the FBI's charter."

"The DEA owns Mexico, Gary," Mike said.

Gary looked at Cheryl and she tipped her head.

"The Ambassador runs all US operations in Mexico. He's the plenipotentiary here, not the DEA Assistant Director."

"The DEA SAC doesn't care." Mike gestured in the direction of the great house.

"The SAC, not the Assistant Director? What am I, second string?"

"The AD is in Washington doing something important."

172

Gary suggested. "Let's go in and let them blow off some steam."

Special Agent-in-Charge Ted Cordia didn't stand when Gary, Oz, Mike and Scooter walked into the room. He had his people strategically stationed against the walls so that no matter where they sat, there were DEA people behind them.

Brief, chilled pleasantries passed quickly and before Ted Cordia could speak and spread his peacock plumage, Gary said, "I really appreciate the opportunity to clarify things and suggest that you worry about the drug situation here and let us try and drag your fat out of the fire without interference."

"You—" Cordia began, "dare?"

"The FBI isn't here and Director Kyle Sanz is the President's point man for murder, mayhem and kidnapping. If you'd been doing your job helping the Mexican Army track down El Macho Gonzales, we wouldn't be in this mess, would we?"

"Granger, aren't you a *contractor*?"

"The one who found the dead US Attorney, yeah, CW5 Olsen and I found him, without any help from *you*."

"I'm acting under the direction of General Barton and Ambassador Loyen."

Oz reached into her purse and produced documentation. Special Agent-in-Charge Cordia motioned to one of his men to take the paperwork and look at it. "I'm operating ex officio for Secretary Nathan Wasliewski, she boasted."

"So it says," Cordia muttered, as he read.

"Now, I've prepared a list of specific tasks for your agents," Gary said humbly.

"Now see here, old man," Cordia protested.

"Or you can be a hero," Gary interrupted. "All the president wants is for the killings and kidnappings to stop. Everybody in this room, including you—unless I presume too much—believes that if Ruben Gonzales is boxed up with a bow on his coffin, that the killings will stop."

"Go on," Cordia prompted.

"Find El Macho, no more screwing around. Don't waste your breath being angry with us. We're nothing. I'm simply a contractor, Oz is a State Department official, Mike and Scooter are military.

You're the DEA Special Agent-in-Charge. Find the biggest drug kingpin in Mexico. The killings will continue, and if I'm right, things will get worse before they get better. You are the man to do something about that, not me."

Cordia said, "Where's the bar?"

Several drinks later, Cordia found that he didn't hate Gary Granger nearly as much as he thought he did. They swapped war stories and played who-do-you-know. Then Gary got serious.

"Do you know what's in Pandora's Box, Ted?" Gary stared hard at Cordia.

"Buried secrets?"

"A mirror. The evil let loose on the world is there for you to see when you pop the lid—and usually we are responsible for most of it. Be sure and kill Ruben El Macho Gonzales when you find him and let the coffin of buried secrets remain with him."

"What's that supposed to mean?"

Gary composed himself, "Just a bit of advice. This guy has all the American dirty secrets cataloged. He can't ever reach the Judge's docket to face a public trial."

"But you're just a fucking contractor."

"Well, that's right, special agent. I'm really only a simple retired man, a civilian."

Gary Granger tossed Cordia a folded newspaper. Cordia opened it and read.

> *America Today News* - Defendant in Gang Racketeering Case Jorge Gonzales Aragon Sentenced to 30 years: "Jorge Gonzales Aragon, also known as El Choco, 33, was sentenced by U.S. District Judge Dale S. Truman, who is presiding over the 51-defendant racketeering indictment that was the centerpiece of 'Operation Knock Down' in 2011.
>
> Operation Knock Down was an investigation into the activities of the Sinaloa Drug Cartel conducted by the Los Angeles High Intensity Drug Trafficking Area (HIDTA) Task Force, which is comprised of agents and officers with the Los Angeles County Sheriff's Department; the Drug Enforcement Administration; the Federal Bureau of

Investigation; the Bureau of Alcohol, Tobacco, Firearms and Explosives; U.S. Immigration and Customs Enforcement's Homeland Security Investigations; and IRS - Criminal Investigation.

Gonzales was the lead defendant in the RICO indictment, a longtime member of the Sinaloa drug gang, and a sometime 'shot-caller' who was able to issue orders to other gang members and collect 'taxes' from drug dealers.

"I know this," Cordia said, with attitude. "I was personally involved in that case. I can quote you chapter and verse on every aspect of it.

"Jorge Gonzales Aragon is El Macho's nephew?"

"Yeah."

"And your fun meter isn't pegged? Am I the only one on the planet who thinks that something really bad is about to happen? 'Cause right about now, my pucker factor is running right at maximum," Gary explained seriously

Special Agent-in-Charge Ted Cordia consulted with Assistant Director (Mexico) Louanne Cogburn and advised her that he had put his entire force on the sole task of locating Ruben (El Macho) Gonzales because in his judgment, things were going to get worse before they got better. A source (not cited) felt that El Macho would up the ante.

27

San Diego International Airport
(Lindbergh Field)
San Diego, California

The airport had been named in honor of Charles Lindbergh, the first man to fly solo across the Atlantic. He used the runway to test his historic aircraft, the *Spirit of St. Louis*. Later, Lindbergh helped campaign for the bond issue that funded the airport, dedicated on August 16, 1928.

Over time the location proved less than ideal, but San Diego and the surrounding area grew and a sufficiently large tract was never available to construct another, larger airport. It is presently ranked the tenth most dangerous airport in the world because of its precarious landing and take off patterns that require airliners to crest skyscrapers on landing and take off to avoid the Point Loma peninsula.

Lindbergh Field currently provides the single busiest single-runway commercial service in the United States with over six hundred arrivals and departures every day, moving 50,000 passengers through its gates to destinations worldwide.

Several alternatives have been suggested including closing Naval Air Station North Island on nearby Coronado Island and using that facility for the purposes of commercial and civil aviation. The US Navy rejected that proposal, though never insultingly. The Navy felt that the needs of San Diego were subordinate to theirs.

Pacific Airlines Flight 281, an Airbus A320, was on time and scheduled to depart at 8:20 am with service to Phoenix.

Security protocols set in place by the United States Department of Homeland Security and its Transportation Safety Administration controlled where passengers could park or how they could arrive at the airport. Curbside loading and unloading of passengers and their luggage was allowed, but frowned upon. Uniformed members of the San Diego Harbor Police provided armed security at the airport once the passengers arrived on airport property. They patrolled the perimeter of the runway, the parking lots, both passenger and commercial terminal areas and had a presence at passenger screening. Generally they dealt with law enforcement officers who flew armed and needed to be cleared.

The United States Transportation Security Administration screened passengers to insure that they had valid identification and that it matched the ticket they purchased. Passengers and their carry-on luggage underwent scrutiny as it and they passed through x-ray and scanning machines. TSA regulations allowed travelers to carry small toiletries of three ounces or less—in a one, quart size, clear plastic, zip-top bag.

Laptop computers, video cameras and electronic devices received additional scrutiny as did shoes, which travelers removed and put into plastic bins.

The Secure Flight program, unseen by passengers, matched their names and biometrics to a watch list. Behind the scenes, TSA's trained bomb and drug K-9s sniffed and barked at suspicious luggage, which was removed from the conveyors and searched by hand.

Having been scanned, partially disrobed, and re-dressed, travelers felt confident that the rules set forth by the security gods were keeping them safe. Those with passage on Pacific Airlines Flight 281 formed a line at Gate 23 and filed from the terminal down the jet way. A flight attendant greeted them individually, directing them down the fuselage to their assigned seats.

With lap belts fastened, seat backs in their full and upright condition and tray tables stowed and latched, the purser advised the captain that the passenger cabin had been secured and that they were ready for take off.

The cheerfully painted Airbus A320-200 began its take-off roll under full power, fully loaded with fuel, 144 passengers and their luggage at just over 155,000 pounds. When the airliner's speed passed 170 mph, the pilot pulled back gently on the yoke and rotated its nose into the air. The Airbus it lifted gently off the runway.

Even though the plane is capable of taking off as soon as the stall speed has been exceeded, the aircraft remains unstable because any change in the configuration of the wing surface will cause it to lose lift, causing it to plunge back to the runway.

Federal Aviation Administration's Regulation Part 25 (FAR25) specifies that take off velocity requirements must be observed by transport aircraft. Through they are set in stone by the federal government, they are also set in stone by immutable laws of physics.

FAR25 requires that the take off climb speed must exceed twenty percent of stall speed to provide an adequate safety margin.

Francisco Sauceda rented a room in an older wood frame home just west of Rosecrans Street with a view of the harbor and a direct line-of-sight to the end of the runway. He'd paid cash, six months in advance. The room had a private stairway entrance that led to the second floor. Francisco didn't care that the paint on the wood slat house peeled or that the owners were potheads. All he really cared about was the location and an unobstructed view.

Pablo Sauceda parked the white delivery truck with a bakery's logo on the slab side, in a large parking lot between Rosecrans Street and Truxtun Road about three blocks from Francisco's apartment. The truck's rear roll-up door faced the end of the airport's runway.

In both the rented room and the back of the truck, sheets scribed with black marker announced that the Sinaloa Federation would no longer tolerate American interference in their commercial affairs, and those of Ruben Gonzales in particular. Further interruptions of the narcotics flow to the United States across the Mexican -American Border would lead to still more dire consequences, and this was only the beginning. The syntax, the penmanship, the threats down to the source of the sheets: a textile mill in Campo El Diez, outside Culiacan, in the heart of Sinaloa—were identical in all respects to every other message that Santiago Iglesias-Aznar sent through his agents.

Both Barrett Model 82A1A rifles tracked the progress of Pacific Airways flight 281 as it rolled almost directly at them. The aircraft filled the impeccable optics integral in their Schmitt and Bender rifle scopes.

The rifles were each loaded with .50 caliber Raufoss cartridges. The bullets, aimed at the spinning hub of the jet engines would explode on contact. One bullet fired accurately into each engine would trash the entire CFM International high-bypass turbofan aircraft engine assembly. Because neither of los Güeros Diablo, Pablo or Francisco Sauceda, were crack shots, they each had ten rounds in their magazines to take out their engine. Pablo tracked the starboard engine and Francisco the engine to port.

They each began their count from nose gear rotation. At twenty seconds they'd both open fire and continue firing until their magazines were empty. Once complete, they'd begin their escape and evasion protocol.

Their firing positions were separated by roughly two hundred meters. Who fired first and who fired last didn't matter much. A trained orangutan could take down the Airbus with the equipment they had at hand.

As it happened, Pablo fired before Francisco did. As he fired, the barrel recoiled for about an inch, held in place by the rotating bolt. A post on the bolt engaged in the curved cam track in the receiver turned the bolt to unlock it from the barrel. As soon as the bolt unlocked, the accelerator arm struck it back, transferring part of the recoil energy from the barrel to the bolt. The barrel's travel stopped and the bolt continued back, to extract and eject a spent case. On its return stroke, the bolt stripped a fresh cartridge from the box magazine, fed it into the chamber and locked itself to the barrel. The striker also cocked on the return stroke of the bolt, and with a new round in battery, Pablo squeezed the trigger again.

The incendiary feature of the Raufoss bullet allowed Pablo to see where his bullet hit. A bright flash marked the impact about a foot right of center. The bullet's incendiary tip flashed first as the armor - piercing core carried it inside the engine. Then the RX51-PETN high explosive detonated, sending steel shards throughout the spinning stator and rotor blades, causing the rapidly spinning blades to break apart and to become part of the shrapnel themselves. He put another three Raufoss rounds into the starboard side turbofan. After that there wasn't much engine left. Francisco's work on the portside engine destroyed it with similar results.

Pablo directed his next half dozen rounds into the aircraft cockpit as the Airbus began a leisurely spiral to the right. Slaughtering the pilots with explosive fifty caliber bullets may have been the kindest thing he could have done because they didn't have to sit holding a dead stick, sitting at the front of a flaming meteor filled with passengers screaming behind them as the aircraft dutifully obeyed Newton's three laws of motion.

The aircrew of five and one hundred forty-four passengers riding the dead Airbus 320A greased into the Famosa Slough, where it came apart, splattering aircraft parts in a debris field that spread in an oblong pattern flanked by the Barnes Tennis Center the Loma Rivera housing development and extending into the Quivira Yacht Basin. If the Airbus hadn't struck the swamp, the loss of life on the ground would have been far worse.

San Diego news choppers were on the scene before the parts stopped tumbling and the President watched the live coverage on Wolf News, where the commentators had been critiquing his new Middle East Initiative. The breaking story preempted and immediately muted criticism as the nation stood still in much the way it had on September 11, 2001.

Shoppers heard the loud report of the .50 caliber rifle from the van. A suspect wearing a nondescript blue hooded sweatshirt and jeans ran from the scene and nobody had much more to report. Some of the curious who approached the white bakery truck were transfixed by the tripod mounted rifle and one of the now infamous bed sheets nailed to the interior wall of the van.

A Wolf News truck beat the police to the scene because the police converged on the crash site to rescue the injured on the ground and protect that crime scene.

Wolf News scooped the other cable channels once again, the American President stewed, as his shrewish wife trilled not about the horrible loss of life, but about Wolf's failure to have an anchor of color reporting the disaster.

Though he considered himself a proponent of Hispanic immigration because they usually voted for him, he began to reconsider the political wisdom of that position as the hot blonde reporter from Wolf News and her camera crew focused on the long, wicked looking black military rifle resting on a tripod with the explicit threat laid out behind it.

Other news crews began to arrive at the crash site and record for all posterity the dismembered passengers and the corpses of those unlucky souls who were in their homes when the airliner struck.

San Diego rested under a clear, azure sky. The rain fell steadily in Mexico City, 1,600 miles to the southeast.

28

Carretera Federal 200
The Tecoman-Ciudad Lazaro Cardenas Road
Near Las Trojitas
Michoacan, Mexico

They listened to the bitter fruit they wrought with their own bloody hands on a news station as they drove down the windy coast road toward El León's 1,000 hectare ranch up the coast from Las Trojitas. There was nothing else on the radio. As the story developed, more information came out, but not the identity of the shooters.

The day that started out blustery with blowing rain cleared as they drove north.

The reaction in Mexico was more violent and angry than either El León or El Indio would have suspected. The talk, even among the old narcos who would have cut their own children's throats before talking to the government, went immediately toward giving up Ruben Gonzales to the hands of justice. Moving drugs north had become a lucrative business and a key part of the Mexican economy, but taking down an airliner full of innocents for the sake of revenge because your nephew was convicted fairly in a court, took things to a surreal level. The Americans and the Mexicans joined together in a sense of national outrage to remove the lead narco from the gene pool once and for all.

"Do we have any loose ends," El Indio asked?

El León rubbed his chin as he drove, "The American snipers who trained won't talk. Their own people will execute them if they do. They're professionals, and there is nothing to link them to us. Los Güeros Diablo worked for the Sinaloa Federation before they came to work for us and if anyone should make the connection, it will only stand to reason that they did what they did at the request of El Macho."

"But…"

"But you can't be too careful," El León stressed, "because there is always something that you overlook. We are about to enter the phase of this plan where we go our separate ways, throw away our cellular telephones and wait for the dust to settle."

"Then when it does?"

El León smiled, "Then when this present angry reaction has passed and El Macho is dead, buried and forgotten, we will take his place as the most powerful cartel in Mexico. The Americans seem to be doing now what they could have done before we had to take drastic measures. It's really *their fault*, you know?"

"The Americans fault?" El Indio had rationalized a great deal in his life, but this seemed to be a radical leap that he found difficult to follow.

"Yes, if they acted decisively when we started murdering their people and if they had killed El Macho earlier, we wouldn't have needed to bring down the airplane."

"Do Los Güeros Diablo live?" El Indio genuinely liked the brothers, who trusted him implicitly.

"Sure, they won't be talking. I don't consider them loose ends that need to be cut. They will be valuable lieutenants joined to me—and you with the blood they took. In a sense, all of the dead were sacrificed to Señora de las Sombras. Haven't you seen her hand in all this? Remember the gun that exploded in El Ingeniero's very hands and sent the bolt through his eye? I keep his skull with me. It's back in the trunk of the car—part of my portable altar to the Saint."

El Indio shuddered involuntarily.

"Señora de las Sombras wants us to be rich, to have cars, fine women, airplanes, yachts, and she wants us to live in mansions. That's why she wrought all of this for us. It's all about Her love for you and me, El Indio."

Once they arrived at El León's rancho, the plan went dark. El Indo took a black Ford pick-up truck back south, retracing his path down the Tecoman-Ciudad Lazaro Cardenas Road. The boss drove north.

There were a few tense moments where El Indio began to take counsel of his fears. He considered the possibility that El León placed a bomb in the truck that would detonate once they separated in time and space but it didn't happen. El Indio reasoned that he'd seen too many movies.

By design, there was a very small group in the center of this new cartel they formed. Killing them all off would mean that El León decided to be a king without a knights to do his dirty work.

29

Jardín Botánico
Coyoacán, Mexico City, Distrito Federal

Track met Gary at the Botanical Gardens, in the rain on a Thursday morning. The grounds were deserted except for the two crazy Americans who didn't have the good sense to remain indoors on a day like this one. Traffic on the streets remained light. Even two days after the airplane went down there was only one story on the news and everyone seemed glued to the television as the horror and body count climbed.

Both men carried umbrellas and sat on a wet park bench made of old, soft, unvarnished wood.

"There are other, possibly better, places to meet," Gary said with a pronounced cadence, feeling irritable.

"I know, but I like it here when it rains. There's a fragrant smell that comes off the tropical plants and the earthy aroma appeals to me."

Gary shrugged; he'd been in the jungle professionally years before and didn't think much of it then or now.

"There is a task force in Op Center on this Mexico situation now. The President signed a lethal finding for Ruben Gonzales and the top members of the Sinaloa Federation, yesterday."

"Did Jim Warren and the Seventh Floor Gnomes say that you could tell me?"

"They told me before Pacific Airways 281 bit it. Back then it was only a contingency plan. For the record, Warren admonishes you to remember that you work for Nathan Wasliewski, not for the CIA."

"I heard that a special helicopter assault group is being cobbled together at Ft. Campbell, Kentucky and sent to a secret air base we're running in the Yucatan Peninsula."

Track blanched, "Where did you hear that?"

"Rumor mill. East Coast: They're sending a mixed force from the 1st and 2nd Battalions from the 160th SOAR and though I haven't heard anything specifically on the matter, it would stand to reason that they'll be flying Delta Force operators and possibly Rangers with that much aviation. West Coast: The Navy and Marine Corps are preparing to float a significant portion of the First Marine Division south and operate from the ships. Don't worry. Nobody at OBI has heard a thing outside of General Barton and Master Warrant Officer Scooter Olsen—and even they aren't completely in the loop. That must mean that there's a bigger general who will be calling the shots and he doesn't like General Barton."

Track smiled, "Major General Ripper Phinizy, an old school Marine is the war planner. Your information is correct. The Marine Corps is sending two battalions from the First Marines with support from the Third Marine Air Wing and will be positioned in the Sea of Cortez. Phinizy will be in overall command, Halls of Montezuma and all that. The Marine Corps cited precedent, even though the most of the American forces who stormed Chapultapec in 1847 were soldiers, not marines. The Marines got the song and that's worked out nicely for Ripper Phinizy.

"The Army will take the eastern and northern portions of Mexico under Operation Vigilant Sword. The Marine Corps will handle the west coast north to south under Operation Vigilant Saber. They'll be on their amphib ships grouped around the USS Carl Vinson carrier battle group."

"Will the Agency be sending Predators or whichever drone of choice they're using now, the Reapers?"

"I don't know."

"Warren didn't say?"

"Nope."

"So it's an open war against the Sinaloa Cartel – mano-a-mano! Doesn't it strike you as strange that these people would provoke that sort of response? Cartel leaders have egos but they're the CEO's of multinational corporations worth billions in commerce each year. Why risk losing it over this kind of senseless bullshit? They know that the Mexican government will step aside and let us in because it's in everyone's interests for them to do so. My God, listen to the news, even the public down here is calling for the Americans to kick cartel ass. They *want* us to invade the narco strongholds."

"It does seem odd, but there are serious political considerations all the way to the White House and the next election—that outweigh my suspicions."

Gary asked, "And when we take out the Sinaloa Federation by decapitating their leadership, who will benefit?"

"The American people?"

Gary snorted, "Of course."

"Other cartels?"

"And the question is which cartel, because when you answer that question, you'll know who has been kidnapping, shooting down and killing."

Track asked, "What do you think the odds are that the Sinaloa Federation has been doing this?"

"What are the odds of finding an ass virgin in the San Francisco City Jail?"

"Long odds."

"Whose secret base is it that the Army is building up?"

"Ours."

"That will make great news in the tabloids when it's leaked."

"Who says it will leak? The base is *black*. Nobody knows about it."

"There wasn't anything more secret than the interrogation centers we ran in Eastern Europe and *that* leaked."

"But the media didn't find about *all* of them."

"No, they did miss *one*, but you get my point."

Track nodded, "Let's get out of this miserable rain."

A thought struck Track as he sloshed through puddled rainwater to his car. He wondered whether or not Lance Parkyn was training up the very people who would use the precision sniping skill sets he taught to blow out the engines of a passenger liner on takeoff. While it might be germane to the issue, he decided to wait and see if Deputy Director Warren thought it was politically important enough to disclose. That the CIA might have known enough to stop the snipers before the disastrous shoot-down could be embarrassing and damaging to the Agency if it came out.

While Gary and Track discussed strategy, Abrille Fuentes combed through Cheryl Osborne's briefcase, and used a hand scanner to transfer data for her father's use later. The first effort was a five page document, captioned *Capitán Segundo Gabriel Aznar * Santiago Iglesias-Aznar Cellular Association Matrix*. It outlined the telephone numbers they both called and represented Oz's personal effort to probe more deeply into the association between the two men, who she had already learned, were cousins.

Abrille did her work quickly and efficiently. Her father trained her thoroughly.

Once she completed that effort, she turned her attention to the apartment and was happy that she did. A key turned in the lock and Oz walked in, carrying groceries.

"Abrille, you don't have to come here on Saturday."

"Señora's brother is staying here and with the two of you here, you need everything made proper."

"Oh, Abrille, you're just the best," Oz exclaimed and put her arms around the ugly, round-shouldered maid. "I don't know what I'd do without you."

She smelled the girl's natural musk and went to a counter and lifted a bottle of Euphoria. "Here, take this perfume. Use it when you're going out with a young man."

Abrille seemed pleased to get the expensive bottle of fine perfume, but Oz privately doubted that there was a young man. If she had a boyfriend, he would have to be somewhere well beyond desperate.

188

30

Office of Bilateral Implementation (OBI)
Mexico City, District Federal, Mexico

Francisco Sauceda smoked a Marlboro light while he waited, separate from the other drivers and bodyguards, who stood together sharing cigarettes and stories.

A pyre of flowers and candles had been assembled in front of the American Embassy a few buildings down the street. Security around the Embassy and around the building that housed OBI increased tenfold after he had personally pulled the trigger on the Pacific Airways jet liner that flew over his head, engines on fire. He thought of the Bible, Romans, Chapter 13, 'Whoever resists authority will bring judgment upon themselves.' The Holy Death, Señora de las Sombras, decreed that they must die—and die they did, according to her holy mind and will.

He didn't feel remorse; only a vague detachment when it came to what he and Pablo did. Part of him felt pride that he'd struck such a blow to a country the size of the United States. Another part registered regret because the passengers on the airplane, some of whom turned out to be Mexican citizens, were innocent of everything except picking an unlucky flight.

Now, in the livery of a chauffer, he watched and waited for Cheryl Osborne-Clarridge, whom he and his brother surveilled many times before. If the pattern remained the same, she'd exit the elevator and walk to her car while he marked her.

The Office of Bilateral Implementation occupied the top three floors of the office building, but the rest of the commercial skyscraper held many other offices. It was for an executive with an office on the sixteenth floor that he purported to work. There was no way to find street parking where you could watch people come and go from OBI.

Standing with the other drivers provided perfect cover. He followed her out of the parking garage driving one of many black Mercedes sedans with darkened windows, on many occasions without rousing the least amount of suspicion.

El Indio said that the lady had a paper linking Capitán Segundo Gabriel Aznar and the boss, Santiago Iglesias-Aznar through telephone calls. If true, she turned out to be a lot smarter than he'd given her credit for being. To him, she was just another woman with a lonely heart who must have landed her job because of family connections or maybe it had been a fluke?

No matter what, at this point, she was worth far more dead to the organization than she was alive. It remained a problem, soon to be resolved.

A few miles distant, El Indio waited patiently in Oz's apartment, stroking the small gray kitten. It purred contentedly and sometimes it mewed. As he sat and petted the kitten, he thought of the hungry ghosts swirling around him in the ether, the gods and demons, not unlike his reflection in a mirror. Sometimes they brought harm, sometimes they brought benefits, but they inevitably acted according to the holy will of Señora de las Sombras. She dolled out riches and possessions like a virulent poison that choked and consumed.

He looked down at his hands, wrapped around the neck of the now lifeless kitten, dead in obedience to the carnal desires of Señora de las Sombras.

El Indio went into the kitchen, found a knife, lifted the kitten against a wooden cabinet door and drove the knife through the body of the lifeless cat into the wood. A sacrifice to the Holy Death needed to be properly displayed.

Francisco Sauceda called when Cheryl Osborne's Volvo made the final turn, approaching her apartment. She turned left and Francisco continued down the street for three blocks before making a u-turn to return to the apartment where he had been instructed to wait for El Indio.

Oz called Gary as she drove down Lomas de Chapultepec to her apartment.

"Hey Oz," Gary answered tensely.

DEA now considered Gary to be their new best friend and he was working with them closely as a treasured advisor in their efforts to narrow down the rat-in-the-hole, as they now tagged El Macho Gonzales. Consequently, she didn't know if he'd be working through the night.

"Do you want me to cook dinner?"

"Do I want *you* to cook?" Gary ate Cheryl's cooking before. It had the uniform characteristic of failing to inspire.

"Yes, *I can cook* and clean up. You just take over the kitchen like a Mongol Chieftain and insist on doing it all—and leaving the dishes for poor Abrille."

"You need to get rid of the maid."

"Why? I like her. I feel sorry for her."

"We'll talk about it when I get home tonight. I won't be late and I'll cook a stroganoff. Decant some wine and don't drink it all before I get there. I don't want it said that I ravished an unresponsive woman. However, the ravishing may have to wait until later. I think I'll bring Andrew Krause home for supper. He needs a good meal."

"I'm always responsive to you, darling, even if I have to wait for Special Agent Krause to leave first."

"Love you Oz."

"Love you Gary."

She ended the conversation and put the cell phone into her purse and fumbled for the apartment key as she ascended the stairs.

The front door was unlocked and she called, "Abrille," as she opened the door and stepped inside.

El Indio whipped a fine strand of piano wire tied at the ends to two wooden toggles. The garrote arced over Cheryl Osborne's head and pulled the toggles tight, dragging her backward off her feet so that her own weight would add to the pressure on the taunt, thin wire around her neck. The wire did its job, cutting through sinew, blood veins and arteries, leaving her dying head attached only by her spinal column.

She dropped like a sack of potatoes at his feet. He stepped carefully over her and walked out to the street where Francisco waited patiently in his black Mercedes.

31

Gary came home as planned, driven by Andrew Krause, the senior DEA man at OBI, who he'd promised a fine dinner with Oz. When they found the front door to the apartment ajar, a cold hand grabbed his stomach and he stopped involuntarily.

Even though neither he nor the DEA man were authorized to carry handguns in Mexico, the cartel war with the United States of America that Ruben Gonzales apparently began, changed everything.

He pulled his Glock Model 21 from his holster and Krause cleared leather when he saw Gary draw and the open door.

Strobeing red and blue lights spun, Mexican military officers, Scooter Olsen, General Barton and a sea of concerned faces revolved around Gary and though he saw, he didn't really see. He felt as if somebody was sitting on his chest, but there wasn't anyone there. The image of Tin Man, the kitten, skewered to the kitchen cabinet remained as his human psyche dealt with the gory sight of Cheryl laying, nearly decapitated in a large pool of her own blood.

USNS Mercy (T-AH 19)
The Sea of Cortez

He woke up in a hospital ward that could have been any place on the planet. The doctors and nurses were US Navy. The dry spider webs in his brain that kept him from thinking clearly caused his balance to be off, but when he looked around and saw a porthole, he connected the dots.

"I'm on a ship?"

A nurse, who had been reading a magazine by his bed, pushed an alarm button and looked over at him, smiling. She laid the magazine on a table next to his bed.

"You're on the *Mercy*, a US Navy hospital ship."

"A dead kitten—Tin Man," Gary mumbled.

"I've called the doctor, Mr. Granger—can I call you Gary?"

Gary blinked his eyes hard two or three times. Time passed and he felt severe disorientation.

An older man wearing a white lab coat suddenly stood next to his bed.

"Where am I?"

"You're on the *Mercy* and I'm Captain Jeff Bradshaw, your attending physician." The navy doctor with a captain's eagle on his nameplate consulted a chart. He knew the doctor hadn't appeared out of thin air, but in his confused state of mind, it seemed like it.

"What happened?"

"You had a mild heart attack and—other trauma. We thought it best to sedate you. The *Mercy* is off the coast of Sinaloa, Mexico right now, standing by to receive military and indigenous civilian casualties. The Ambassador called in your med-evac personally and the Marine Corps flew you in from Mexico City.

"A hospital ship?"

"We came back from Pacific Partnership to support Operation Vigilant Saber."

"Ah." Gary recalled the plan for the Marine Corps to flush out Sinaloa State. "The war—I had a dream about Oz.

The doctor exchanged a concerned look with the nurse.

"We have counselors embarked and some," Doctor Bradshaw cleared his throat, "other counseling staff enroute from the East Coast to make sure that you have everything you need."

"CIA?"

The doctor nodded.

"Fuck 'em."

The doctor smiled, "They said you'd take that position."

Gary's head cleared quickly and most of what happened before he discovered Cheryl came back to him. After he found her—well most of that seemed to be missing.

"How long?" He tried to sit up and the nurse plunged a syringe into the IV tube.

"Three days, Gary. You just take it easy. We're here to help you."

Everything went black.

193

When he woke up, Scooter Olsen, in Army Blue Class B Service Uniform, sat in the chair that had been occupied by the navy nurse. He turned the pages on a *Penthouse* magazine.

Gary laughed but it came out as a dry croak.

"Did you get my stuff?"

Scooter nodded and put his finger to his lips. "I was one of the first ones there from the Army. Krause did a great job coordinating things, but there was nothing that could be done for her."

"Or for Tin Man."

"Yeah, the cat too."

"The nurse drugged me. I can't remember anything about Oz except that she was messed up somehow. Is she ok? Is she *here*?"

"You're pretty fucked up."

"Not that bad, Scooter."

"You need to consider standing down for a bit, Gary."

"Maybe, once I sort things out."

"The Agency sent a team to help you and the Secretary of State wants to meet you when you're feeling better. He's in Mexico City smoothing over ruffled feathers at the moment."

"What happened?"

"They found El Macho in the basement of the Royal Viper Casino in Sinaloa after the Marine Corps worked the casino and half the town over."

"Dead?"

"El Macho? Yes, very dead. There are a number of dead civilians too, and a lot of dead narcos who decided to shoot it out with the Marines. They're mopping up the other people on the list, and the army is royally pissed because they're on the other side of the country without as many targets. That's what caused the problem on the east coast. Some of the Zetas took potshots at 'em and the Army was a little enthusiastic in their pursuit of the criminals. Quite a few neighborhoods in San Fernando were leveled. Not just there, anywhere there was resistance These guys were used to dealing with the local troops, not with us."

"When will they let me out of here?"

"I don't know. Once you've talked to the shrinks, and the croakers decide that you won't die if they let you stand up, they should let you go if that's what you want."

Scooter took Gary's hand. "I'm so sorry."

"I know, Scooter. I remember what happened to Oz now and I have business to attend to and I can't do it here." Gary's voice was cold, hard and brittle as slate.

Scooter Olsen changed the subject. "A few marine casualties have come in from Los Mochis, where the US Marines are doing what the Mexicans should have done a long time ago. It seems as though the cartels felt that our people would be a push over."

"We've been fighting in shit hole towns in the third world since September 11, 2001."

"Yeah, well the narcos didn't figure on that." Scooter shrugged. "The fighting was intense but brief. There are neighborhoods in Los Mochis that you can see from the deck of the *Mercy* that are smoking ruins. Maybe they'll let you up on deck and you can watch some of the payback. The locals seem to have caught the vision and those criminals we didn't catch or smoke on our own have been surrendered to us."

"How long have you been here on the ship, Scooter?"

"Two days. It's been about a week since Cheryl died, Gary."

"Did they ever figure out whether or not it really was El Macho who was behind Pacific Airways 281?"

"Well, yes, sure he was. Everyone says so. He sent you that 'fuck you' note written in pig's blood. That's been on television but they never mentioned you by name."

32

Tláhuac
Zona Metropolitana de la Ciudad de Mexico

A location in Tláhuac sat high on his list and it surprised him that El Indio felt comfortable in that neighborhood. The people of that district in Mexico City had a reputation of dealing harshly with outsiders, and Felix Ochoa was an outsider.

When Gary had been in Mexico on his previous tour, with the CIA, residents of the San Juan Ixtayopan village in Tláhuac, lynched a detachment of undercover federal police officers. Two of the policemen were burned alive and a third was badly mauled by the mob. The officers, on an antidrug patrol, were apparently confused with child abductors. Gary always harbored the suspicion that they were setting somebody up to be kidnapped when they suffered their fate. It schooled anyone interested in getting up to mischief in that village.

Because some of the electronic bread crumbs that the airborne surveillance assets pulled from the ether led to Tláhuac, Gary wondered whether or not the people who killed Cheryl and Tin Man, the kitten, lived in there. Maybe they were friendly with El Indio?

Gary's new cell phone vibrated softly. Track was the only person who had the number.

"Where are you, Gary?" Track's voice brimmed over with emotion.

"Don't pick a fight with an old man. If he's too old to fight, he'll just kill you. There are some people who picked a fight with an old man's girlfriend and it's all the same. Meet me at one of the places, later, if you want."

He pushed the disconnect button on the cell phone, pulled out the battery and threw both into a garbage heap in the alley where he stood.

Trash and dead animals lay in random clumps along the narrow roadway that occupied the space between crumbling brick industrial buildings. It took Gary the better part of an hour to cross a hundred feet, but he did it silently in the darkness.

A heavy roll-up metal door scraped and squeaked ahead of him. Fluorescents flickered on. A blue Toyota rested up on a rusted hydraulic lift and a man began to tinker with his tools, looking up at something near the engine compartment.

A section of the garage had been portioned off by heavy steel sheeting with a padlocked door in the middle. Gary stood in the shadows close enough to see that the lock hung open in the hasp.

The RC-12 Utes targeted this location with their cellular telephone tracking electronics suites and told the story. Felix Ochoa came here before the airliner had been shot down in San Diego. After that, the cell phones went dark and Gary had to rely on the Neanderthal throwback's historical movements for tracking purposes.

A moped turned into the alley and sputtered its way, weaving to avoid trash heaps. As it came into the light of the open garage, Gary saw Abrille Fuentes, the maid who bore such a striking resemblance to her father. She struck up a brief conversation with the mechanic that led to a romantic embrace. The mechanic reached down and wedged his hand between the fabric of her corduroy trousers and her flesh.

Gary reached behind him and pulled the crossbow from where he'd strapped it onto his back. He left it cocked because it took time to pull the bow cord back to the trigger group and occasionally drawing it made the tiniest creaking noise.

All of the energy of the bow lay in the steel prods, pulled back and held in place by his braided wire bowstring. Gary pulled a steel crossbow bolt with a wicked barbed head from a padded case and placed the shaft carefully. The garage had enough light that he turned off the low-light feature of the telescope sight and put the crosshairs in the middle of the mechanic's back. He watched as the mechanic broke his clinch and lifted Abrille onto a shop table, holding her in place with one hand and clumsily unbuckled his belt with the other.

Gary raised the crosshairs slightly, centering them between the mechanic's shoulders, but not too high—so that the bolt would take them both. Light pressure, the swish and twang of the string and the short shaft disappeared into the mechanic with a pink halo spray of blood. He toppled backward, hand still on his buckle, revealing Abrille, pinned to the metal interior wall of the garage. The prod took her through the center of her chest; a heart shot.

The mechanic hadn't been so lucky. It cut his spine and left him sputtering slimy red foam from his dying mouth. Gary admired the art for a moment. The razor sharp broadhead severed his spine, shot through his heart, clearly nicked a lung, and completely cleared his ribcage before passing through the woman.

The kinetic force impressed him—as it usually did—but a double heart shot? Well, *that* was a first. He hadn't set it up the way it turned out, but Abrille looked a lot the way that Tin Man, the kitten looked, nailed to Cheryl's door—in the house of Oz.

Gary turned and walked away, not nearly as quietly as he'd come. He believed that El Indio would put a hunting pack on his tail if the big thug ever figured out who skewered his daughter, but not for a while and by then, it might not be important.

Track looked for Gary from behind the wheel of an old rusted 1972 Plymouth Barracuda with all of the window glass missing. He drove the throw-away car through the deep night, passing from a district of quaint old Mexico City neighborhoods into a rabbit warren of filth and decay. Working through the maze of poverty, he checked two likely spots with no luck. The only positive seemed to be that he'd dry-cleaned his tail of any possible ground surveillance.

Arriving at the third possible spot, he parked the car as Gary previously directed and opened the hood. The worn, greasy distributor rotor went into his pocket as a measure of security against theft.

Descending more deeply into hell, Track walked carefully into a labyrinth of packing-crate houses on car-tire foundations. The pathways, between what passed for residences was an open sewer. Eyes looked out at the tall golden man as he gingerly navigated the footpath. Sometimes he looked back at them. The eyes that followed his progress were those of poverty, mostly women, children and the very old and infirm.

Gary told him about a bar and went to the point of providing instructions as to the best and safest way to approach it. If Track went there, Gary instructed, he should make his way though the barrio on foot to dry-clean once more. The bar was a hideout where the police, the army and even the narcos hesitated to come but if somebody followed him, it could still be trouble.

Emerging from the neighborhood, he entered the bar, past a blue Coupe de Ville, which had seen better days.

Empty restaurant, chairs rested on tables with what appeared to be a waiter standing in a shadow in the darkness. An exterior streetlight, the only one in the neighborhood, cast harsh contrasting light the darkness. But nothing more. He consulted his wristwatch. 0200 HRS, the witching hour arrived.

The waiter, who said that he owned the bar, led Track down a row of empty booths to the very back of the restaurant. A line of dim light showed under a door. He motioned to the door and Track opened it. Gary sat in a chair on a wood slat balcony that overlooked a neighborhood. Until that moment, Track didn't realize that they were on the top of a mesa.

"Bring food for my friend, please," Gary ordered in a warm and friendly voice.

"What are you eating?"

"Pollo Pibil. It's made from chicken and chorizo sausage. They marinate it in lemon and orange juice. It's a stew that you can fork into tortillas. It's not bad, but I think I could make it better."

Gary poured a shot for Track from a bottle of Viajero Luis Tequila. "Rumor has it that a narco bought the agave fields and now he has his own label. He's said to travel some between Mexico and Europe, expanding the trade in coca. I don't know if that's true but the tequila isn't too bad."

199

"You seem calm—I thought that after—what happened, that you might want to—I'm sorry about your, uh—"

"Cheryl. Yeah, me too."

"I thought that you might have gone off the reservation, unauthorized lethality and all that. The brass all think you were a cowboy back when you were in harness but they couldn't ever catch you doing anything wrong. Nothing wet—"

"I don't work for the government anymore, Track. When that bastard Ochoa killed my girlfriend, my boss—my love, it ended my work for the United States Department of State. I don't have to worry about a polygraph, I can do most anything that I want to do.

"How do you know it was Ochoa?"

"He didn't wear gloves. He wanted everyone to know who did that. The President of Mexico personally gave me a green light to do whatever the fuck I want in this matter. And he's promised to give General Barton another medal to assuage his angst at having the Marine Corps lift El Macho's scalp. That means Barton has my back too."

"You know I can't help you."

"Did I ask?" Gary forked the meat into a small corn tortilla and bit into it. "I sent a calling card to the bastard who killed her with one of my little spikes."

"Oh, Christ, the crossbow."

Gary tipped his head, confirming. "I hoped I'd get Felix Ochoa in my sights, but I had to settle. From a symmetrical point of view it worked out better but I'd have loved to have sent a bolt through that fucker's head and watch it explode like a rotten melon."

"What are you going to do now?"

"Mossad has a file on Felix Ochoa from the old days. I talked to a Jumper Katsa that I've known for more than a few years. She handles the turf from Mexico to the Southern Cone. She said Ochoa was in Mozambique with the Cubans. It seems that the guy is allergic to onions. It's a rare food allergy. If he eats them, there's an asthma attack. He carries an epi-pen to keep from going into anaphylactic shock. I doubt that he tells many people about that. I had the notion to poison him with onions and onion extract to make his death look natural."

Track smiled, "Just like in the old days."

"When wet work was authorized for our friends in Al Qaeda. Strictly speaking I never did go Cowboy, but I did innovate. The bastard dies and nobody can attach it to anyone."

Gary made another taco from the meat as another platter of Polo Pibil arrived. He spoke to the owner who waited on him, "Pancho, we'll need more tequila."

Pancho smiled with a mouth full of gold teeth. "Si senior Gary."

"Pancho Cortez runs this barrio, he's the patron and he's a mean son-of-a-bitch. This bar is his headquarters.

"And I take it you met him during your tour here six years ago?"

"Closer to seven if we're counting. I simply helped him with a problem he had and he's willing to do me a favor or two in return."

"He's the one who's going to help you find Ochoa?"

"Now he is. I thought it might be time to activate him. Ochoa won't return to the place where his daughter died. And you're here to meet Cortez and to do another favor for him in case I don't make it. The Bundespolizei arrested his son for narcotics possession in Frankfurt and we need to see the charges dropped and the boy released. You have contact with the same people at the Bundesnachrichtendienst that I do. The German Service owes me a dozen favors. Call Otto Langer and use my name."

"Otto retired."

"That's right. Call Ernst Hauser and remind him about Hong Kong."

"What happened in Hong Kong?"

"You don't need to know all of the details, he'll remember—but if he doesn't—tell him you know about the egg beater, the carrot and the underage hooker."

"You don't have to go through with this," Track said with resignation.

Gary ignored him. "I'm not sure who Felix Ochoa works for. Everyone says he was in the employ of the Sinaloa Federation when El Macho lived, but I'm not so sure." He shrugged to a black Pelican rifle case in the darkness behind the table.

"What's in that?"

"A JP LRP-07 – Long Range Precision Rifle, the best shooting semi-auto rifle in the world. This one is chambered for the .260 Remington."

"Where did you get that?"

"A Candy store. Every town in Mexico has one if you know which door to bang on."

Track reminded Gary, "This is me you are talking to. No Mexican arms merchant stocks an LRP-07 in .260 Remington."

Gary raised his hands in mock surrender. "I called in a favor from the same woman who told me about Ochoa's food allergy. Apparently he has Jewish blood on his hands and they'd like to see a forced disappearance almost as much as I would. They just never were able to rally enough manpower to close the deal. Mexico is not their prime area of concern and the cave man wasn't that high on their list."

"You weren't a wanton murderer in the old days, Gary."

"Not then. Now I am. Just because the President of the United States put his pen to paper doesn't cleanse what we did back then, even though it was legal. No, at this stage, it's all on me. I don't need support, don't need a Presidential Finding, and I don't need somebody to wink and nod in a direction. I'm retired, unemployed, and—" Gary broke down just briefly and sobbed, "I loved that woman and I will have justice in this matter. And when I'm done with Ochoa, I'll take out General Brigadier Jorge Villanueva Sanchez, the prick who ordered the death of Jason Carter."

Track stared through the darkness at Gary's face trying to read it. "There is a move afoot to deal with Brigadier Villanueva Sanchez."

Gary laughed, "I thought that was why you were down here bouncing around. It took me some time to figure that one out. Well, you don't have to worry about it because I knew and liked Carter. He had a lot of promise, a wife and a young child. "

"General Villanueva Sanchez needs to be put on trial."

"If I miss with any of these fuckers, I'll be dead and you can haul whoever you want back to the US to be tried and put up in splendor at Club Fed."

"So you're going after the cave man, El Indio?"

"And everyone he loves."

"His mother should have thrown him away and kept the stork."

Gary didn't say anything.

Track said, "You were never really an assassin, Gary. You didn't have the temperament, crossbow notwithstanding."

"That's changed. I'm an old man now and the one person I thought I had to live for isn't in the land of the living. Now I'm going to do what I do, and you should get out of here so that you're not tempted to do something that will screw with your next flutter."

"My next polygraph has nothing to do with it."

"It has *everything* to do with it, Track. Protect your 201 file. The Seventh Floor," Gary said, referring to the executive level at CIA headquarters, "has kissed all this off now that El Macho has been planted. The gnomes and mandarins will read the tealeaves and will pronounce it a job well done. Unfortunately it's not done and I'm going to put things right."

33

The Butcher's Club
Carretera Mexico-Toluca 2000

They began by drinking Johnny Walker Green Label and the party continued from there. El Indio had not seen Francisco Sauceda since the airplane disaster. After the Airbus augured into the residential neighborhood of Point Loma, the Millennium Organization had gone completely dark by design.

The bright steel arrow that killed his daughter almost a week before sent him into the sort of depression that he hadn't known before. He thought himself immune and detached from that sort of grief at death and loss. He had hoped that the Holy Death would have interceded to relieve a measure of his anguish, but she had not. The tarot cards were ambiguous – Six of Swords/Six of Pentacles/Knave of Swords/Justice/Eight of Wands.

Hanging with a coterie of friends from the old days reminded him of past glory. When combined with the Johnny Walker and the abundance of pretty dancers and waitresses in the club that catered to the higher rung of narcos, it became a party.

All of the pleasure that the expensive Scottish bust-head pumped through Felix's veins was about to be wasted because Pancho Cortez, patron of the barrio, and a man you simply didn't mess with, marked Felix Ochoa and the drinking companion who paid him such homage seated next to him. Old Pancho didn't know that the man who drank with Felix Ochoa was Francisco Sauceda, oldest of los Güeros Diablo, nor would he have cared. Señor Gary told him to wait for the moment and seize the opportunity if it happened. If not, they would wait for another time. It wasn't the murder that counted, but the art of the execution would matter to a man like El Indio.

Fate took control of the matter in the form of a weak bladder and Francisco Sauceda stood to relieve the pressure. Pancho Cortez followed him into the men's room and took him with a thin piano wire garrote as soon as Francisco unzipped. As it usually happened, the wire pulled clear through the tissue and gristle to the backbone, creating quite a mess as free flowing arteries flooded the wall, urinal and tile floor. Pancho smiled to himself. This little prick wouldn't be the first man to be killed in the men's room of the club.

Francisco Sauceda sagged. Pancho knelt down next to the body and propped him up like a tailor's dummy against the white tiled wall. Then he pulled his white, blood stained shirt off, buttons popping and scattering on the floor leaving only his black t-shirt that matched the black trousers that he wore out of the club and into a waiting car with Gary Granger seated behind the wheel.

Three Weeks Later

Gary's own parents wouldn't have recognized him as he walked down the street pushing a tamale cart wearing clown-sized jeans, a black Hilfiger polo two sizes too small, and cheap red Korean sneakers. His gray hair, now dyed black, lay dank, greasy and slick, combed harshly from left to right. Brown contact lenses and six day's growth of gray beard completed the picture.

Track said good-bye to him, commenting that Gary was a vision of savoir-faire, as he trundled the cart south, around a corner, and out of sight.

Track had a bridge officer coming in from headquarters with a read-then-destroy note on the plan to kidnap and remit Brigadier Jorge Villanueva Sanchez to the United States. They expected Track to meet the courier at the airport and put him on the first available airplane back to Washington.

Track thought the move to be overly dramatic, but that's how the bureaucracy worked sometimes.

He thought of Gary and of the gray man's life he'd led. Gary had been a meticulous and compassionate trainer, sharing tradecraft with Track that he'd developed on his own and never shared with anyone before. The man in the goofy clothing, pushing the hot tamale cart was by no means unique in the company of spies, but he was one of the best Track knew of, from any nation.

205

He opened the door of his car and turned the ignition. Acting on an impulse, he drove past where Gary shuffled the cart, ringing a bell, and adjusted the mirror by way of a farewell wave.

Gary rang the tamale cart bell three times in rapid succession.

Four blocks away, an intense handball game with big money stakes unfolded behind high stone ramparts, topped with rusting concertina wire that surrounded a mansion in a neighborhood populated by diplomats. A sea of criminal faces from the bleachers cheered on the sweating, heavily tattooed gangsters competing below in a closely matched contest. Currency changed hands rapidly to those holding the stakes as the game reached a crescendo.

None bellowed louder than Felix Ochoa, El Indio, who had been invited as a matter of course by the Cuban Ambassador. The Ambassador had been one of many old soldiers who served with El Indio in the struggle to free the oppressed nations of Africa from the grip of the Imperialists and the Reactionary Forces of the West.

The Cuban Ambassador's compound had the latest protection measures in place with three rings of security extending out nearly a quarter of a mile in all directions. A mixture of uniformed and nondescript security guards formed the outer perimeter. A roving patrol on motorcycles and cars moved between the outer perimeter and the stone walls. Finally, at the mansion, the walls themselves provided a barrier and there were armed official Cuban cadre inside to deal with any issue.

El Indio invited Pablo Sauceda, who grieved the loss of his brother and had sworn revenge against the man who killed him with a wire around his neck. Venom spurted from Pablo's mouth when he damned the man who shed his brother's blood that drained through a hole in the floor of a shitty men's room in a titty bar.

The party with the Cubans offered an opportunity for both of them to drink and relax surrounded by the unparalleled security offered by El Indio's old masters.

A semi-derelict church within a gated compound sat within the first ring of security, three hundred meters to the north. Gary pushed his cart past the hired Cuban security guard to a solid metal gate with a speakeasy slit in the door and pulled on a rope attached to a bell.

"Free Tamales for the servants of God."

No more than a minute later, a metal slit clacked open and eyes narrowed at the sight of the cart. A fat Cuban priest in a filthy cassock pulled the gate open, groaning on rusty hinges. "Come in my son!"

Gary pushed the cart in, head lowered in humility, and the priest closed the gate behind him, lowering a metal bar and then a restraining bar to keep it secure.

When the priest turned, Gary shot him in the throat with a silenced pistol. The hollow point round exited through the side of his skull and the Brother of Penance died before he hit the paving stones.

The CIA had known about the radio mast concealed within the church spire for the past thirty years and the fat 'monastic' pederast who ran the broadcast/receive station for Dirección de Inteligencia, the Cuban State Intelligence Agency. Gary looked down at the round, flaccid face of the assassin known as Antonio Tonto, CIA Cryptonym BCTRUCK. Antonio took the cloth as part of his cover, delighting in whatever young flesh he could lure into the church. Gary spit. BCTRUCK had raped his last little boy.

He left the cart and conducted a quick recon of the small church. Antonio Tonto had been the only one there, as prior intelligence indicated. He pushed the cart through the doors of the church and into the nave.

The greasy aluminum sheet walls of the cart slid aside and he slipped the black case from inside, lifting five plastic latches that held the lid closed. The JP LR-07 rifle with its telescope sight had been embedded in foam, but came free with a light tug.

Gary inserted a twenty-round magazine and walked quickly to the stairs that led to the tall radio mast inside the tower.

The whole place was filthy, and had been unattended for decades. Pigeon droppings caked the stone floor. Under other circumstances, the corruption might have repelled Gary slightly. Under these circumstances, he disregarded them completely.

The tower provided a complete and unobstructed view of the handball court.

Flipping up the telescope sight's covers, he shouldered the rifle from deep within the shadows cast by the bell tower and cranked it up to twenty power. At that range, he could nearly read the time on El Indio's Rolex. A young man who Gary didn't know, Pablo Sauceda, sat next to El Indio. The remaining Güero Diablo kissed the caveman on the cheek as his handball-smacking warrior won the match. El Indio looked pleased at the attention and tossed the younger man's long hair with affection.

Gary planned to end it then because so much effort had gone into the planning, but his mind drifted back to Oz and his eyes flooded momentarily. Dropping the sight back, he moved it from El Indio to his companion.

The flat, sharp crack made by a .260 Remington doesn't sound like anything else. The distinctive barrel report had been muffled further by a muzzle break on the end of the barrel and by the hollow chambered bell tower so by the time the sound reached the drunken, cheering narcos, it didn't sound like much at all.

The Israeli Service provided 140-grain Boat Tail solid point Vital Shok bullets that had been hand loaded. Gary used ten cartridges to confirm that the rifle had been sighted, and made minor adjustments so that it would be dead-on at 300 meters. That left him thirty remaining cartridges. More than enough.

The first bullet tore through Pablo Sauceda's hand, shredding it, leaving only a stump, spurting blood. The partially spent round continued on and struck another spectator in the leg, evoking a reaction that Gary couldn't hear, but clearly saw.

Sauceda just looked at the hand-that-once-was, as realization dawned on Felix Ochoa, who had been misted over by his friend's blood.

The semi-automatic rifle could fire as quickly as Gary pulled the trigger and the LR-07 had no appreciable recoil to take him off target. Once he had Felix's attention, he sent the next round through Sauceda's right ear. He watched for an exit wound, but didn't see one. However, Sauceda died at that instant with hemorrhaged eyes that literally popped out of his head when the bullet hit. The now lifeless body slumped onto the lap of the howling El Indio.

Thirty seconds later, Gary pushed his cart through the squeaking metal door and into the street. Nobody stopped him or noticed anything amiss.

34

El Indio went to ground after the second Sauceda brother took a bullet. It's difficult to stick your head out of the hole when they can take somebody sitting next to you in a location such as the Cuban Ambassador's residence in Mexico City.

The Cubans did a little math and figured out where the shot came from. Father Antonio Tonto's corpse confirmed trigonometry. They tried to get to Felix Ochoa. They had questions about why his friend had been targeted but he didn't make himself available to anyone.

As he camped from his pick-up truck near Volcán de Fuego de Colima, the larger of the two Colima Volcanoes, he decided that the Americans had been a bit cleverer than he gave them credit for. More disturbingly, the move to shoot down the airplane loaded with women, children and the innocent angered Niña Negra Santa.

From where he sat, eating a tortilla he'd recently heated on a paraffin burner, filled with cold beans, the Holy Death toyed with him like a cat with a mouse. Maybe the Americans would take El León last of all? Or perhaps the boss lived with the Niña Negra Santa now? The depression, brought on with the realization that he would be sent to hell without Her presence to warm his soul, created profound regret that he didn't think he was capable of—until now. The blood of the innocent cried from their grave and death stalked him.

On an impulse, he threw all of his camping gear into the back of the black Ford pick-up that El León gave him for his use and drove back in the direction of the last place he'd seen the boss. Suddenly, it became very important for him to know whether or not El León still lived.

Carretera Federal 200, the narrow, twisty coastal road, ran a long distance. Before long, driving down the highway with the window down, the smell of salt air awakened a powerful hunger in El Indio.

Fishing villages abounded on the coast. Some were crabbers, others took the big fish in larger pangas. He turned off the highway and drove to a cluster of brightly painted fishermen's huts that looked as if they might contain a restaurant. He didn't find a restaurant per se, but one of the fisherman's homes had an open veranda that served the purpose. He'd seen many like it in other places. The veranda would serve as a gathering place where men from the village would gather, drink, smoke, chat of the day's catch and of strategy for the following morning.

El Indio's new Ford truck attracted a lot of attention. These people were poor crab fishermen and a rig like his was far beyond their means—but not their dreams.

He walked onto the tiled veranda in a foul mood and shouted to a young boy that he was hungry and wanted to see some food. The boy ran to his grandmother, who expected a decent payday from the rich stranger who drove such a grand automobile – with Mexico Distrito Federal license plates.

She walked out of the kitchen with a large bowl of ceviche and looked at the man in person. In all her life, she had never seen anyone as ugly and forbidding. Her grandson, six years old played hide-and-peek at with the ugly stranger. The man seemed to be irritated by the game because he pegged a loose piece of concrete masonry at the little boy, missing him by a small margin and making him yelp.

"Just because we are poor and because we take our living from the sea is no reason to behave like a brute," she scolded, setting the bowl in front of the large, shaggy man.

"I want cerveza."

Yes they had beer but she felt concerned that they had no refrigeration for it. What would she do if he rose up and attacked her for serving warm beer?

"Old woman!"

She turned.

"What is in this ceviche?"

"Mostly crab, octopus, filets of small corbina, juice of the lemon, cilantro, pepper and salt."

"That's all?"

"Yes, that's all. I made it myself." As she said that, she thought to herself that she had seen the photo of such a man before, in the school when she was young. This was one of the men who lived in

211

caves many thousands of years before. How remarkable that one of his kind would drive into their little village in a beautiful truck and throw rocks at her grandson—and order ceviche.

He picked over the food briefly and then began to devour it, placing the fish and crab it into his mouth with his fingers in a fierce and predatory way that reminded her of a wild dog, bolting down meat.

She brought the warm beer and he gulped it with the same haste and anger that he'd been eating his cold fish stew. As she watched, he began to slowly stop eating. He'd found something in the stew that caught his attention.

"Onion?"

"Yes, there is onion in the ceviche."

"I asked what you put into it."

"I always add onion."

Felix Ochoa reached for his pocket and just as suddenly, realized that the Epi-Pen was in his truck. He had difficulty breathing as his airways constricted.

Looking through blurring vision at the old woman he said, "Bitch, get my bag. It's inside of my truck. I need it now."

"Do you worship the Holy Death?"

He wondered why she would ask such a question while he felt such distress. "Yes, I am a *high priest* of Niña Negra Santa!"

She began to scream and she kept screaming to the fishermen who were still looking at and admiring the fancy black Ford pick-up. They came running and saw the old woman's eyes rolled back in her head as she keened to the fishermen, inciting them to action.

"He is of the Devil! He is here to take our souls! After eating the food of honest men, taken from the sea with toil and sweat, look at how he suffers. It is said that Satan can not eat at the table of people of God!"

The fishermen looked at the ugly man, now sinking to his knees, pleading for them to get his bag from the truck.

"You must kill him," the old woman pleaded with her son, "while he has been weakened by the honest food!"

Her son took a shark club and swung it at El Indio's head. It killed many sharks and would have killed a normal man, but El Indio only seemed to be stunned while he struggled to breathe.

"Maybe he can't be killed, mother," the fisherman reasoned with the old woman.

She thought for a few seconds while blood started to flow from the wound in El Indio's head.

"Maybe we can't kill him because it is a sin for us to take the life of even one so evil—wrap him in a net and take him down *to the shore.*"

All of the fishermen were there now and they did as the old woman directed. The stranger from Mexico City proved to be a heavy load, but together they wrapped him in a net and carried him as directed to the high tide mark and pegged the net into rocks, wedging the staves firmly in place.

El Indio did not expect that sort of reaction. Through his entire life, people feared him, and some avoided him. None with the exception of these simple fishing folk every treated him this way. He gagged most of the ceviche back up and shook off the blow to his head but it still bled. He had only one remaining problem. The net held him fast no matter how he struggled and his eyesight remained blurred.

The clicking and sounds of scuttling along the rocks and sand didn't alarm him until the first crab took a small bite-sized piece of skin from his ankle with a razor sharp claw and then another tangled in his hair, the claw incising from his ear.

His vision had begun to clear and what he thought to be red stones on the beach, were in fact crabs. Large red crabs. Thousands and thousands of red crabs crawling relentlessly toward him.

El Indio screamed and he howled.

Back on the patio, the fishermen, led by the old woman, prayed as they listened to what they thought to be the same pitiful cries as the damned souls uttered in hell.

Epilogue

Gary Granger sits on a barstool that he's come to think of as *his* barstool at the Old Dominion Club on Wisconsin Avenue, just down from the Naval Observatory. Missy, the cocktail waitress, brings him complimentary bar burgers but he waves her off, preferring to drink his lunch, alone.

Santiago (El León) Gustavo Iglesias-Aznar runs a very large narcotics cartel, but does so with great unease. Heavy is the head that wears the crown. One can outrun everything but the clock and sand through the hourglass, as he is reminded constantly like a hag-ridden man.

CW5 Scott (Scooter) Olsen US Army (Armor), retired from the Army and was noticed by a reality television producer. Today, he spends his days as talent in front of the camera on the Fishing Channel.

Though **Lance Parkyn** suspected his own involvement in events that led to the Pacific Airlines crash in San Diego, he continues to take the opportunity to train people with money to spend, to shoot accurately at long range. He, his wife and their two sons relocated to the Prescott Valley in Arizona.

Brigadier General Darrell H. Barton, US Army (Infantry) went on to earn his second star and serves in a major Army Command.

During the dry season six months later, on another continent, **Llewellyn (Track) Ryder**, planted a bomb in a water cistern in a valley where people depended on it for survival. He left and the bomb went undetected until the rainy season arrived. The water level lifted a float, attached to a trigger that detonated the explosive. Without the cistern, people left the valley and it is now available for others to use for their own purposes.

The polls tracking presidential popularity rose over twenty points following the administration's 'decisive response' to narco-terrorism and all further inquiries into who may have pulled the trigger (and why) were promptly discontinued. Pundits agreed that taking out El Macho Gonzales would comfortably propel what had been an unpopular president, into his second term.

General Brigadier Jorge Villanueva Sanchez, Ejército Mexicano, (CIA Cryptonym: DMGATOR), the murderer of CIA Branch Chief Jason B. Carter, was found dead in his car near a bar in Tuxtla Gutiérrez where he'd been drinking with friends. The state judicial police investigation determined that a wicked looking, viciously barbed crossbow bolt, fired at short range, pierced the windshield of his Renault Clio and then punched through the unfortunate general officer's long and prominent nose. The force of the impact took his nose and much of his face with it, pushing it out the back of his skull. The proposed extradition to the United States to stand trial was no longer necessary and the file was closed.

Acknowledgements

I appreciate the diligent efforts of Dr. Jack Hermansen, Thong Cao, and Jeff Harr, my editors, who went after and seized errata like terriers after rats.

Thanks go out to colleagues and friends from Mexico who fight the cartel wars every single day. Some work in the 'alphabet agencies' of the United States Government. Others, unheralded, do what they do simply for the right reasons. They are hereafter, nameless but they know who they are.

The late Detective Sergeant Tom Perdue, San Francisco Police Department Intelligence Unit, deserves honorable mention here. He died with his boots on, was loved and respected by all who knew him and remains a legend as well as a credit to his profession.

Though it may be far too little, too late, thank you to William L. Cassidy, and the effort he put out to stop a large quantity of high order explosives and sophisticated detonators from crossing the Mexican Border and entering the United States at the hands of Middle Eastern terrorists in the wake of the World Trade Center attack. There are no bands, no reviewing stands, no cheering crowds and no grateful, adoring government.
—this will have to serve as your bright medal, your trumpet and your parade.

About the Author

Having spent his entire adult life in the service of government, the author has had the opportunity to travel and to operate in places and in situations denied to many people.

7648804R0

Made in the USA
Charleston, SC
27 March 2011